THE ADVENTURESS

'THE DETECTIVE STORY CLUB is a clearing house for the best detective and mystery stories chosen for you by a select committee of experts. Only the most ingenious crime stories will be published under the THE DETECTIVE STORY CLUB imprint. A special distinguishing stamp appears on the wrapper and title page of every THE DETECTIVE STORY CLUB book—the Man with the Gun. Always look for the Man with the Gun when buying a Crime book.'

Wm. Collins Sons & Co. Ltd., 1929

Now the Man with the Gun is back in this series of COLLINS CRIME CLUB reprints, and with him the chance to experience the classic books that influenced the Golden Age of crime fiction.

THE DETECTIVE STORY CLUB

FURTHER TITLES IN PREPARATION

THE
ADVENTURESS

A STORY OF CRIME

BY

ARTHUR B. REEVE

WITH AN INTRODUCTION BY
DAVID BRAWN

COLLINS
CRIME
CLUB

COLLINS CRIME CLUB
An imprint of HarperCollins*Publishers*
1 London Bridge Street
London SE1 9GF
www.harpercollins.co.uk

This edition 2017

First published in Great Britain by
W. Collins Sons & Co. Ltd 1918
Published by The Detective Story Club Ltd 1930

Introduction © David Brawn 2017

A catalogue record for this book is available from the British Library

ISBN 978-0-00-813765-6

Typeset in Bulmer MT Std by
Palimpsest Book Production Ltd, Falkirk, Stirlingshire
Printed and bound in Great Britain by Clays Ltd, St Ives plc

MIX
Paper from
responsible sources
FSC™ C007454

INTRODUCTION

'The name's Kennedy. Craig Kennedy.'

The twenty-first century crime reader might be forgiven for replying, 'Who?' But a hundred years ago, Craig Kennedy, 'scientific detective', needed no introduction. He was a household name on both sides of the Atlantic, acquiring the impressive tagline 'The American Sherlock Holmes' and conquering newspapers, magazines, books, comic strips, stage, films—silent and spoken—and early television, destined, or so it seemed then, for literary immortality.

Kennedy's creator, Arthur Benjamin Reeve, was born in the New York town of Patchogue on 15 October 1880. A gifted academic and polymath, he graduated from Brooklyn's exclusive Boys' High School in 1899 and went to Princeton University, studying 'about everything with an 'ology or an 'onomy at the end of it', inspiring and even tutoring fellow students. Law School beckoned, and although fascinated by the subject of criminal law Reeve had no appetite to compete when he discovered that there were 16,000 lawyers in New York and dropped out to pursue his first love: writing. Various editorial posts led to freelance journalism and some short stories, his first in *Argosy* magazine, before his big break came with *Cosmopolitan* in 1910.

Cosmopolitan, the magazine that had premiered H.G. Wells' *The War of the Worlds* in the US in 1897, was at that time a monthly literary publication with nearly a million readers. Reeve's story, 'The Case of Helen Bond', introduced Craig Kennedy, 'the Professor of Criminal Science', and was followed the next month by 'The Silent Bullet' (January 1911), which became the titular chapter of the first hardback when the first dozen stories were collected and published by Dodd, Mead in 1912. The adventures of Craig Kennedy were a constant monthly fixture in *Cosmopolitan* for two years before becoming less regular items, and more than 80 were published altogether by 1918.

The innovation of Reeve's stories was that Kennedy, a chemistry professor based in New York, would apply scientific methods to the detection of crime. The fictional narrator was Walter Jameson, a newspaper reporter whose bemused interpretation of Kennedy's wild experiments gave the reader's eye view of events, recalling Sherlock Holmes' Dr Watson. The stories contained more than a little science fiction, from developments in chemistry and medicine to speculative communication devices and weaponry, but these were not tales of fantasy: the scientific theories were perceptive and up to date. Reeve prided himself on keeping abreast of the science journals and plundered them for story ideas, with scientists like Tesla and Edison complimenting him on his technological intelligence, and readers thrilled at the possibilities that were envisioned in the Craig Kennedy tales. As John Locke observes in his invaluable biography, *From Ghouls to Gangsters: The Career of Arthur B. Reeve* (Off-Trail Publications, 2007), the inventions had mysteriously evocative names like the 'vocaphone', the 'sphygmograph' and the 'optophone', but Reeve was not a research scientist or a soothsayer of future-truth and did not restrict himself to hard sciences. He was writing detective stories, and it was his entertaining storytelling and mastery of the puzzle-solution structure that ensured his continuing popularity.

In addition to *Cosmopolitan*, Reeve wrote stories in the early years for *McClure's*, *Hearst's*, *The Popular*, *The Red Book*, *Pearson's* and *Adventure* magazines, also creating new principal characters—Guy Garrick, an enlightened young detective who had studied criminal science, and Constance Dunlap, a relative rarity in 1913 being a woman detective. There were more books, all bind-ups of the short stories, although they began to be presented as novels, with additional linking material and chapter breaks to disguise the original short story format. The first full-length Craig Kennedy novel, *The Gold of the Gods*, was published in 1915 by Hearst's International Library.

It was at this point that the movie industry, a fertile ground for dramatic writers with its requirement for cliffhanger serials, lured Reeve and his fictional brainchild to the silver screen. *The Exploits of Elaine* (1914), a formulaic follow-on from that year's *The Perils of Pauline*, featured Craig Kennedy heroically deploying science against the menace of the villainous Clutching Hand. Two sequels swiftly followed, as did novelisations, which were published by Hearst's in 1916 and separately in the UK by Hodder & Stoughton. Meanwhile, Craig Kennedy also made his stage debut, with the first play opening in Hartford, Connecticut, in 1915.

Despite a general curtailment in Reeve's short story output during his film writing years, a new full-length novel commissioned by the respected New York publishing house Harper & Brothers was published in 1917 as part of their centenary year celebrations. *The Adventuress*, concerning a murder in a munitions firm and the theft of a new invention, the 'telautomaton', was serialised initially in the *Chicago Examiner* for, they claimed, 'the highest price ever paid this author for a novel'. UK rights were sold to Harpers' future sister company, William Collins, who also bought the final two collections of *Cosmopolitan* shorts, *The Treasure-Train* and *The Panama Plot*. Meanwhile Harpers went on to publish ten more books with Reeve, plus an impressive twelve-volume reprint collection, *The Craig Kennedy Stories* (1918), which included the bulk of the *Cosmopolitan* shorts (although not the newly released *The Panama Plot*), the novel *The Gold of the Gods*, the Elaine novelisations and the two non-Kennedy books, *Guy Garrick* and *Constance Dunlap*. The widespread success of this set at the time has ensured that the early Craig Kennedy books have remained relatively easy to track down, whereas *The Adventuress* and the novels that followed it remain generally much harder to find.

With his *Cosmopolitan* run having ended in 1918, the 1920s saw Reeve diversifying. More film work included writing for stage sensation Harry Houdini, with their first movie, *The*

Master Mystery, also having the distinction of featuring the first on-screen robot, Automaton 'Q'; he even wrote Westerns. A return to magazines, newspapers and lucrative pulps saw Craig Kennedy appearing in both cosier romantic mysteries and stories set in the country as well as harder-edged gangster stories and syndicated comic strips. Technology remained a constant theme—the film serial *Craig Kennedy: Radio Detective* (1926) capitalised on a very topical medium, and the novel *Pandora* (1926) featured synthetic fuel and an atomic bomb.

By the end of the decade Reeve was focusing more on real-life criminology. He became 'radio detective' himself when NBC signed him in 1930 to write and host *Crime Prevention Program*, an advisory series in conjunction with the NYPD. It rejuvenated his journalistic career: more radio followed, he published his first non-fiction book, *The Golden Age of Crime*, an examination of racketeering and other consequences of Prohibition since its introduction in 1920, and he covered high-profile crime cases in newspapers, including the Lindbergh kidnapping case that had inspired Agatha Christie's *Murder on the Orient Express* (1934).

Reeve's final novel, *The Stars Scream Murder* (Appleton-Century, 1936), was in terms of the science one of his least plausible—astrology!—and was also Craig Kennedy's swan song. The flap of the dust-wrapper bore an enthusiastic summary of Reeve's achievements since creating his scientific detective a quarter of a century earlier:

'More than a million copies of Arthur B. Reeve's "Craig Kennedy" books have been sold in the United States to date and almost as many in Great Britain.* They have been translated into practically every language, including one book into ancient Korean.

---

* This figure is more conservative than the claim on the jacket of *The Clutching Hand* (Reilly & Lee, 1934): 'His books have sold 2,000,000 copies in the United States, 1,000,000 in Great Britain.'

'*The Stars Scream Murder*, probably the first astrological detective novel ever published, maintains Mr Reeve's long record of firsts. His first story employed the use of tire treads in detection, a method which has now borne fruit in the Federal Bureau of Investigation of the U.S. Department of Justice, with its astounding file of the treads of all tires manufactured. The first story ever to use the now well-known dictagraph was written by Mr Reeve even before the scientific journals had described it. He also wrote the first story based upon the Freudian theory and psychoanalysis. Pioneering in this manner, he has created a new type of detective story with a host of imitators. He himself considers his most important influence the helping along of the creation of a scientific department in every one of the country's modern detective headquarters.

'It is hardly necessary to recount the innumerable titles which have made his name a household word as a master of detective fiction, nor to recall his various motion picture serials, such as *The Exploits of Elaine*, *The Master Mystery*, *Terror Island*, etc., which so many of us remember. He was in radio in the days of its infancy, his N.B.C. Crime Prevention Program having achieved particularly wide attention.'

Arthur B. Reeve died just four months later, on 9 August 1936, of cardiac asthma, aged only 55. As John Locke wryly observes, 'Reeve all but took Kennedy to the grave with him. Most of the books were already out of print; the remainder soon joined the silence. Reeve went from American institution to forgotten man of antiquity virtually overnight.' The only reprieve was a 26-part television series starring Donald Woods, *Craig Kennedy, Criminologist* in 1952, although it was pretty generic and largely ignored the science angle that had distinguished the original Craig Kennedy from his peers.

Reeve had undoubtedly struck a chord with readers and had modernised crime fiction to make it feel relevant and exciting; but sadly nothing dates quite as quickly as yesterday's cutting-edge science. Craig Kennedy now reads more like a parody than a visionary detective. But if you can transport your mind back 100 years, *The Adventuress* might still 'unfold new delights to readers of exciting mysteries', as the review in the London *Globe* newspaper maintained, and will hopefully inspire readers to investigate more of the forgotten work of Arthur B. Reeve and his 'American Sherlock Holmes'.

DAVID BRAWN
October 2016

CONTENTS

EDITOR'S PREFACE

To the real reader of detective fiction the name of Craig Kennedy must be almost as well known as that of Bulldog Drummond, or Sherlock Holmes himself. He has taken his place among the great crime investigators of our literature, not simply because he is the 'hero' of some of the world's best mystery novels, but because he is distinctly an individual. His personality and his methods are his own, and except perhaps in his success as a solver of crimes he cannot be said to resemble any other detective hero. He is essentially the scientific sleuth; not only in his logic, but in the more melodramatic sense of the word—in his laboratory experiments.

Mr A. B. Reeve, the creator of Craig Kennedy, seems to be a very mine of ingenuity. He introduces into his stories strange cyphers, diabolical machines, subtle poisons, and a hundred and one new weapons for his murderer, but he never becomes cheaply sensational. His farthest flights of imagination appear rational to his readers, for he unfolds his story so cunningly and with such a conviction of truth.

At the present time, when the crime novel is at the height of its popularity and authors vie with each other in turning out more and more complex plots, it is refreshing to find someone like A. B. Reeve, who is content to entertain and mystify us without putting us through an examination in mathematics or psychology.

One need only read *The Adventuress* to test the truth of this assertion; it is of the author's best and, unlike many of Craig Kennedy's cases, is a full-length novel and not a short story; but the one admirable feature of an A. B. Reeve book is that it makes one forget office, household duties, everything one wants to forget, for several glorious hours in a new world of romance and mystery.

CHAPTER I

A REVOLVER-SHOT followed by the crash of glass sounded in our hall.

At the same instant the laboratory door burst open and an elderly, distinguished-looking man stumbled in on us, his hat now off, his coat and collar awry, his hair rumpled, and his face wearing a dazed, uncertain expression, as though he did not yet comprehend what had so suddenly taken place.

'My God!' he exclaimed, gazing about in a vain effort to restore his dignity and equilibrium. 'What was that? I hardly had my hand on the knob when it happened.'

A glance was enough to assure Kennedy that the man was unhurt, except for the shock, and in a moment he dashed out into the hall.

The front door of the Chemistry Building had been shattered by a revolver-shot. But not even the trace of a skulking figure could be seen on the campus. Pursuit was useless. There was, apparently, no one to pursue.

Pale and agitated still, the man sank limply into a chair as I forced a stimulant into his trembling lips.

Kennedy closed the door and stood there a moment, a look of inquiry on his face, but without a word.

'Someone—must have—shadowed me—all the way,' gasped the man as he gulped hard, 'must have seen me come in—tried to shoot me before I had a chance to tell you my story.'

It was some minutes before our strange visitor regained his poise, and Craig refrained from questioning him, though I was consumed with curiosity to know the reason of his sudden entrance.

1

When at last he did speak, his first words were so different from anything I had expected that I could hardly believe him to be the same person. In spite of his nervousness, his tone was that of a hard, practical man of business.

'I suppose you know something of Maddox Munitions, Incorporated?' he inquired, somewhat brusquely.

I did not quite understand a man who could be himself so soon after an episode such as he had been through, nor do I think Kennedy did, either.

'I have no interest in "war brides",' returned Craig coldly.

'Nor have I—as such,' the man agreed, apparently rather pleased than otherwise at the stand-off attitude Kennedy had assumed. 'But I happen to be Maxwell Hastings, attorney for Marshall Maddox, who was—'

Kennedy wheeled about suddenly, interrupting. 'Whose body was found floating in Westport Bay this morning. Yes, Mr Jameson and I have read the little five-line despatch in the papers this morning. I thought there was something back of it.'

As for me, I was even more excited now than Kennedy, and I could see a smile of satisfaction flit over the face of Hastings. In a few sentences the clever lawyer had extracted from us what others took all manner of time and art to discover. He knew that we were interested, that he could depend on Kennedy's taking the case.

Kennedy and I exchanged a significant glance. We had discussed the thing cursorily at the breakfast-table as we did any odd bit of news that interested us.

Already I knew, or fancied I knew, something of the affair. For it was at the time when explosions in munitions plants had furnished many thrilling chapters of news.

All the explosions had not been confined to the plants, however. There had been and still were going on explosions less sanguinary but quite as interesting in the Maddox family itself.

There was a hundred million dollars as the apple of

discord, and a most deadly feud had divided the heirs. Together they had made money so fast that one might think they would not feel even annoyance over a stray million here and there. But, as so often happens, jealousy had crept in. Sudden wealth seemed to have turned the heads of the whole family. Marshall Maddox was reported to have been making efforts to oust the others and make himself master of the big concern.

'Maddox had had some trouble with his wife, hadn't he?' I asked, recalling scattered paragraphs lately in the papers.

Hastings nodded. 'They were separated. That, too, was part of the family disagreement. His sister Frances, took the part of his wife, Irene, I believe.'

Hastings considered a moment, as though debating how far he should go in exposing the private affairs of his client, then caught the eye of Kennedy, and seemed to realise that as long as he had called Craig into the case he must be frank, at least with us.

'At the Westport Harbour House,' he added deliberately, 'we know that there was a little Mexican dancer, Paquita. Perhaps you have heard of her on the stage and in the cabarets of New York. Marshall Maddox knew her in the city.'

He paused. Evidently he had something more to say and was considering the best way to say it.

Finally Hastings leaned over and whispered, 'We know, too, that Shelby Maddox, his brother, had met Paquita at the Harbour House just before the family conference which brought them all together.'

It was evident that, at least to Hastings, there was something in the affair that looked ugly to him as far as Shelby was concerned.

'It's not at all strange,' he added, 'that two men as unlike as Marshall and Shelby should disagree. Marshall was the dominating type, eager for power; Shelby easy-going, more interested in having a good time. In this affair of Paquita—

whatever it amounted to—I'm not at all surprised at Shelby. He is younger than Marshall was—and inclined to be a sport. Still, there was a vein of susceptibility in Marshall, too. There must have been.'

Hastings paused. Human frailties were out of his ken as a lawyer. Property he understood; passions, no. With him the law had been a jealous mistress and had brooked no rival.

'It was on Shelby's yacht, the *Sybarite*, was it not, that the tragedy occurred?' ventured Kennedy.

It was a leading question and Hastings knew it. He drew in a long, contemplative breath as he decided whether he should consent to be led.

'Yes—and no,' he answered finally. 'They were there on the yacht, of course, to agree to disagree and to divide the family fortune. Shelby Maddox went to Westport on the yacht, and it was so hot at the Harbour House that they decided to hold the conference on the *Sybarite*. Marshall Maddox and I had motored out from town. The sister, Frances, and her husband, Johnson Walcott, live on the other side of the island. They motored over, also bringing with them Johnson Walcott's sister, Winifred, who stayed at the Harbour House. Johnson Walcott himself went ashore from the yacht early in the evening, having to go to the city on business. That was all right, for there was Bruce, the lawyer who represented Frances Maddox—I mean Mrs Walcott, of course. You see, I've known the family so long that I often forget that she is married. Shelby had his lawyer, also, Mr Harvey. That was the party. As for the tragedy, I can't say that we know positively that it took place on the yacht. No. We don't *know* anything.'

'Don't know anything?' hastened Kennedy. 'How's that? Wasn't the conference amicable?'

'Well,' temporised Hastings, 'I can't say that it was especially. The division was made. Marshall won control of the company— or at least would have done so if the terms agreed on had been signed in the morning. He agreed to form a syndicate to buy the others out, and the price at which the stock was to be sold was fixed.'

'But did they dispute about anything?' persisted Kennedy, seeing how the lawyer had evaded his question.

Hastings seemed rather to appreciate the insistence than to be annoyed by it. So far, I could see that the great corporation lawyer was taking Kennedy's measure quite as much as Craig was doing the same by him.

'Yes,' he answered, 'there was one thing that occasioned more dispute than anything else. Maddox Munitions have purchased a wonderful new war invention, the telautomaton— wireless control of submarines, torpedoes, ships, vehicles, aeroplanes, everything—the last word in the new science of telautomatics.

An exclamation of surprise escaped Kennedy. Often he and I had discussed the subject and he had even done some work on it.

'Of course,' resumed Hastings, 'we have had to acquire certain rights and the basic, pioneer patents are not ours. But the manner in which this telautomaton has been perfected over everything yet devised by inventors renders it the most valuable single piece of property we have. At last we have an efficient electric arm that we can stretch out through space to do our work and fight our battles. Our system will revolutionise industry as well as warfare.'

It was not difficult to catch the enthusiasm which Hastings showed over the telautomaton. There was something fascinating about the very idea.

Kennedy, however, shook his head gravely. 'Too big a secret to be in the hands of a corporation,' he objected. 'In warfare it should only be possessed by the Government, and in industry it is—well, it is a public service in itself. So that went to Marshall Maddox also?'

Hastings nodded.

'There will be trouble over that,' warned Kennedy. 'Mark my

words. It is too big a secret.' For a moment he pondered, then changed the subject. 'What happened after the conference?'

'It was so late when we finished,' continued Hastings, 'and there were still some minor details to be cleared up in the morning. We all decided to stay on the yacht rather than go ashore to the Harbour House. The *Sybarite* is a large yacht, and we each had a cabin, so that we all turned in. There wasn't much sociability in a crowd like that to keep them up later than was necessary.'

'Yes,' prompted Kennedy as Hastings paused. 'Marshall Maddox seemed all right when he retired?'

'Perfectly. I went into his cabin and we chatted a few moments before I went to mine, planning some steps we would take in the morning to clear things up, especially to release all claims on the telautomaton. I remember that Maddox seemed in very good spirits over the way things had been going, though very tired. To my mind, that removes the possibility of its having been suicide.'

'Nothing is impossible until it is proved so,' corrected Kennedy. 'Go on. Tell me how it was discovered.'

'I slept later than usual,' replied Hastings, seeking to get everything in order. 'The first thing I heard was Shelby's Jap, Mito, rapping on all the doors to make sure that we were awake. We had agreed to that. Well, we gathered on the deck, all except Mr Maddox. We waited, no one thinking much about it except myself. I can't say why it was, but I felt uneasy. Mr Maddox had always been so punctual and I had known him so long. It was not like him to be the last on an occasion like this.

'Finally someone, I think it was Shelby, suggested that inasmuch as I was in a sense his representative, I might go and hurry him up. I was only too glad to go. I walked forward to the cabin he occupied and rapped on the door. No answer. I tried the handle. To my surprise it turned and I pushed the door open.'

'Don't stop,' urged Kennedy eagerly. 'What did you see?'

'Nothing,' replied Hastings. 'There was nothing there. The bed had been slept in. But Mr Maddox was gone!'

'How about his clothes?'

'Just as he had left them.'

'What did you do next?'

'I shouted an alarm and they all came running to me. Shelby called the crew, Mito, the steward, everyone. We questioned them all. No one had seen or heard anything out of the way.'

'At least that's what everybody said,' observed Craig. 'What then?'

'No one knew what to do. Just about that time, however, we heard a horn on a small boat tooting shrilly, as though for help. It was an oysterman on his way to the oyster beds. His kicker had stopped and he was signalling, apparently for help. I don't know why it was, but Mrs Walcott must have thought something was wrong. Even before one of the crew could find out what was the matter she picked up a marine glass lying on a wicker chair.

'"It—it's a body!" she cried, dropping the glasses to the deck.

'That was enough for us. Like a flash it went through my mind that it could be no other than Mr Maddox.'

'What did you do then?'

'The most natural thing. We did not wait for the oysterman to come to us. We piled into one of Shelby's tenders and went to him. Sure enough, the oysterman had found the body, floating in the bay.'

There was a trace of a tear in Hastings's eye, and his voice faltered a bit. I rather liked him better for it. Except for fear at the revolver-shot, I had almost begun to think him devoid of feeling.

'So far as we could see,' he resumed, as though ashamed to show weakness even over one whom he had known so long, 'there was nothing to show whether he might not have got up, fallen overboard in some way, and have been drowned, or might have been the victim of foul play—except one thing.'

'What was that?' inquired Kennedy eagerly.

'Maddox and I had taken out with us, in a brief-case which he carried, the plans of the telautomaton. The model is in the company's safe here in New York. This morning when we went back to Maddox's room I found that the brief-case was missing. The plans are gone! You were right. There has been trouble over them.'

Kennedy eyed Hastings keenly. 'You found nothing in the room that would give a hint?'

'I didn't look,' returned Hastings. 'I sealed the door and window—or port-hole—whatever you call it—had them locked and placed a wax seal bearing the impression of my ring, so that if it is broken, I will know by whom. Everything there is just as it was. I wanted it that way, for I had heard of you, and determined to come to town myself and get you.

'The body?'

'I had the oysterman take it to an undertaking establishment in the town so that we would have witnesses of everything that happened after its discovery.'

'Did any of them suggest a theory?' asked Kennedy after a moment's thought. 'Or say anything?'

Hastings nodded negatively. 'I think we were all too busy watching one another to talk,' he ventured. 'I was the only one who acted, and they let me go ahead. Perhaps none of them dared stop me.'

'You don't mean that there was a conspiracy?' I put in.

'Oh, no,' smiled Hastings indulgently. 'They could never have agreed long enough, even against Marshall Maddox, to conspire. No, indeed. I mean that if one had objected, he would immediately have laid himself open to suspicion from the rest. We all went ashore together. And now I must get back to Westport immediately. I'm not even going to take time to go down to the office. Kennedy, will you come?'

'An unnecessary question,' returned Craig, rising. 'A mystery like this is the breath of my life. You could scarcely keep me away.'

'Thank you,' said Hastings. 'You won't regret it, financially or otherwise.'

We went out into the hall, and Kennedy started to lock the laboratory door, when Hastings drew back.

'You'll pardon me?' he explained. 'The shot was fired at me out here. I naturally can't forget it.

With Kennedy on one side and myself on the other, all three of us on the alert, we hurried out and into a taxicab to go down to the station

As we jolted along Kennedy plied the lawyer with a rapid fire of questions. Even he could furnish no clue as to who had fired the shot at him or why.

CHAPTER II

HALF an hour later we were on our way by train to Westport with Hastings. As the train whisked us along Craig leaned back in his chair and surveyed the glimpses of water and countryside through the window. Now and then, as we got farther out from the city, through a break in the trees one could catch glimpses of the deep-blue salt water of bay and Sound, and the dazzling whiteness of sand.

Now and then Kennedy would break in with a question to Hastings, showing that his mind was actively at work on the case, but by his manner I could see that he was eager to get on the spot before all that he considered important had been messed up by others.

Hastings hurried us directly from the train to the little undertaking establishment to which the body of Marshall Maddox had been taken.

A crowd of the curious had already gathered, and we pushed our way in through them.

There lay the body. It had a peculiar, bloated appearance and the face was cyanosed and blue. Maddox had been a large man and well set up. In death he was still a striking figure. What was the secret behind those saturnine features?

'Not a scratch or a bruise on him, except those made in handling the body,' remarked the coroner, who was also a doctor, as he greeted Kennedy.

Craig nodded, then began his own long and careful investigation. He was so busily engaged, and I knew that it was so important to keep him from being interrupted, that I placed myself between him and those who crowded into the little room back of the shop.

But before I knew it a heavily veiled woman had brushed past me and stood before the body.

'Irene Maddox!' I heard Hastings whisper in Kennedy's ear as Craig straightened up in surprise.

As she stood there there could be no doubt that Irene Maddox had been very bitter toward her husband. The wound to her pride had been deep. But the tragedy had softened her. She stood tearless, however, before the body, and as well as I could do so through her veil I studied her face. What did his death mean to her, aside from the dower rights that came to her in his fortune? It was impossible to say.

She stood there several minutes, then turned and walked deliberately out through the crowd, looking neither to the right nor to the left. I found myself wondering at the action. Yet why should she have shown more emotion? He had been nothing to her but a name—a hateful name—for years.

My speculation was cut short by the peculiar action of a dark-skinned, Latin-American-looking man whose face I had not noticed in the crowd before the arrival of Mrs Maddox. As she left he followed her out.

Curious, I turned and went out also. I reached the street door just in time to see Irene Maddox climb into a car with two other people.

'Who are they?' I asked a boy standing by the door.

'Mr and Mrs Walcott,' he replied.

Even in death the family feud persisted. The Walcotts had not even entered.

'Did you know that the Walcotts brought Mrs Maddox here?' I asked Hastings as I returned to Kennedy.

'No, but I'm not surprised,' he returned. 'You remember I told you Frances took Irene's part. Walcott must have returned from the city as soon as he heard of the tragedy.'

'Who was that sallow-faced individual who followed her out?' I asked. 'Did you notice him?'

'Yes, I saw him, but I don't know who he can be,' replied Hastings. 'I don't think I ever saw him before.'

'That Latin-American?' interposed Kennedy, who had completed his first investigation and made arrangements to co-operate with the coroner in carrying on the autopsy in his own laboratory. 'I was wondering myself whether he could have any connection with Paquita. Where is she now?'

'At the Harbour House, I suppose,' answered Hastings—'that is, if she is in town.

Kennedy hurried out of the establishment ahead of us and we looked down the street in time to see our man headed in the direction the Walcott automobile had taken.

He had too good a start of us, however, and before we could overtake him he had reached the Harbour House and entered. We had gained considerably on him, but not enough to find out where he went in the big hotel.

The Harbour House was a most attractive, fashionable hostelry, a favourite run for motor parties out from the city. On the water-front stood a large, red-roofed, stucco building known as the Casino entirely given over to amusements. Its wide porch of red tiles, contrasting with the innumerable white tables on it, looked out over the sheltered mouth of Westport Bay and on into the Sound, where, faintly outlined on the horizon, one saw the Connecticut shore.

Back of the Casino, and on a hill so that it looked directly over the roof of the lower building, was the hotel itself, commonly known as the Lodge, a new, up-to-date, shingle-sheathed building with every convenience that money and an expensive architect could provide. The place was ideal for summer sports— golf, tennis, motoring, bathing, boating, practically everything one could wish.

As we walked through the Lodge we could almost feel in

the air the excited gossip that the death of Maddox had created in the little summer colony at Westport.

Vainly seeking our dark-skinned man, we crossed to the Casino. As we approached the porch Hastings took Kennedy's arm.

'There are Shelby Maddox and Winifred Walcott,' he whispered.

'I should like to meet them,' said Kennedy, glancing at the couple whom Hastings had indicated at the far end of the porch.

Following the lawyer, we approached them.

Shelby Maddox was a tall young chap, rather good-looking, inclined to the athletic, and with that deferential, interested manner which women find almost irresistible.

As we approached he was talking earnestly, oblivious to everything else. I could not blame him. Winifred was a slender, vivacious girl, whose grey-blue eyes caught and held yours even while you admired her well-rounded cheeks, innocent of make-up. Her high forehead denoted an intellect which the feminine masses of puffy light-brown hair made all the more charming. One felt her personality in every action. She was not afraid of sun and air. A pile of the more serious magazines near her indicated that she was quite as much alive to the great movements that are stirring the world today as she was to the outdoor life that glowed in her face. It was easy to see that Shelby Maddox was having a new experience.

'Good morning,' greeted Hastings.

Winifred smiled, but Shelby was plainly annoyed at the intrusion of the lawyer. I could not make out whether there was an aversion to Hastings behind the annoyance or not.

The introductions over, we sat down for a moment. Hastings had been careful not to say that Kennedy was a detective, but to hint that he was a friend and, by implication, a lawyer.

'It must have been a severe shock when you heard what had happened,' he began, speaking to Winifred.

'It was, indeed,' she replied gravely. 'You see, I stayed here at the Harbour House while my brother and sister-in-law were on the yacht. Johnson came off early because he had to go to the city, and telephoned up to the room that they were going to be late and Frances would stay out on the yacht. Then when I came down this morning they were just bringing the body ashore.'

She shuddered at the recollection and Shelby flashed a look at Kennedy as though he could knife him for bringing up the distasteful subject. It seemed as though Shelby Maddox was pretty unconcerned about his brother's death.

'Strange that you heard nothing on the yacht,' switched Kennedy, looking full at Shelby.

'We didn't,' returned the young man, but in a tone that showed his attention was somewhere else.

I followed the direction of his eyes.

A petite, frilly, voluptuous figure stood in the doorway. She had an almost orchid beauty that more than suggested the parasite. Of a type quite the opposite of Winifred, she had nevertheless something interesting about her. For the born adventuress is always a baffling study.

Even before Hastings whispered I knew it must be Paquita.

She passed across the porch toward a flight of steps that led down to the shore, and as she did so nodded to Shelby with a smile, at the same time casting a look at Winifred such as only one woman can when she is taking in another at a glance. Winifred was first of all a woman. Her face flushed almost imperceptibly, but her own glance of estimation never faltered. I felt that there was a silent clash. Winifred was the antithesis of Paquita.

Shelby failed even with his cigarette to cover up his confusion. But as I searched his face I thought I saw one thing at least. Whatever might or might not have been the truth in Hastings's story of Shelby's acquaintance with Paquita once, it was evident now that Winifred Walcott quite filled his eye.

As she paused before going down the steps Paquita darted

back one more look at Shelby. Had he once felt the lure? At least now he made no move. And Paquita was insanely jealous.

'I should like to have Mr Kennedy look over the *Sybarite*, especially the room which I sealed,' suggested Hastings in a tone which was not peremptory, but nevertheless was final.

Shelby looked from Hastings to Winifred. The passing of Paquita seemed to have thrown a cloud over the sunshine which had brightened the moments before. He was torn between two emotions. There was no denying the request of Hastings. Yet this was no time to leave Winifred suspicious.

'I think you had better go,' she said finally, as Shelby hesitated.

'Would you not be one of the party?' he asked eagerly.

'I don't think I could stand it,' she replied hastily.

It was perfectly natural. Yet I could see that it left Shelby uncertain of her real reason.

Reluctantly he said goodbye and we four made our way down the dock to the float where was moored a fast tender of the yacht. We climbed aboard, and the man in charge started the humming, many-cylindered engine. We darted off in a cloud of spray.

Once I saw Kennedy looking back, and I looked back also. In the far corner of the Casino stood the sallow-faced man, watching us intently. Who and what could he be?

Westport Bay is one of those fjords, as they almost might be called, which run in among the beautifully wooded hills of the north shore of Long Island.

The *Sybarite* was lying at anchor a mile or so off-shore. As we approached her we saw that she was a 150-foot, long, low-lying craft of the new type, fitted with gas engines, and built quite as much for comfort as for speed. She was an elaborately built craft, with all the latest conveniences, having a main saloon, dining-room, library, and many state-rooms, all artistically decorated. In fact, it must have cost a small fortune merely to run the yacht.

As we boarded it Shelby led the way to the sheltered deck aft, and we sat down for a moment to become acquainted,

'Mito,' he called to a Japanese servant, 'take the gentlemen's hats. And bring us cigars.'

The servant obeyed silently. Evidently Shelby spared nothing that made for comfort.

'First of all,' began Craig, 'I want to see the state-room where Marshall Maddox slept.'

Shelby arose, apparently willingly enough, and led the way to the lower berth deck. Hastings carefully examined the seal which he had left on the door and, finding it intact, broke it and unlocked the door for us.

It was a bedroom rather than a state-room. The walls were panelled in wood and the port-hole was finished inside to look like a window. It was toward this port-hole that Kennedy first directed his attention, opening it and peering out at the water below.

'Quite large enough for a man to get through—or throw a body through,' he commented, turning to me.

I looked out also. 'It's a long way to the water,' I remarked, thinking perhaps he meant that a boat might have nosed up alongside and someone have entered that way.

'Still, if one had a good-sized cruiser, one might reach it by standing on the roof of the cabin,' he observed. 'At any rate, there'd be difficulty in disposing of a body that way.'

He turned. The wind had swung the yacht around so that the sun streamed in through the open port. Kennedy bent down and picked up some little bright slivers of thin metal that lay scattered here and there on the carpet.

He looked about at the furniture, then bent down and examined the side of the bedstead. It seemed to be pitted with little marks. He rose, and as he did so his gaze fell on one of the brass fittings of the cabin. It seemed to have turned green, almost to be corroded. With his penknife he scraped off some of the corrosion and placed it on a piece of paper, which he folded up.

The examination of the state-room completed, Shelby took us about the boat. First of all, he showed us the handsomely furnished main saloon opening into a little library, almost as if it were an apartment.

'It was here,' he volunteered, 'that we held the conference last night.'

For the first time I became aware, although Kennedy had noticed it before, that when we boarded the *Sybarite* Mito had been about. He had passed twice down the hall while we were in the state-room occupied by Marshall Maddox. He was now busy in the library, but on our entrance had withdrawn deferentially, as though not wishing to intrude.

Henceforth I watched the Japanese keenly as he padded about the boat. Everywhere we went I fancied that he turned up. He seemed ubiquitous. Was it that he was solicitous of the wants of his master? Had he received instructions from him? Did the slant-eyed Oriental have something hidden behind that inscrutable face of his?

There did not seem to be anything else that we could discover aboard the yacht. Though we interviewed the officer and those of the crew who had been on watch, we were unable to find out from them that anything unusual had been observed, either as far as any other boat was concerned or on the *Sybarite* itself. In spite of them, the affair was as completely shrouded in mystery as ever.

Having looked the yacht over, Kennedy seemed now to be eager to get ashore again.

'I hope you are satisfied, gentlemen?' asked Shelby at last as our tour brought us to the mahogany steps that led from the outside of the white hull to the tender which had brought us out.

'Very well—so far,' returned Kennedy.

Maddox looked up quickly, but did not ask what he meant. 'If there is any way in which I can be of service to you,' he continued, 'you have only to command me. I have as much reason as anyone to clear up the mystery in this unfortunate affair. I believe I will go ashore with you.'

He did not need to say that he was eager to get back to see

Winifred Walcott, any more than Kennedy needed to tell me that he would like to see our sallow-faced friend again.

The tender skimmed over the waves, throwing the spray gaily as we sped back to the Harbour House dock.

We landed and Maddox excused himself, repeating his desire to aid us. Down the beach toward the bathhouses I could make out the frilly Paquita, surrounded now by several of the bathers, all men. Maddox saw her, but paid no attention. He was headed for the veranda of the Lodge.

The day was growing older and the Casino was beginning to liven up. In the exquisitely appointed ballroom, which was used also for morning and afternoon dances, strains of the one-step attracted some dozen couples. Kennedy sauntered along, searching the faces we passed in the hope of seeing someone who might be of value to know on the case, now and then reminding Hastings not to neglect to point out anyone who might lend aid. Hastings saw no one, however, and as we mounted the steps to the Lodge excused himself for a minute to send some telegrams to those of the family whom he had forgotten.

We had promised to meet him in the lobby by the desk, and thither Kennedy bent his steps.

'I think I'll look over the register,' he remarked, as we approached the busiest part of the hotel. 'Perhaps, too, some of the clerks may know something.'

There was nothing on the register, apparently, for after turning it around and running through it he merely laid his finger on the name 'Señorita Paquita Gonzales, Maid and Chauffeur, New York,' written under the date of the day before the arrival of the Maddoxes for the conference, and among the last of the day, showing that she had arrived late.

As we were looking over the names we were startled by a voice softly speaking behind us.

'Well, I should have known you fellows would be out here before long. It's a big case. Don't notice me here. I'll see you in the writing-room. It's empty now.'

We turned in surprise. It was our old friend Burke, of the Secret Service.

He had already lounged off, and we followed without seeming to do so, stopping only for a moment at the news-stand.

'Why are you here?' demanded Craig, pointedly, as we three settled ourselves in an angle of the deserted writing-room.

'For the same reason that you are,' Burke returned, with a smile; then added gravely, 'I can trust you, Kennedy.'

Craig was evidently much impressed by the low tone and the manner of the detective, but said nothing.

'They tell me Hastings was in town this morning, at your laboratory,' went on Burke. 'Too bad he didn't take the time to call up his office. But he knows something now—that is, if he has that note I left for him.'

'Why, what is that?' chorused both Craig and I.

Just then Hastings himself almost ran into the room as if his life depended on finding us.

As he saw us he darted over to our corner.

'You are Mr Burke, of the Secret Service?' he queried as Burke nodded. 'Kennedy, the safe in the office of Maddox Munitions in New York was robbed late last night or early this morning and the model of the telautomaton is stolen!'

CHAPTER III

THE CABARET DANCER

WE could only stare from Burke to Hastings, startled at the magnitude of the affair as it developed so rapidly.

For a moment Hastings was at a loss, then darted quickly into a telephone-booth to call up his office on long distance for confirmation of the news.

As we waited I happened to glance out into the lobby. At the far end, in an angle, to my surprise I saw Shelby and Paquita. Evidently she had hovered about, waiting for a chance to find him alone, and had at last succeeded.

Already Kennedy and Burke had seen them.

Paquita was talking earnestly. Of course, we could not over-hear what was said, and they were so placed that even if we moved closer to them they would be likely to see us. Still, from our corner we could observe without being observed.

It seemed as if Paquita were making a desperate effort to attract Shelby, while, on his part, it was quite evident that he was endeavouring to get away.

Paquita was indeed a fascinating figure. From what I had already observed, a score of the young fellows about the Harbour House would have given their eyes to have been in Shelby's place. Why was he seeking so to avoid her? Was it that he did not dare to trust himself with the little dancer? Or was there some hold that she had over him which he feared?

The interview had not proceeded long when Shelby delib-erately seemed to excuse himself and walked away. Paquita looked after him as he hurried off, and I would have given much to have been close enough to observe her expression. Was it one of fury, of a woman scorned? At any rate, I would have wagered that it boded no good for Shelby.

I turned to say something to Kennedy and found that he was looking in another direction. We were not the only observers. From a window outside on the porch the sallow-faced man was also watching. As Shelby walked away the man seemed to be very angry. Was it the anger of jealousy because Paquita was with Shelby or was it anger because Shelby had repulsed her advances? Who was the fellow and why was he so interested in the little dancer and the young millionaire?

Hastings rejoined us from the telephone-booth, his face almost pale.

'It's a fact,' he groaned. 'They have been trying to reach me all day, but could not. The secret of the telautomaton stolen—the secret that is too terrible to be in the hands of anyone except the Government. How did you hear of it?' he asked Burke.

Burke answered slowly, watching the expression on Hastings's face. 'When the cashier of the company arrived at the office this morning he found the safe had been rifled. It seems an almost incomprehensible thing—as you will understand when you see it for yourself. The cashier telephoned at once to the Secret Service in the Custom-House, and I jumped out on the case. You did not go to your own office. I did a little hasty deduction—guessed that you might have gone to see Kennedy. At any rate I wanted to see him myself.'

Kennedy interrupted long enough to tell about the revolver-shot and the attack on Hastings at our very door.

'Whew!' exclaimed Burke, 'just missed you. Well,' he added, with a dry sort of humour, 'I missed you, too, and decided to come out here on the train. Kennedy, you must go back to town with me and look at that safe. How anybody could get into it is a mystery beyond me. But the telautomaton is gone. My orders are simple—get it back!'

For a moment neither Kennedy nor Hastings spoke. It was

most peculiar—the plans gone in Westport, the model gone in New York.

'Who could have stolen the model?' I asked finally. 'Have you any theory, Burke?'

'A theory, yes,' he replied slowly, 'but no facts to back it. I suppose you know that the war has driven out some of the most clever and astute crooks that Paris, Vienna, London, and other capitals ever produced. The fact is that we are at present in the hands of the largest collection of high-grade foreign criminals that has ever visited this country. I think it is safe to say that at present there are more foreign criminals of high degree in New York and at the fashionable summer resorts than could be found in all the capitals of Europe combined. They have evaded military service because at heart they are cowards and hate work. War is hard work. Then, there is little chance of plying their trade, for their life is the gay life of the cafés and boule-vards. Besides, America is the only part of the world where prosperity is reigning. So they are here, preying on American wealth. Suppose someone—some foreign agent—wanted the telautomaton. There are plenty of tools he could use for his purpose in obtaining it.'

The countenance of the sallow-faced man recurred to me. It was an alarming possibility that Burke's speculation raised. Were we really not involved in a pure murder case, but in the intricacies of the machinations of some unknown power?

Burke looked at his watch, then again at Kennedy. 'Really, I think you ought to go back to town,' he reiterated, 'and take the case up there.'

'And leave these people all here to do as they please, cover up what they will?' objected Hastings, who had tried to prevent just that sort of thing by bringing Kennedy out post-haste.

'My men are perfectly competent to watch anything that goes on at Westport,' returned Burke. 'I have them posted all about and I'm digging up some good stuff. Already I know just what happened the night before the conference. That cabaret dancer, Paquita, motored out here and arrived about the time the *Sybarite* cast anchor. She met Shelby Maddox at the Casino and they had a gay supper party. But it ended early. She knew that Marshall Maddox was coming the next day. I know he had known her in the city. As to Shelby we don't know yet. The meeting may have been chance or it may have been prearranged.'

I recalled not only the little incident we had just seen, but the glance of jealousy Paquita had given Shelby when she saw him with Winifred. What did it mean? Had Shelby Maddox been using Paquita against his brother, and now was he trying to cast her off? Or was Burke's theory correct? Was she a member of a clever band of super-criminals, playing one brother against the other for some ulterior end? Was the jealousy feigned or was it real, after all?

'What I am endeavouring to do now,' went on Burke, 'is to trace the doings of Paquita the night of the murder. I cannot find out whether she came out at the invitation of Marshall Maddox or not. Perhaps it was Shelby. I don't know. If it was Marshall, what about his former wife? Did he suppose that she would not be here? Or didn't he care?'

'Perhaps—blackmail,' suggested Hastings, who, as a lawyer, had had more or less to do with such attempts.

Burke shook his head. 'It might have been, of course, but in that case don't you think you, as Maddox's lawyer, would have heard something of it? You have not—have you? You don't know anything about her?'

Burke regarded the lawyer keenly, as though he might be concealing something. But Hastings merely shook his head.

'Mr Maddox did not confide his weaknesses to me,' Hastings remarked coldly.

'If we are going back to the city,' returned Burke, cheerfully changing the subject, to the evident surprise of Hastings, 'I must find my operative, Riley, and let him know what to do while we are gone.'

'Look,' muttered Kennedy under his breath to us and nodding down the lobby.

Shelby Maddox had sought and found Winifred, and was chatting as animatedly as if there had been no Paquita in the world less than five minutes before.

As we watched, Hastings remarked: 'It was only the day before the murder that Shelby first met Winifred Walcott. I believe he had never seen his brother-in-law's sister before. She had been away in the West ever since Frances Maddox married Walcott. Winifred seems to have made a quick conquest.'

Remembering what had happened before, I took a quick look about to see whether anyone else was as interested as ourselves. Seeing no one, Kennedy and I strolled down the corridor quietly.

We had not gone far before we stopped simultaneously. Nestled in the protecting wings of a big wicker chair was Paquita, and as we watched her she never took her eyes from the couple ahead.

What did this constant espionage of Shelby mean? For one thing, we must place this little adventuress in the drama of the Maddox house of hate. We moved back a bit where we could see them all.

A light footfall beside us caused us to turn suddenly. It was Mito, padding along on some errand to his master. As he passed I saw that his beady eyes had noted that we were watching Shelby. There was no use to retreat now. We had been observed. Mito passed, bestowing a quick sidewise glance on Paquita as he did so. A moment later he approached Shelby deferentially and stood waiting a few feet away.

Shelby looked up and saw his valet, bowed an excuse to Winifred, and strode over to where Mito was standing. The conversation was brief. What it was about we had no means of determining, but of one thing we were certain. Mito had not neglected a hasty word to his master that he was watched. For, an instant later when Mito had been dismissed, Shelby returned to Winifred and they walked deliberately out of the hotel across a wide stretch of open lawn in the direction of the tennis-courts. To follow him was a confession that we were watching. Evidently, too, that had been Shelby's purpose, for as he chatted he turned half-way, now and then, to see if they were observed. Again Mito padded by and I fancied I caught a subtle smile on his saturnine face. If we were watching, we were ourselves no less watched.

There was nothing to be gained in this blind game of hide-and-seek, and Kennedy was evidently not yet prepared to come out into the open. Paquita, too, seemed to relinquish the espionage for the moment, for she rose and walked slowly toward the Casino, where she was quickly joined by some of her more ardent admirers.

I glanced at Kennedy.

'I think we had better go back to Burke and Hastings,' he decided. 'Burke is right. His men can do almost as much here as we could at present. Besides, if we go away the mice may play. They will think we have been caught napping. That tel-automaton robbery is surely our next big point of attack. Here it is first of all the mystery of Marshall Maddox's death, and I cannot do anything more until the coroner sends me, as he has promised, the materials from the autopsy. Even then I shall need to be in my laboratory if I am to discover anything.'

'Your sallow-faced friend seemed quite interested in you,' commented Burke as we rejoined him.

'How's that?' inquired Kennedy.

'From here I could see him, following every move you made,' explained the Secret Service man.

Kennedy bit his lip. Not only had Mito seen us and conveyed a warning to Shelby, but the dark-skinned man of mystery had been watching us all. Evidently the situation was considerably mixed. Perhaps if we went away it would really clear itself up and we might place these people more accurately with reference to one another.

Burke looked at his watch hurriedly. 'There's a train that leaves in twenty minutes,' he announced. 'We can make the station in a car in fifteen.'

Kennedy and I followed him to the door, while Hastings trailed along reluctantly, not yet assured that it would be safe to leave Westport so soon.

At the door a man stepped up deferentially to Burke, with a glance of inquiry at us.

'It's all right, Riley,' reassured Burke. 'You can talk before them. One of my best operatives, Riley, gentlemen. I shall leave this end in your charge, Val.'

'All right, sir,' returned the Secret Service operative. 'I was just going to say, about that dark fellow we saw gum-shoeing it about. We're watching him. We picked him up on the beach during the bathing hour. Do you know who he is? He's the private detective whom Mrs Maddox had watching her husband and that Paquita woman. I don't know what he's watching her yet for, sir, but,' Riley lowered his voice for emphasis, 'once one of the men saw him talking to Paquita. Between you and me, I wouldn't be surprised if he was trying to double-cross Mrs Maddox.'

Hastings opened his eyes in wonder at the news. As for me, I began to wonder if I had not been quite mistaken in my estimate of Irene Maddox. Was she the victim, the cat's-paw of someone?

Riley was not finished, however. 'Another thing before you leave, Mr Burke,' he added. 'The night watchman at the Harbour House tells me that he saw that Japanese servant of Shelby Maddox last night, or, rather, early this morning. He didn't go down to the dock and the watchman thought that perhaps he had been left ashore by mistake and couldn't get out on the *Sybarite*.

'That's impossible,' cut in Hastings quickly. 'He was on the yacht last night when we went to bed and he woke me up this morning.'

'I know it,' nodded Riley. 'You see, I figure that he might have come off the yacht in a row-boat and landed down the shore on the beach. Then he might have got back. But what for?'

The question was unanswered, but not, we felt, unanswerable.

'Very well, Riley,' approved Burke. 'Keep right after anything that turns up. And don't let that Paquita out of sight of some of the men a minute. Goodbye. We've just time to catch the train.'

Hastings was still unreconciled to the idea of leaving town, in spite of the urgency of the developments in New York.

'I think it's all right,' reassured Kennedy. 'You see, if I stayed I'd have to call on an agency, anyhow. Besides, I got all I could and the only thing left would be to watch them. Perhaps if I go away they may do something they wouldn't dare otherwise. In that case we have planted a fine trap. You can depend on it that Burke's men will do more for us, now, than any private agency.'

Hastings agreed reluctantly, and as we hurried back to New York on the train Kennedy quizzed Burke as he had Hastings on the journey out.

There was not much that Burke could add to what he had already told us. The robbery of the safe in the Maddox office had been so cleverly executed that I felt that it would rank along with the historic cases. No ordinary yeggs or petermen had performed this operation, and as the train neared the city we were all on edge to learn what possibly might have been uncovered during the hours that we had been working on the other end of the case out at Westport.

CHAPTER IV

As we crossed the city Hastings, remembering the sudden attack that had been made on him on the occasion of his last visit, looked about nervously in the crowds.

Sometimes I wondered whether the lawyer had been frank with us and told all he knew. However, no one seemed to be following him and we lost no time in hustling from the railroad terminal to the office of Maddox Munitions.

The office was on the top floor of the new Maddox Building, I knew, one of the recent tower skyscrapers down-town.

As we turned into the building and were passing down the corridor to the express elevator a man stepped out from behind a pillar. Hastings drew back nervously. But it was Burke that the man wanted to see. He dropped back and we halted, catching only the first whispered sentence.

'We've been watching Randall, sir,' I overheard the man say, 'but he hasn't done anything—yet.

There was a hasty conference between the man and Burke, who rejoined us in a few seconds, while the man went back to his post of watching, apparently, every face of the crowd that thronged forward to the elevators or bustled away from them.

'My men have been at work ever since I was called in on the case,' explained Burke to Kennedy. 'You see, I had only time to map out a first campaign for them, and then I decided to hurry off to find you and later to look over the ground at Westport. Randall is the cashier. I can't say that I had anything on him—really—but then you never can tell, you know.'

We rode up in the elevator and entered the imposing offices of the great munitions corporation, where the executive business was conducted for the score or more plants owned or controlled by the company in various parts of the country.

Hastings led the way familiarly past the girl sitting at a desk in the outside office and we soon found ourselves in the section that was set apart for the accounting department, over which Randall had charge.

It seemed that the lawyer was well acquainted with the cashier as he introduced him to us, and we noted that Randall was a man approaching middle age, at least outwardly, with that solid appearance that seems to come to men who deal with numbers and handle large sums of money.

While we talked I looked about curiously. Randall had an inner office, though in the outer office stood the huge safe which was evidently the one which had been rifled.

The cashier himself seemed to have lost, for the time, some of his customary poise. Trying to make him out, I fancied that he was nearly frantic with fear lest he might be suspected, not so much, perhaps, of having had anything to do with the loss of the telautomaton as of being remiss in his duties, which included the guardianship of the safe.

The very anxiety of the man seemed to be a pretty good guarantee of his honesty. There could be no doubt of how deeply he felt the loss, not only because it was of such vital importance, but from the mere fact that it might reflect on his own management of his department.

'It seems almost incredible,' Randall exclaimed as we stood talking. 'The most careful search has failed to reveal any clue that would show even how access to the office was gained. Not a lock on any of the doors has been tampered with, not a scratch indicates the use of a jimmy on them or on the windows. In fact, entrance by the windows at such a height above the surrounding buildings is almost beyond the range of possibility as well as probability. How could it have been accomplished? I am forced to come back to the explanation that the outer office doors had been opened by a key!'

'There were keys—in the hands of several people, I suppose?' inquired Kennedy.

'Oh, yes! There are in every large office like this,' hastened Randall.

'Mr Maddox had a key, of course?'

'Yes.'

'And you?'

'Certainly.'

'Who else?'

'The agent of the building.'

'I mean who else in the office?'

'My assistant—oh, several. Still, I am sure that no one had a key except those whom we could trust.'

'Did Shelby Maddox ever have a key?' cut in Hastings.

The cashier nodded in the negative, for the moment surprised, apparently, at the very idea that Shelby would ever have had interest enough in business to have such a thing.

I saw Burke looking in covert surprise at Hastings as he asked the question. For the moment I wondered why he asked it. Had he really thought that Shelby might have a key? Or was he trying hard to make a case? What was his own connection with the affair? Kennedy had been looking keenly about.

'Is that the safe over there?' he indicated. 'I should like to examine it.'

'Yes, that's it, and that's the strangest part of it,' hastened Randall, as though eager to satisfy us on all points, leading the way to a modern chrome-steel strong-box of a size almost to suggest a miniature bank vault: surely a most formidable thing to tackle.

'You see,' he went on nervously, as though eager to convince us, 'there is not a mark on it to show that it has been tampered with. Yet the telautomaton is gone. I know that it was there last night, all right, for I looked in the compartment where we keep the little model, as well as the papers relating to it. It is a small model, and of course was not charged with explosive. But it is quite sufficient for its purpose, and if its war-head were actually filled with a high explosive it would be sufficiently deadly against any ordinary ship in spite of its miniature size.'

Kennedy had already begun his examination, first of all assuring himself that it was useless to try to look for finger-prints, inasmuch as nearly everybody had touched the safe since the robbery and any such clue, had it once existed, must have been rendered valueless.

'How did you discover the loss?' I ventured as Craig bent to his work. 'Did anything excite your suspicion?'

'N-no,' returned the cashier. 'Only I have been very method-ical about the safe. The model was kept in that compartment at the bottom. I make it a practice in opening and closing the safe to see that that and several other valuable things we keep in it are there. This morning nothing about the office and certainly nothing about the safe suggested that there was anything wrong until I worked the combination. The door swung open and I looked through it. I could scarcely believe my own eyes when I saw that that model was gone. I couldn't have been more astonished if I had come in and found the door open. I am the only one who knows the combination—except for a copy kept in a safety deposit box known only to Marshall Maddox and Mr Hastings.

Before any of us could say a word Kennedy had completed his first examination and was facing us. 'I can't find a mark on it,' he confessed. 'No "soup" has been used to blow it. Nitroglycerin enough might have wrecked the building. The old "can-opener" is of course out of the question with a safe like this. No instrument could possibly rip a plate off this safe unless you gave the ripper unlimited time. There's not a hint that thermit or the oxy-acetylene blow-pipe have been used. Not a spot on the safe indicates the presence of anything that can produce those high temperatures.'

'Yet the telautomaton is gone!' persisted Hastings.

Kennedy was looking about, making a quick search of the office.

As his eye travelled over the floor he took a step or two forward and bent down. Under a sanitary desk, near a window, he picked up what looked like a small piece of rubber tubing. He looked at it with interest, though it conveyed no idea to me. It was simply a piece of rubber tubing. Then he took another step to the window and raised it, looking out. Far below, some hundred or more feet, was the roof of the next building, itself no mean structure for height.

'Have you searched the roof below?' he asked, turning to Burke.

Burke shook his head. 'How could anyone get in that way?' he negatived.

'Well—search the roof below,' repeated Kennedy.

Even though he did not understand what good might come of such a strange request, Burke had known Kennedy long enough not to question his actions. He moved away, seeking one of his men whom he could send on the errand.

While we waited Kennedy continued to question Randall.

'Mr Maddox was very careful of his key, I suppose?' he ventured.

'Yes, sir, very careful. So we all were of the combination, too. Not even my assistant knows that. If I should drop dead, there would be only one way to get it—to open that safety deposit box, and that must be done by someone with the proper authority. It has all been carefully safeguarded.'

'You know of no one intmate with Mr Maddox—who might have obtained the key—or the combination?'

I wondered at what Kennedy was driving. Had he the little dancer, Paquita, in mind? Did he suspect that she might have wormed from Maddox the secret? Or was he, too, thinking of Shelby?

Randall shook his head, and Kennedy continued his quick examination of the office, questioning the assistant, who was unable to add anything of value.

So far there had been nothing to show that the robbery might not have been an inside job. As Kennedy was still pondering on the new mystery that confronted us Burke approached with the man whom he had sent to make the search.

His face indicated that he was puzzled. In his hand he was holding a disc that was something like the flat telephone receivers one sees often on interior office telephones. To it was attached a rubber tube like that which Kennedy had picked up in the office a few minutes before.

'My man found this thing on the roof below,' explained Burke, with a look of inquiry. 'What do you suppose it is? How did it get there?'

Kennedy took the disc and began examining it carefully, fitting on the other rubber tube.

'Perhaps it had served its purpose—was no longer of use,' he meditated. 'At any rate, if someone had to get away with that telautomaton he would not want to burden himself with anything else that was unnecessary. He might very well have discarded this.'

What the thing was I could not imagine. We all crowded about, examining it, not even Burke offering an explanation.

Suddenly Craig's face lightened up. He thrust the tubes into his ears and walked over to a smaller safe that was still locked. As he turned the combination handle he held the black disc up close to the safe. The intent look on his face caused us all to watch without a word. Around and around he turned the handle slowly. Finally he stopped. Then, with a few quick turns, he gave the door a pull and it swung open on its oiled hinges.

We fairly gasped. 'What is it?' I demanded. 'Magic?'

Kennedy smiled. 'Not magic, but black science,' he replied. 'This is a burglar's microphone.'

'A burglar's microphone?' I repeated. 'What's that?'

'Well,' he explained, 'the microphone is now used by burglars for picking combination locks. When you turn the lock a slight sound is made when the proper number comes opposite the working part. It can be heard by a sensitive ear, sometimes, I am told. However, it is imperceptible to most persons. But by using a microphone it is an easy matter to hear the sounds. Having listened to the fall of the tumblers, the expert can determine what are the real numbers of the combination and open the safe. That is what happened in this case.'

We followed Kennedy speechless. What was there to say? We had already seen him open a safe with it himself.

Though we were thus far on our way, we had not even a clue as to the identity of the criminal or criminals.

I recalled Burke's own theory as he had expressed it. Could it be that someone had betrayed to a foreign government agent the priceless secret of the telautomaton?

CHAPTER V

THE WHITE LIGHT CAFÉ

'As long as I am back in the city,' continued Kennedy, while we stared at one another, wondering what next move to make, 'I think that I had better take the opportunity to make some investigations in my laboratory which would be impossible out at Westport.'

In the meantime Burke had been examining the burglar's microphone, turning it over and over thoughtfully, as if in the hope that it might furnish some clue.

'It might have been possible,' he ruminated, 'for someone to get into the building at night if the night watchman was off his guard and he had a key to the building. I suppose he might get out again, too, under the same circumstances.'

'A good lead,' agreed Kennedy. 'While you are finding the night watchman and getting anything else along that line of reconstructing what actually did take place it will give me just the chance I need. Let us meet in two or three hours—say, at Mr Hastings's office. Let me see, I believe your firm is Hastings and Halsey, isn't it?'

'Hastings and Halsey,' repeated the lawyer. 'You are quite welcome to meet again there. You know where it is, on Wall Street?'

We noted the number and Kennedy and I hurried up-town to the laboratory which we had left only a few short hours before.

Already there were waiting for him, by special messenger, the materials from the autopsy which had been promised by the Westport coroner, who for once had appreciated the importance of a case and had acted with speed and decision.

Kennedy lost no time in throwing off his coat and donning his acid-stained smock. For some minutes I watched him in silence as he arranged his jars and beakers and test-tubes for the study which he had in mind. He had taken some of the material and placed it over a Bunsen burner in an apparatus which looked like a miniature still. Another apparatus which he took from a cabinet was disposed on a table. It seemed to consist primarily of three tubes. In one was a slit, and through the slit evidently rays of light were caused to stream. Inside I saw a lens. Each of the tubes seemed to radiate from a triangular prism of some substance that looked like glass. Two of the radiating tubes had an eye-piece and on one was a sort of scale.

As Kennedy made these rapid preparations he paused now and then to study carefully the slivers of bright metal he had picked up from the carpet in the state-room, while on a porcelain plate he placed the powder which he had scraped from the brass fittings.

'I'm not doing you a bit of good here, Craig,' I remarked, at length. 'Isn't there something I can do while you are working? I can come back here in time to go down and meet Hastings and Burke with you.'

He paused a moment. 'Yes,' he replied, 'there is something that you might be doing. I have been wondering just how intimate that little Mexican dancer was with Marshall Maddox and whether Shelby actually knew her in New York before he met her out at Westport the other night. I think you might make some inquiries along that line, and by the time you find anything you may find me more interesting also.'

Glad of the opportunity to be of service, for anything was better than to sit about idle in the present high-keyed state of my nerves, I started out.

My first impulse was to visit the New Amsterdam Club, one of the oldest clubs in the city, of which I knew that Maddox had been a member.

I knew several men who were members, and I was sure that

among them I might find someone at the club at that time, and perhaps either from him learn something of Maddox or at least obtain an introduction to someone who did know.

I found that I had not acted without reason. In the big window that overlooked Fifth Avenue, ensconced in the deep leather chairs, looking out on the fashionable throng of shoppers who passed up and down the Avenue, I found several men, among whom was Conigsby, whom I had known for some time as assiduous first-nighter and man about town.

Conigsby welcomed me and I soon saw that the topic of conversation was the reports that all had been reading in the papers about the mystery that shrouded the death of Marshall Maddox.

'Peculiar fellow, Maddox,' commented Conigsby. 'What do the boys down on the *Star* have to say about the case, Jameson?'

I had no desire to commit myself, yet I wanted to glean as much as I could. For although we are prone to accuse the ladies of gossip, I think most men will back me up when I say that there is no place for the genuine article that cannot be beaten by a comfortable window in a club where congenial spirits have gathered over a succession of brandies and soda.

'It promises to be the great case of the year,' I returned guardedly. 'So far, I understand there is much more in the life of Maddox than even some of his friends suspect.

At the mere suggestion of scandal all eyes were fixed on me. Yet I was determined to speak in riddles and betray nothing, in the hope that some of them might open up a rich vein of inquiry.

Conigsby laughed. 'Perhaps more than *some* of his friends imagined—yes,' he repeated.

'Why, what was it?' inquired one of the group. 'Is there another woman in the case? I thought Maddox was divorced.'

'So he was,' returned the clubman. 'I knew his wife, Irene, before they were married. Really, it was a shame the way that man treated her. I can claim no special virtue,' he added, with a shrug, 'but then I haven't a wife—not so much as a friend who would care whether I was here or in No Man's Land. But Maddox—well, he was one of those men who have worked hard all their lives, but in middle age seem to begin sowing the wild oats they failed to sow in youth. You know the kind. I guess he must have reached the dangerous age for men, if there is such a thing.'

'What was it—chorus girls?' chimed in the other, ever ready for a spicy bit of gossip.

'Yes—lately cabaret dancers—one in particular—at The White Light—a little Mexican—Paquita.

'What—Paquita?' chorused the group, and I could see by the inflection that she was not unknown to several of them. 'You don't say. Well, you must admit he was a good picker.'

'I rather suspect that his acquaintance cost him high, though,' persisted Conigsby. 'Paquita has a scale of prices. It costs so much to take dinner with her. She'll drive out of an afternoon with you—but you must pay. There's a union scale.'

'It takes dough to make tarts,' frivolously suggested another of the group, forgetful of the tragedy that they were discussing.

Indeed, I was amazed at the nonchalant attitude they took. Yet, on analysis, I concluded that it also might be significant. No doubt the estimate of Maddox by his club members was more accurate than that of the world at large.

'If it had been Shelby,' put in another man, 'I wouldn't have been surprised.'

'Don't worry,' interposed Conigsby. 'Shelby Maddox is clever. Remember, Shelby is young. Underneath his wildness there is ambition. I think you'll hear more of that boy before we are through. I know him, and he's likely to prove a chip of the old Maddox block. Nothing that Shelby does would surprise me.'

'How about the other sister, Frances?' inquired another. 'Do you know her husband, Walcott?'

'Not very well. You're more likely to find him on Broad Street than Broadway. You know what I care for Broad Street. I'd never visit it if my bankers were not down there. Walcott has a deuced pretty little sister, though. I hear that Shelby is quite smitten.'

'Well, whatever you may think of him, I have seen Shelby Maddox with Paquita, too. I'll lay you a little bet that that little baggage knows something about the case. Remember, the murder was on Shelby's yacht.'

Conigsby shrugged. 'Quite possible—another case of notoriety for The White Light.'

'Notoriety for Paquita, you mean,' corrected another. 'I hear she plans to get back into musical comedy this fall. She's not at The White Light any longer.'

'Well, I think she'll make good,' agreed Conigsby. 'I wonder who the angel is for her new show?'

The conversation was now hopelessly drifting, and I excused myself. At least I had learned enough to give me an insight into another phase of the life of Marshall Maddox.

Pondering what I had just heard, I decided to wander over towards the café and theatre district, and drop into the cabaret which they had mentioned—The White Light.

As I entered the place in broad daylight I was struck by the sordidness of it. Deserted except by those who were cleaning up for the coming late afternoon and evening, it was positively tawdry. It needed the glamour of bright faces and night life, and even then it must be viewed through the bottom of a glass to wear even the semblance of attraction.

In the main dining-room of the café, grouped about the little dancing floor before the platform on which sat the orchestra when things were in full swing, stood innumerable little white tables. Just now there seemed to be no one there except a man at the piano and a girl who was evidently rehearsing her dance steps.

I paused for a moment and a waiter who had been arranging the tables for the coming crowd moved over to tell me that the place was not yet open.

I satisfied him that it was on other business that I had come, then asked him whether Paquita was at The White Light any more.

'No, sir,' he replied brusquely. 'She hasn't been here for several days. I've heard that she has gone away to the country—has another contract. It is a rehearsal for the girl who is to do her number that is going on now. Is there anything I can do for you?'

I thanked him. It was not the waiter I wanted, but the proprietor, Henri.

In a little office in the rear I at last discovered him, a rather stout, genial Frenchman, who had made a reputation as one of New York's restaurateurs to the *risqué*. I had known Henri once when I had the assignment on the *Star* that covered the theatre and hotel district, and I had no fear that he would not talk.

'Well, Henri,' I began cautiously, 'I suppose you saw in the papers this morning about your friend, Marshall Maddox?'

Henri, who was matching up cheques showing the business done up to an early hour of the morning, shrugged. 'Monsieur was more the friend of La Paquita than of me,' he returned, still matching cheques.

'Still, he came here a great deal,' I asserted, taking a chance.

'*Oui*,' he agreed, 'but it was not to see us. Always La Paquita, La Paquita. So different from his brother.'

'Indeed?' I queried, quite overjoyed at the turn the conversation was taking. 'Then you know Shelby, too?'

'Ver' well. Oh, yes. He has been here. A fine fellow, but—it is all right. Business is not for him. He is always ready for the good time—a sport, you call it?'

I smiled. 'Was he a friend of Paquita's, too?' I hazarded, watching Henri's face.

He lifted his eyebrows a fraction of an inch. 'No more than of the rest,' he returned, with a deprecating gesture. 'Pretty faces and figures all look good to Shelby,' he added, with a smile; then, seriously: 'But he will settle down. We will see him here no more, some day. Also I know his brother-in-law, Messtair Walcott. I do not like him.'

'Why?' I asked, somewhat amused at getting his point of view.

'Too quiet. He will come in, not often, perhaps, bow, maybe speak, then go away.'

I thought I 'got' him. One must be a good spender to appeal to Henri. I could not imagine Johnson Walcott as such. In fact, I could scarcely imagine him coming to Henri's at all.

'Paquita was quite intimate with Marshall Maddox, wasn't she?' I ventured again.

Henri brought into play his ready shrug. It was not for him to say anything about his patrons, much less about the dead. Still, his very manner gave the impression that his lips would not frame.

'Did anyone ever seem to be watching him here?' I asked, the thought of the sallow-faced man at Westport recurring to my mind.

Henri stopped matching his cheques and looked up. Was he growing suspicious of my disinterestedness?

'Such things are not unusual,' he answered, showing a fine assortment of ivory beneath his black moustache.

I met his eye frankly. He seemed to understand.

'Not for the *Star,* you understand?' he nodded, still looking at me fixedly.

'Oh, no, no!' I hastened, truthfully. 'I am not playing reporter now, Henri.'

He appeared to be satisfied, and it did not occur to him to inquire why else I should be interested.

'Yes,' he went on slowly, 'he has been watched. I have seen it myself. Several times there was a man who came in, Spanish-looking.'

'Did Mr Maddox know it?' I inquired, more eager than ever.

Henri shook his head negatively. 'Not until one day when La Paquita was talking to the man. Monsieur came in unexpectedly.'

The manager laughed a little to himself.

'Why do you laugh?' I asked. 'What happened?'

'Nothing,' he returned. 'It was not what happened. It was what she told him. So clever, too. She said it was a detective set to trail him by Mrs Maddox, that she had flirted with the man and found out.'

'Then you do not think he was a detective?' I asked, puzzled.

'How should I know?' replied Henri, with another question. 'It might have been. It might not have been. She is clever.'

'What did Maddox do?' I persisted. Was he more cautious?'

Again Henri shook his head. 'He gave orders that the man was not to be admitted. And we? He was a ver' wealthy man, Mr Maddox. We could not afford to lose him.'

'But this Spaniard,' I reiterated, convinced it was the same man whom we had seen at Westport, 'isn't it possible that Mrs Maddox really did pick him out as a detective in the hope that he might get acquainted with Paquita and so report on her husband?'

'We are just guessing, monsieur,' dodged Henri. 'I speak only of the things I know—and not all of them.'

He had evidently told me in substance about all that he was sure of. I knew him of old. Even after he had told his story he liked to leave a sort of 'continued in our next' at the close of it, just so that you would not think he was not what Broadway calls a 'live one.' I had absorbed about all that he had at first hand. It was enough. It gave me a view of the characters of the chief actors, from an angle which others did not know. I rose nonchalantly, thanked Henri, and sauntered out as I had in the old days when the *Star* picked on me to expose some new society scandal.

The visit to Henri's White Light cabaret had shown me one very important thing, however. Shelby Maddox had known Paquita before the night of the gay dinner party preceding the arrival of the Maddox family for the conference on the yacht.

What that might indicate I did not yet venture to guess. And yet I felt sure that it must prove significant. Else why had Paquita arrived at Westport at just that particular time? It seemed as though it must have something to do with the calling of the family conference.

Above all, however, stood forth the strange coincidence of the murder of Marshall Maddox, head of the family, and the stealing of the telautomaton, the most valuable single piece of property that the family owned. There was mystery enough in this case to satisfy even Kennedy.

CHAPTER VI

THE POISON GAS

A GLANCE at my watch was sufficient to assure me that I should have no time for further inquiries if I wanted to meet Kennedy before going down to the office of Hastings. I wanted to do that, too, for I felt sure that Craig would talk more freely to me than to the rest, and my interest in the affair had by this time become insatiable.

Accordingly, I retraced my steps to the laboratory. Kennedy was still at work, partly over some reactions in test-tubes, but mostly using the strange three-tubed instrument I had noted. As I outlined to him rapidly what I had discovered and the plain inferences to be drawn from it, he listened attentively, still working.

'Very good,' was Kennedy's sole comment as I concluded my story. 'That's very interesting—possibly very important. It begins to look as though Maddox had been in someone's way and that that someone was taking no chances in order to "get" him.'

'What have you discovered so far?' I hesitated, not sure yet whether he was willing to talk, for Kennedy never said anything, even to me, until he was perfectly sure of his ground.

'Marshall Maddox was not drowned, at least,' he vouchsafed.

'Not drowned?' I repeated, more to lead him on than because I was surprised.

'No. Whatever was the cause of his death, he was not killed by drowning. The lungs and stomach show that. In fact, I knew at Westport that he might have died a natural death or might even have been a suicide. But he certainly did not die of drowning. Only more careful tests than either the coroner or I could make at Westport were necessary.'

'How did it happen, then?' I continued, emboldened by his apparent readiness to talk.

Kennedy took a bottle with a ground-glass stopper and held it up so that I could see its greenish-yellow contents. Then he pulled out the stopper, covered with vaseline, for an instant and shoved it back again.

The instant was enough. A most unpleasant odour filled the laboratory. I felt a sense of suffocation in the chest, an irritation in the nose and throat, as though by the corrosive action of some gas on the air passages.

'If we could only have seen him before he died,' continued Kennedy, 'I suspect we should have found his face as blue as it was when we did see him, his lips violet, his pulse growing weaker until it was imperceptible, and perhaps he would have been raising blood. It would have been like an acute bronchitis, only worse. Look.'

From a little pin prick which he made on his own thumb Craig squeezed out a drop of blood into a beaker containing some distilled water.

'This is a spectroscope,' he explained, touching the instrument I had noticed. 'I think you are acquainted with it in a general way. Blood in water, diluted, shows the well-known dark bands between what we call "D" and "E." These are the dark bands of oxyhaemoglobin absorption. Now, I add to this, drop by drop, the water from that bottle which I uncorked. See—the bands gradually fade in intensity and finally disappear, leaving a complete and brilliant spectrum devoid of any bands whatever. In other words, here is a substance that actually affects the red colouring matter in the blood, bleaches it out, and does more—destroys it.'

I listened in amazement at the fiendish nature of his discovery.

'Marshall Maddox was overcome by the poison gas contained in a thin-shelled bomb that was thrown through his state-room window. The corrosion of the metal in the room gave me a clue to that. Then—'

'But what is this poison gas?' I demanded, horrified.

Kennedy looked at me fixedly a moment. 'Chlorine,' he replied simply; adding, 'the spectroscope shows that there is a total absence of pigment in the blood. You can readily see that it is no wonder, if it has this action, that death is sometimes so rapid as to be almost instantaneous. Why, man alive, this thing destroys without the possibility of reconstitution! It is devilish in the quantity he inhaled it.'

I could only gasp with surprise at the discovery.

'But how was it done?' I repeated. 'You think a bomb was thrown through the open port?'

'Without a doubt. Perhaps, as you guessed, from a boat outside, the roof of a cruiser, anything, as far as that end of it goes. Whoever did it might also have entered the room in the same way.'

'Entered the room?' I asked.

'Yes, wearing a mask composed of several layers of gauze impregnated with glycerinated solution of sodium hypophosphate. That is one of many substances used. All that was necessary was to wet the mask with water and adjust it. It would have served a double purpose—to protect the wearer's life as well as his identity.'

Amazed at Kennedy's powers of reconstruction from evidence that looked so slender, I merely waited for him to proceed.

'Then whoever it was probably rifled his clothes and so obtained the keys to the building and the office. From the briefcase they must have extracted the copies of the telautomaton plans. After that it was a simple matter to throw the body overboard in the hope that the affair might possibly be covered up as an accident or suicide. In the course of the night the wind cleared the room of the gas. They did not reckon, however, on what science can discover—or if they did, cared little. After that, I suppose, someone went to New York, perhaps in a high-powered car.'

'Mito couldn't have gone to New York—and got back again,' I exclaimed impulsively, recalling that Mito had been ashore that night without apparent reason.

'Mito may or may not have played his part,' was all that Kennedy would comment.

He left me wildly speculating. Was Mito a cog in the wheel, of which Paquita and the gang suspected by Burke were other cogs? Was Shelby Maddox also a cog, willingly or unwillingly? Could he have got away from the yacht and got back again? A host of unanswered questions raced through my mind. But Kennedy had said all that he was prepared to say now.

'We had better be going,' he remarked calmly, 'if we are to keep that appointment with Hastings and Burke.

He was evidently much more interested in what Burke might turn up than in his own investigation, which was quite natural, for what he had told me was already an old story to him, and his restless mind craved to be speeding toward the solution of the mystery.

Half an hour later Kennedy and I entered the office of Hastings. I looked about curiously. There were, as in many lawyer's offices, two private offices for the members of the firm, while outside was a large room for the clerks, the stenographers, and the telephone girl.

As we were welcomed by Hastings in his own office I wondered what the walls might have heard. Marshall Maddox and his lawyer must have had many conferences there during the time that Maddox was planning his great coup in the munitions company.

'Burke hasn't arrived yet,' remarked Hastings nervously. 'I've been expecting him any moment. I wonder what is keeping him?'

There was no way of finding out, and we were forced to sit impatiently.

A few moments later we heard hurried footsteps down the hall and Burke burst in, his face flushed with excitement.

'This thing is devilish,' he exclaimed, looking keenly at Hastings. 'I must be in your class.'

'How's that? Did someone shoot at you?' queried the lawyer.

'No, but I came within an ace of being poisoned.'

'Poisoned?' we inquired incredulously.

'Yes. You know I started to find that night watchman. Well, I found him. He knows nothing—and I think he is telling the truth. But after I had questioned him I made him admit that sometimes he takes a meal in the middle of the night. Of course he has to leave the front hall of the ground floor unguarded to do so. I figured that the robber might have got in and got away during that time. And I guess I'm right.

'After that I saw the policeman who walks the beat at night. I thought he was going to prove a better witness. He remembers, under questioning, seeing a speedster that stopped around the next corner and was left there standing some time—about the time that the robbery must have taken place, if I am right. He thought it was strange, and hung about.

'When the fellow who drove the car came back the policeman walked over. The fellow offered no explanation of leaving his car on the street at such an hour, except that he had stopped to shift a shoe that had blown. Then he asked where there was an all-night lunch-room. The policeman directed him and the fellow thanked him and drove off in that direction.'

'But the poisoning,' prompted Craig. 'How did that happen?'

'I'm coming to it. Well, I thought at once of going to the lunch-room and inquiring. You see, I thought I might check up both the night watchman's story and the cop's. So I went in and it happened that the night man was just going to work. I hadn't had anything to eat since this morning and I ordered a sandwich and a cup of coffee. I left the coffee standing on a little table while I talked to the man behind the counter.

'I found out from him that the night watchman had been there, all right. But he didn't remember anyone in a speedster.

In fact, I hadn't expected that he would. I don't believe the fellow went there.

'Anyhow, when I went to look for my coffee I noticed something on the lip of the cup. It looked like sugar, and I recollected that I hadn't put any sugar in the coffee. Besides, this looked like powdered sugar, and I wouldn't have put powdered sugar in when there was lump sugar. I tasted a bit of it. It was bitter—very bitter. Here's some of it.'

Kennedy took from Burke a few particles of a white powder which he had carefully preserved in a piece of paper and began examining the particles closely.

'There were lots of people coming and going at the lunch-room,' went on Burke, 'but I didn't pay much attention to any of them.'

Kennedy had placed just a particle of the powder on his tongue, and was now making a wry face. As he turned toward us he exclaimed, 'Strychnine!'

'See?' nodded Burke excitedly. 'I thought it was some poison. I knew there was something wrong.'

Burke looked at Kennedy fixedly. There could be no doubt now that we were watched. Someone was evidently desperate to prevent discovery. First the attack had been levelled at Hastings. Now it was Burke. Who would be next? I think we all realised that we were marked, though none of us said anything at the time.

Burke looked over questioningly at Kennedy.

'I've found out how Maddox was killed,' volunteered Craig, understanding the query implied in his glance.

'Indeed—already?' interrupted Hastings, to whom Kennedy was already frankly incomprehensible.

'How?' demanded Burke, checking himself in time to protect himself from setting forth a theory of his own, for Burke was like all other police detectives—first forming a theory and then seeking facts that confirmed it.

Eagerly both Burke and Hastings listened as Kennedy

repeated briefly his discoveries of the spectroscopic tests which he had already told me.

'Gassed, by George!' muttered Burke, more puzzled than ever. 'I may as well admit that I thought he had been thrown overboard and drowned. The shot at Mr Hastings rather confirmed me in the rough-neck methods of the criminal. But this burglar's microphone and the strychnine have shaken my theory. This fellow is clever beyond anything I had ever suspected. And to think of his using gas! I tell you, Kennedy, we don't know what to expect of criminals these days.'

Burke shook his head sagely. At least he had one saving grace. He realised his own shortcomings.

'How about the speedster?' reverted Kennedy, passing over the subject, for both Craig and I had a high regard for Burke, whatever might be his limitations. 'What did the patrolman say the fellow in the speedster looked like?'

Burke threw up his hands in mock resignation. 'As nearly as I could make out, he looked like a linen duster and a pair of goggles. You know that kind of cop—doomed always to pound pavements. Why, it might have been anybody—a woman, for all he knew.'

'I think we've been away from Westport long enough,' concluded Kennedy. 'Perhaps our unexpected return may result in something. A speedster—h'm. At least we can look over the garage of the Harbour House.'

I remember that I thought the words of little consequence at the moment. Yet, as it proved, it was a fateful statement made at this time and place.

CHAPTER VII

THE DIVORCE DETECTIVE

AT the Westport station, when our train pulled in, there was the usual gathering of cars to meet the late afternoon express from the city.

As we four were searching for a jitney 'bus to take us down to the Harbour House I caught sight in the press of cars of the Walcott car. Sitting in the back were Winifred and her sister-in-law, Mrs Walcott, sister of the murdered man. They had come up to meet her husband, Johnson Walcott, who now came down the platform from the club car, which had been well forward.

The train was pulling out, clearing the road across the track, and as it did so there flashed past a speedster with a cream-coloured body, a shining aluminium hood, and dainty upholstery. No one could have failed to notice it. As if the mere appearance of the car was not loud enough, the muffler cut-out was allowing the motor to growl a further demand for attention.

In the speedster sat Paquita, and as we looked across from our jitney I caught sight of Winifred eyeing her critically, turning at the same time to say something to Mrs Walcott.

Paquita saw it, too, and shot a glance of defiance as she stepped her dainty toe on the gas and leaped ahead of all the cars that were pulling out with passengers whom they had met.

'Did you get that?' whispered Kennedy to me. 'Not only have we a mystery on our hands, but we have something much harder to follow—conflict between those two women. Shelby may think he is a principal in the game, but one or the other of them is going to show him that he is a mere miserable pawn.'

'I wonder where she could have been?' I speculated. 'That

road up past the station leads to the turnpike to the city. Could she have been there, or just out for a spin?'

Kennedy shook his head. 'If we are going to follow that colour-scheme about the country we'll need to get a car that can travel up to the limit.'

'Well,' snorted Burke, 'it does beat all how these dancers can sport cars with special bodies and engines that would drown out the hammers of hell; but—I suppose it would cut down the work of us detectives by half if it weren't so.'

Hastings said nothing. Perhaps he was calculating the cost of the outfit that had just passed, and wondering whether the bill had been paid by his client—or someone else.

The Walcott car had got away and we were now jolting along in our more modest flivver, eager to get back to the scene of our labours, and learn what had taken place in our absence.

Back at the Harbour House Burke's man, Riley, was waiting, sure enough, with a full budget of news as we entered quietly by another than the main entrance and drew him off in a corner.

'What's happened?' demanded Burke.

'Plenty,' returned Riley, his reticence before us now overcome. 'You remember that dark-skinned fellow?' he asked excitedly.

'An unnecessary question,' returned Burke. 'He has not been out of my thoughts since I left. I hope you've watched him closely. We saw Paquita. She must have slipped through your fingers. You'll have to get a car that can keep up with her, Riley, if we are going to handle this affair successfully.'

'Yes, sir,' agreed Riley, evidently relieved that his chief had not administered a severer rebuke. 'I was about to tell you of how she slips away from us in that car, sir. Well,' he graced on, as though eager to change the subject, 'we have not only found out who that spiggoty chap is, but that he has reported to Mrs Maddox finally, today. It seems as though she has paid him for his work of watching her husband, and now that Mr Maddox is dead has no further use for him.'

'And he has gone away?' asked Craig.

'No,' replied Riley quickly, 'that's just the point. Even though she has discharged him—at least that is what it looks like—he is sticking around. At first I thought he was watching Paquita—and he is. But twice I have caught him talking to her. It may be that it's all right. I don't get it at all. I can't make out yet whether he is with her or against her.'

'That's strange,' agreed Burke, turning to Kennedy. 'I don't understand that. Do you? Do you suppose the fellow has been double crossing Irene Maddox all the time? These divorce sleuths are an unprincipled lot, usually.'

Kennedy shook his head non-committally. 'I think it will be worth looking into,' he considered. 'Has anything else happened?'

'Plenty,' replied Riley cheerfully. 'Since you went away Shelby Maddox has given up living out on the *Sybarite*, I understand. He is to live at the Harbour House all the time, and has brought his stuff ashore, although he hasn't been about much. He is another one who has a speedster that can do some travelling.'

'What do you make of that move?' encouraged Hastings.

Riley shrugged. 'Sometimes,' he remarked slowly, 'I think he is watching the others. I don't know yet whether he does it because he suspects something of them, or because he thinks they suspect something of him. Anyhow, he has brought that Jap, Mito, ashore, too. Is he afraid of him? Has Mito something that gives him a leverage on Shelby Maddox? I don't know. Only, it's mighty strange.'

'Has Mito done anything suspicious?' asked Kennedy.

'His whole conduct is suspicious,' asserted Riley positively. 'Why was he in town so late last night? Besides, the fellow is well educated—too well educated to be a servant. No, sir, you can't make me believe that he is here for any good. He's clever, too. They tell me he can run a motor-boat or a car as well as the best. And he's quiet. There's something deep about him. Why, you can see that he knows that he is being watched.'

'But what has he done?' emphasised Kennedy.

'N-nothing. Only he acts as though he was covering up something. I know the symptoms.'

I tried to analyse our feelings toward Mito. Was it merely that Riley and the rest of us did not understand the subtle Oriental, and that hence we suspected everything we did not understand? There was no denying that Mito's actions out on the *Sybarite*, for instance, had been open to question. Yet, as far as I knew, there was nothing on which one could place his finger and accuse the little man, except his alleged presence in town so late the night before.

From the corner in which we were sitting we could see through an open window the porte-cochère beside the hotel at which guests were arriving and departing.

'Look!' pointed out Riley. 'There's Shelby Maddox now.'

His motor had purred up silently around the corner of the road that led about the shore, and as he pulled up before the door the omnipresent Mito appeared from nowhere. Shelby crawled out from under the steering-wheel and turned the car over to Mito to run around to the hotel garage. For a moment he stood talking to the Jap, giving him some parting instructions, when another car tooted its horn and came up to the steps. It was the Walcott car. Evidently they had not come directly from the station, but had taken a little ride along the shore to get the stuffy air of the railroad train out of Johnson Walcott's lungs.

It was just the opportunity Shelby wanted. He quickly waved to Mito to pull away and turned to the new arrival, opening the rear door before the officious starter could get to it, and handing out Winifred Walcott most attentively—so much so that he forgot all about his own sister and Johnson Walcott.

He and Winifred stood talking, evidently about Shelby's own departing roadster, for they were looking after Mito as he shot up the road to the garage.

'Do you guess what they are talking about?' queried Kennedy to me. 'I would be willing to wager that I can reproduce at least a part of the conversation. As they watched the speedster get away she spoke first, and he nodded his head in the negative as he replied. She spoke again, and she nodded in the affirmative—and smiled.'

'What was it?' I asked.

'Remember Paquita? So does Winifred. First she asked Shelby if his roadster was hard to drive—or something of the sort. He said it was not. Then she asked whether he would show her some of the fine points of driving it—I am sure that Winifred Walcott can drive, for she looks like that sort of a girl. Shelby fairly leaped ahead like his motor does when he feeds it gas. That was easy long-distance eavesdropping.'

'What are they talking about now?' I demanded, rather spoofing him than serious, for Shelby was standing on the steps yet, quite oblivious to everything about him except Winifred.

'I don't know,' he confessed, 'but I can predict that something will happen in thirty seconds. Look up the road.'

I glanced away. Paquita in her speedster was shooting down as though she had a fourth speed. A second, and she had pulled up, leaping lightly to the ground. She nodded gaily to the starter to take her car for her to the garage, and bounded up the steps, not neglecting to display a generous vision of a trim ankle that almost caused the starter to turn the car up the steps instead of wide from the Walcott car.

Deliberately she passed close to Shelby, as though to show him the contrast between the fluffy little girl of the morning and the motor girl of the afternoon. She smiled sweetly at Shelby, not neglecting a quick glance of superciliousness at Winifred, such as only a true actress can give.

At that moment Irene Maddox appeared in the door, to greet Johnson and Mrs Walcott. Paquita had not seen her, nor if she had would she probably have avoided the dramatic meeting.

For an instant the two women were face to face. Men would have been at each other's throats in a brutal grip. Paquita was no less brutal. Without turning an eyelash she looked steadily into the face of the woman who had been so grievously wronged, and for all the surprise or emotion she displayed she might have been gazing at a bisque ornament. Irene Maddox, stately in her black suit of mourning, drew herself to her full height and the colour in her cheeks deepened as her eyes flashed at the other woman.

Paquita swept on gaily. She was supremely happy. She had gone up-stage and had thrown two bombs.

From our coign of vantage I saw that another was watching. It was our sallow-faced friend, who smiled darkly to himself as he watched, then, a moment later, was gone, observed by none of them.

Paquita had passed. One might have easily paraphrased 'Pippa Passes,' and it was not God who was in his heaven, either, nor was all right with the world.

The group at the porte-cochère glanced at one another, and for the moment each was reminded of his own particular hate and rivalry. Shelby was plainly chagrined. He had been getting along famously with Winifred, when a cold shower had been plunged over him. Irene Maddox had received a sharp reminder of her trying position. Frances Walcott was again a Maddox, unsoftened by the tragedy. Winifred listened while Shelby tried to finish what he had been saying, but nothing was the same as before. Only Johnson Walcott seemed able to remain the unconcerned outsider.

All turned into the hotel now, and as they separated and disappeared I wondered whether Paquita had been trailing about and had deliberately framed the little incident. What was the meaning of the continued observation by the man of the sallow face?

Just then one of the boys came through the lobby, where we were sitting in the angle, calling 'Mr Sanchez! Mr Sanchez!'

From around the angle, where he could not have seen us, appeared the sallow-faced individual who had so disturbed our thoughts. He took the telegram which the boy carried, tore it open, and read it. As he did so his face, lined with anger, happened to turn in our direction and he saw us. Without appearing to notice us, he slowly tore the telegram as well as the envelope and stuffed the pieces into his pocket. Then he turned and coolly sat down again as though nothing had occurred.

'At least we know that one of his names is Sanchez,' commented Kennedy. 'I'd like to see that message.'

'You're not likely to see it now, unless we can pick his pocket,' returned Burke. 'Don't look around. There comes Mito.'

The Japanese padded silently past, unconcerned, casting no look at either our party or Sanchez. But I knew that his beady eyes had already taken us in. I felt that he was watching us. But was it for his own or someone else's benefit?

I determined that, given an opportunity, I would try to find out two things—what the telegram contained and why Mito had been in town the night before.

It was the dinner hour, and the guests of the Harbour House, either singly or in groups, were stringing into the brilliantly lighted dining-room, where the orchestra had already tuned up. We moved over, nearer the door, as Shelby Maddox, all alone, placed his hat on the rack and entered, allowing the head waiter to seat him.

'Let us go in and observe them,' decided Kennedy. 'Hastings, you brought us out here. It will look queer if we all go in together. So I think that you, Burke, and Riley had better sit at another table in another part of the room; then we won't appear to be all together and we may get more, too.'

Accordingly, Hastings, Kennedy, and I entered, and by a little manœuvring managed to get ourselves placed by a window where we could see pretty much everything that went on.

Winifred Walcott was already there, at a table with her brother, her sister-in-law, and Irene Maddox. They did not seem to be talking much. I wondered what could be the matter. Perhaps it was fancy, but it seemed as if the two older women were not quite so friendly as they had been when I saw them in the automobile in the morning. Johnson Walcott also said little, but appeared to be engrossed in reading the despatches from Westport in the papers. None of them ate as though they enjoyed it, and all seemed preoccupied, especially Winifred, who let dish after dish go untasted. What had she on her mind? Was it solely Paquita?

I looked over at a table on the other side of the room where there was a lone diner, Shelby Maddox. He, too, was preoccupied. He had placed himself so that he could catch the eye of Winifred whenever she chose to cast it his way. But though he was never off guard, she did not choose. Something, too, was seriously affecting his appetite. As far as food was concerned, his presence was a mere formality.

'There's something strange going on in that family,' I commented at length.

Hastings smiled dryly. 'They can't agree, even on a tragedy,' he returned. 'What you have seen so far today was merely a lull in the storm. And now, if that is complicated by outsiders—well, we shall need all Mr Kennedy's acumen if we are to untangle the snarl.'

Kennedy appeared oblivious to the compliment, which was something for Hastings to pay, for very little in this mundane sphere met the approval of his legal mind. Craig was studying a large mirror at the end of the dining-hall thoughtfully. I turned and placed myself as nearly as possible in the same angle of vision.

'Please, Walter,' he cautioned, 'your head is opaque—I mean to the human eye, old man.'

My one glance had been sufficient to whet my curiosity. By means of the mirror he could see around an 'L' in the dining-room, and there, at a little table, alone, was seated Paquita. She had chosen the coign of vantage quite apparently because it put her in range of Shelby, without its being apparent to the other guests. But Shelby was busy. He had not even noticed Paquita, in his eagerness to catch the crumb of a glance from Winifred's table.

Not being able to watch Paquita without interfering with Kennedy, and finding the strained relations of the others rather tiresome, I glanced out on the veranda by the window where our table stood. Someone was pacing quietly up and down. Almost with a feeling of certainty I strained my eyes in the darkness.

'That Sanchez is outside, watching everything,' I called Craig's attention.

He nodded.

At the other end of the dining-room Burke and Riley were quite as busy as we were, observing how those whom we were watching acted when they were all together.

The Walcott party finished dinner first and soon afterward rose and left the room. Down in the Casino there was dancing every night, but, of course, they did not go there. Instead, they chose a secluded corner of the porch at the Lodge. Though there was no lost cordiality, apparently they did not want to separate. At least they had their conflicting interests in common.

Shelby needed nothing but a finger-bowl in order to finish his dinner, and left hurriedly, much to the astonishment of the waiter.

Burke and Riley had already gone out and had disappeared when we followed shortly.

Prompted by Kennedy, Hastings sauntered around to the end of the porch which the Walcotts and Mrs Maddox had occupied. Shelby Maddox had already joined them, unable to keep away from Winifred longer.

One could feel the constraint of the party, although to an outsider it might readily have been accounted for by the tragedy. However, we knew by this time that there was something deeper.

Shelby was apparently endeavouring to overcome the impression which the appearance and smile of Paquita had produced, but I could see that Winifred was not yet entirely mollified.

The Maddox party welcomed us—not cordially, but at least

not coldly, for it was no part of their character ever to betray their real feelings before one another.

As we drew up chairs I could feel the close scrutiny to which we were being subjected.

'Well?' queried Shelby at length, after we had talked about several inconsequential things, 'what have you found out, Hastings?'

He said it in a tone that was meant to imply that he knew that some kind of investigation was on. Was it bravado?

'Oh, several things,' returned Hastings, turning to Kennedy as if to leave the answer to him.

'For one thing,' shot out Kennedy, taking advantage of the opportunity, 'we have determined that your brother died from the effects of a poisonous gas—I won't say yet what it was or how administered.'

The light from a window was shining full on Shelby's face as Craig said it, and he knew that we were all watching intently the effect it would have.

'Is that so?' he replied, with an interest this time unfeigned. 'I suppose you know who did it?'

'I have an idea,' replied Kennedy, 'a theory on which I am proceeding. But it is too early to talk about it yet.'

If Shelby had been trying to 'pump' us he was getting something to think about, at least. I felt sure that Craig was telling the family this much in the hope that it would spur them to some action, or at least reach ears that would be affected.

It was while Kennedy was talking that I noticed that Winifred showed her first real interest in what was going on about her. She was about to ask a question when the sound of footsteps on the veranda interrupted. If I had wondered what the cause of the coolness between Shelby and Winifred was I had here a partial answer at least.

Again, as though to foment trouble, Paquita crossed the veranda and walked slowly down the steps to the Casino, whence floated the rhythmic strains of the orchestra. Though she did not know it, she produced the result she sought. A few minutes later Winifred excused herself to retire to her room, her question still unasked and unanswered.

Shelby bowed a reluctant goodnight, but I could see that inwardly he was furious. And I felt impelled to ask myself, also, why Paquita was so apparently dogging Shelby's every step. Could it be that the notorious little heart-breaker was actually in love with him—or had she some darker motive?

CHAPTER VIII

THE PULMOTOR

SHELBY was plainly angry and disconcerted. For the moment he seemed to hesitate between hurrying after Winifred and striding down the steps toward Paquita, as though to demand an explanation of her haunting appearances and disappearances.

In the moment that elapsed during his indecision he seemed to think a second time and to check both impulses. Better, he evidently considered, to affect to ignore the matter altogether.

Still, he could not conceal his chagrin. Nor was it lost on the others. The Maddox family were watching one another like hawks. Each knew that the other knew something—though not how much.

Winifred's desertion seemed to throw a damper on the entire group. As for Shelby, life had lost its attraction for him with Winifred Walcott gone. He was about to make some excuse to leave the party, then decided that perhaps he might better stay. If anything was going to be said or to happen, at least he would learn it. Meanwhile I noticed that Johnson Walcott was covertly observing Shelby, who seemed to be aware of the scrutiny of the brother of the girl with whom he was in love. I felt that Shelby would not antagonise Walcott at least.

'Then you are getting closer to the truth of the death of my brother?' inquired Shelby.

'Step by step,' replied Kennedy. 'I am trying now to recon-struct what might have been hidden in his private life.'

Irene Maddox gave a quick glance at Kennedy. The others were silent. It was a queer family. There was no word of grief for Marshall Maddox. Each seemed merely to consider what bearing the tragedy might have on his own fortune.

A moment later Walcott excused himself, pleading that he had some letters to write, and passed slowly down the porch in the direction of the office and writing-room. His wife, however, and Irene Maddox showed no disposition to move. None of us said anything about the incident, but I know that I did a lot of wondering why the mere appearance of Paquita seemed to break up the party each time as though a shell had burst. Was there something lying back which neither Kennedy nor myself knew anything about? Was it more than revenge or jealousy?

As for myself, somehow I had become mightily interested in the drama of the little Mexican dancer and Shelby, whatever it might be. How did Sanchez complicate it? Could it be that Burke was right and that he was an international crook? Besides, Mito was on my mind now more than any of the Maddoxes in the group, anyhow.

Accordingly, I leaned over and whispered to Kennedy. 'I'd like to follow that girl Paquita and watch her a bit.'

'Very good, Walter,' he whispered back. 'See if you can find her. I want to stay here with Hastings and talk to them. Molasses will catch more flies than vinegar. I will stick along until there is an open break.'

Glad of the release he had given me, I made some excuse to the party, and without seeming to do so wandered off from the Lodge toward the Casino in the direction taken by Paquita. As I approached the Casino, which was now ablaze with lights and gaiety, I paused outside in the shadow to survey the long line of snowy white tables on a balcony whose outlook was directly on the dark-blue waters of the bay and out between the two necks of land into the Sound. It seemed a veritable fairyland.

One after another, I scanned the faces of the parties at the tables in the hope of catching a glimpse of Paquita, but she was at none of them.

As I stood in the shadow of a clump of shrubbery I was

suddenly aware that someone had crossed the thick grassy carpet and was standing almost directly behind me. I turned to find Burke.

'I don't suppose you have seen that Jap, Mito, about?' he asked, modulating his voice.

'No,' I replied. 'I just came down here. Kennedy and Hastings are on the porch with the Maddoxes and I thought I might do some investigating on my own account. Why? What has Mito been doing?'

Burke shrugged. 'Perhaps nothing—perhaps much. Riley and I have been strolling about the outside, on a chance. Once we found Mito sitting apart, apparently looking out over the harbour, although I am sure that that was not all he was doing. For when he saw Paquita coming down the path, almost before we knew it he had given us the slip in the darkness. I think he had been waiting for her to appear.'

'Where is she?' I asked. 'It was really to follow her that I came down here.'

Burke nodded toward the dancing-floor of the Casino. 'I suppose she is in there,' he replied. 'At least she was a moment ago. I would feel a great deal safer in putting my finger on her than on that Jap. He is eely. Every time I think I have caught him he gets through my grasp. It may be that he is only a faithful servant to his master, although I would like to be convinced of it. All the time that you and Kennedy were up there on the veranda he was watching. I don't know what Paquita did, but when she walked down he spotted her in a moment—and was gone.'

'That's just the point,' I hastened. 'She didn't do a thing except pass near us and bestow a sweet smile on Shelby. It's the second time since we got back from the city. I can't make out what she is up to, unless it is to separate the lovers.'

'I think I shall try to see Kennedy,' concluded Burke.

'All right,' I agreed as he turned away. 'You'll find him at the Lodge on the porch. I am going to stay here awhile and see what Paquita does. How about Sanchez?' I recollected.

'Nothing at all,' imparted Burke as he left me. 'Since dinner he seems to have dropped out of sight entirely.'

Burke having left me, I sauntered into the light, and, being alone, chose a table from which I could see both the dancers and the gay parties at the other little round tables.

Intently my gaze wandered in toward the dancing. The lively strains of a fox-trot were sending the crowded couples ricocheting over the polished floor. It was a brilliant sight—the myriad lights, the swaying couples, the musical rhythm pervading all.

Sure enough, there was Paquita. I could pick her out from among them all, for there was none, even among these seasoned dancers, who could equal the pretty professional.

Dancing with her was a young man whom I did not recognise. Nor did it seem to matter, for even in the encore I found that she had another partner. Without a doubt they were of the group of the younger set to whom Paquita was a fascinating creature. What, if anything, her partners might have to do with the Maddox mystery I was unable to determine, though I inclined to the belief that it was nothing. Sophisticated though they may have thought themselves, they were mere children in the hands of Paquita. She was quite apparently using her very popularity as a mask.

From my table on the terrace over the bay I caught sight of a face, all alone, which amazed me. Johnson Walcott was quite as much interested in Paquita as any of the younger set.

It was too late for me to move. Walcott caught sight of me and soon had planted himself in the chair opposite.

'What do you make of that girl?' he asked finally, as though frankly confessing the object of his visit to the Casino.

I was on guard. I did not want to admit to any of the family that neither Kennedy nor myself had fathomed her. 'I don't know,' I replied, carefully avoiding the appearance of having come down solely to watch her. 'She seems to be quite interested in the Maddox family.'

Walcott laughed as though to indicate to me that he under-stood that I knew the scandal. Just then Paquita caught sight of us together. I thought she seemed distrait. She rose and a moment later disappeared through the French window.

Inwardly I cursed Walcott for his intrusion at that moment, for under the circumstances I could not abruptly jump up and leave him to follow her. Yet it was just that second in which she was gone.

The dancing seemed to have no attraction for her tonight. Evidently there was something lying back in her strange actions. More than likely she had come down to the Casino for the sole purpose of passing Shelby again when Winifred was present.

As soon as I conveniently could I managed to detach myself from Walcott, but, as I had expected, by the time I got around to the French window through which Paquita had gone she was nowhere about.

What of Sanchez? Where was he? I loitered about for a moment, then slowly mounted the steps that led back to the Lodge, intending to rejoin Kennedy and Hastings.

When I reached the porch again all were gone. Shelby had got away, and the others had either gone to their rooms or to the more lively corridor of the hotel. I looked about, but could see neither Kennedy nor Hastings. They, too, seemed to have disappeared on some mission.

What I would do next I did not know. Suddenly there flashed through my mind the thought of the high-powered car that the policeman had told Burke of seeing near the Maddox Building the night before.

I wondered whether there might not be some clue that I might obtain from the garage back of the Lodge. There must be at least two speedsters there, Paquita's and Shelby's. Perhaps there were others. At least I might find out whether either of them had been out the night of the murder. Having nothing better to do, I determined to make a little tour of investigation in that direction myself.

As I made my way to the rear of the hotel I saw that there were indeed two garages, one large one that was most generally used and a smaller one that looked as though it might have been built as an afterthought to accommodate an overflow of cars. The smaller one was near and I determined to examine it first. It was dark, too, as though not being used except over weekends, when the hotel was crowded.

Almost before I was aware of it it seemed as if I saw a figure flit past a window. Perhaps it was my imagination. At any rate I would not have conscientiously sworn to it, for my attention at the time was directed at the other, lighted, garage.

The impression was enough, however. I quickened my pace until I came to the dark building. Mechanically I tried the door, fully expecting that it would be locked. To my surprise, it was open, and before I realised it I had swung the door and my foot was on the threshold.

'Who's—'

The words were scarcely out of my lips when a spit of fire in the blackness of the interior replied. For a moment my head seemed in a whirl. Sight and hearing left me.

That is all I remember.

An hour later, vaguely, indistinctly, as though far away, I heard a familiar voice calling me.

It seemed to be far off, and I struggled after it, blindly groping. There seemed to be something over my face, something that covered my eyes. I felt that if I could only get it off I would be all right. But try as I would, I had not the strength.

Still, I was encouraged. The voice seemed nearer, more distinct. Was it Kennedy's? It sounded strangely like it.

I clawed again at the thing that seemed to keep me from him. To my surprise it came off itself, leaving me blinking in a flood of light.

'Walter—are you all right?' I now heard the voice distinctly.

'Wh-where am I? What happened?' I gasped, feeling still a suffocating sensation in the throat and chest, my mouth parched, dry and irritated, and my nose tingling as though afire.

'Here in the garage,' replied Craig, holding a peculiar rubber face mask in one hand, while Burke stood beside a sort of box about the size of a suit-case from which rubber tubes ran to the mask. 'I thought the pulmotor would do the trick.'

'It's lucky you are that there was a gas company in town that's up-to-date and has one of the things,' returned Burke, breaking back into a vernacular more natural than that veneered on his honest tongue. 'Praise be that he's all right. A night's sleep will do him good, don't you say, Mr Kennedy?'

'But—but what is it all about?' I choked, striving to get my feet, but finding myself still a bit weak. My eye caught the motors and pumps and tubes in the pulmotor, but that conveyed no idea to me. 'Tell me—Craig—who was it?'

'I wish I could, old fellow,' replied Craig, smoothing back my hair. 'We were just a bit late for that—heard the shot—dashed in, and found you, of all people. How did you come here?'

Propped up gently by Craig, I told what I could of the story, though there was next to nothing to tell.

'Whoever it was,' I concluded, pressing my aching temples ruefully, 'he had just time to get away. You heard a shot? Am I wounded? What's that pulmotor for?'

'Not wounded,' Craig returned. 'But you can be thankful we had that thing and that the gas in this asphyxiating pistol was not chlorine. I don't know what it was—possibly sabadilla vera-trine, some of those things they're using abroad in asphyxiating bombs.'

'Whoever it was, he was prepared for us here,' called Burke, who, now that I was out of danger, had turned his attention to the garage itself. 'He's removed whatever might be incrimin-ating. It's all as clean as a whistle here. Someone expected us.'

'I knew that all along,' returned Craig quietly. 'Walter blun-dered into a trap that was set for me.'

I felt the pressure of his hand on mine. It was worth it all to know that I had at least saved Kennedy something, even if I had accomplished nothing.

'But who could have known that we were going to the garage?' I asked.

Kennedy was silent a moment.

'Someone is spying on us—knows our movements, must know even what we talk about,' he said slowly.

We looked at one another blankly. It was uncanny. What could we do? Were we in the hands of a power greater than any of us had imagined?

CHAPTER IX

THE TRAILING OF PAQUITA

RAPIDLY recovering now from the effects of the asphyxiating gun, thanks to the prompt aid of Kennedy, I was soon able to sit up in my improvised bed on the garage floor. As well can be imagined, however, I did not feel like engaging in very strenuous activity. Even the simple investigation of Burke, as he explored the garage, seemed like a wonderful exhibition of energy to me.

'Well, there certainly is no car here now,' he remarked as he surveyed the obvious emptiness of the place.

'Which is not to say that there has not been one here recently,' added Kennedy, who was now dividing his attention between me and the building. 'Someone has been here with a car,' he added, pointing to some fresh oil spots on the floor, and bending down beside them. 'Jameson's inhospitable host has evidently taken the pains to remove all traces that might be of any value. See—he has obliterated even the tyre tracks by which the car might have been identified.'

'Must have had great respect for your ability,' remarked Burke, also examining the marks that showed how carefully the floor had been gone over to guard against leaving a clue. 'Whoever it was was clever enough to keep just a jump ahead of us. Not a single trace was left. I wonder who it could be?'

'I've narrowed it down to two theories,' interposed Burke's Secret Service man, Riley, always fertile with conjectures, 'but I can't say which I prefer. To my way of thinking, either the presence of Mito in the town last night would explain everything, or else this all has something to do with the telegram that we saw the sallow-faced Sanchez receive.'

Either conjecture was plausible enough, on the face of it. Kennedy listened, but said nothing. There seemed to be no reason for remaining longer in the garage.

'How do you feel now, Walter?' asked Craig. 'Do you think you could stand being moved to the hotel?'

An oppressive dizziness still affected me, but I knew that I could not continue to lie on the damp floor. With Kennedy's aid, I struggled to my feet.

Barely able to walk, and leaning heavily on his arm, I managed to make my way from the garage and across the bit of lawn to the side veranda of the Harbour House. Still weak, I was forced to drop into a wicker chair to recover my strength.

'Why, Mr Jameson, what is the matter?' asked a woman's voice beside us.

I looked up to see Winifred Walcott. Evidently when she left us she had not gone to her room.

As Craig told her briefly what had happened, she was instantly sympathetic.

'That's strange,' she murmured. 'I felt restless and I was strolling about the paths back of the Lodge. I heard the shot—thought it was an automobile tyre or a back-fire. Why, not ten minutes before, I am sure I saw Paquita with Shelby's valet, Mito.'

Burke whispered to Riley, who nodded and disappeared with alacrity.

I thought of the cordiality I had often observed between Mexicans and Japanese. Was that the case in this instance? Could it be that Paquita knew something about the attack on me? Was Mito the mysterious attacker?

It was scarcely a moment later that Johnson Walcott appeared round the corner, evidently seeking his sister.

Just then Riley returned, dragging the reluctant Mito.

'Where have you been?' bellowed Burke.

The little Jap's face was impassive.

'I was sitting just outside the servants' quarters, sir, most of the evening,' he returned, in bland surprise.

'Think a moment,' shouted Burke, advancing close to him and peering into his face. 'Who have you been talking to? Tell me, and mind you tell the truth—or it will go hard with you.'

'With no one, sir,' asserted Mito, positively.

Burke was by this time red in the face with rage as all that he had ever learned in his third-degree days came to the surface.

'You lie!' he exclaimed. 'I saw you with—'

'Well,' demanded a voice, interrupting, 'what's all this? What has Mito been doing?'

It was Shelby Maddox, who had been attracted from the lobby by the loud voices.

'Doing enough,' returned Burke. 'Someone's taken a shot at Mr Jameson in the garage. Now, look here, you little brown brother. Do you mean to tell me that you haven't been with anyone all the evening? Think—think hard?'

Mito protested, but Burke was not satisfied.

'Don't try to hide it,' he urged. 'This lady saw you.'

Shelby gave a quick glance at Winifred. Then he turned to Mito. 'Tell him,' he commanded.

'Only Miss Paquita passed me once,' replied the Jap. 'She did not say anything. I saw Mr Jameson, too, before, on the shore by the Casino.'

It was clever, whatever else it might be. No matter what either Paquita or I might say later, Mito had protected himself. He had admitted everything and confessed nothing.

Burke was far from satisfied. He was about to turn to Winifred when her brother interposed.

'Winifred,' interrupted Johnson Walcott in a tone approaching authority, 'I think you had better not get mixed up in this affair.'

'Quite right,' agreed Shelby. 'I see no reason why Miss Walcott should be annoyed by this cross-examination.'

Winifred looked open defiance at her brother's interference.

'I can promise you that if I find that Mito has been doing anything he should not, I shall be responsible for him,' smoothed Shelby.

A moment later both Winifred and her brother left. She still resented his brotherly interference.

Burke had not got anywhere with his questioning and Kennedy apparently believed that the time for such a course was not yet ripe.

'I think the best thing we can do is to get Jameson to his room,' he suggested, by way of cutting off an unprofitable examination before any damage was done.

Burke accepted the broad hint. While Shelby and Mito withdrew, Hastings and Craig between them managed to get me up to our room and to bed.

As I lay there, glad enough to be quiet, we held a hasty conference to consider the strange attack that had been made.

'What I don't understand,' I repeated, 'is how anyone should know that we ever thought of visiting either that garage or the other.'

Kennedy had been saying very little. As Hastings and I talked he seemed to be thinking over something deeply. Suddenly his face registered the dawn of an idea.

'Tomorrow, Hastings,' he exclaimed, 'we must go into town. I want to go to your office. As for tonight, there doesn't seem to be anything more that we can do. Burke and Riley are on guard downstairs. I think Walter needs a good rest. So do we all. Goodnight, Mr Hastings. I will see you tomorrow early.'

A night's rest fixed me up all right and I was anxiously down in the lobby early next morning.

Fortunately nothing further of any great importance had happened during the night and I felt a sense of satisfaction at not having missed anything. Among us all we had been able to keep a pretty close surveillance on those in Westport whom we suspected might have any information. The day before had brought with it a grist of new mystery instead of clearing up the old, but Kennedy was happy. He was in his element, and the harder it was to crack the nut the more zest he put into the cracking of it.

To my surprise, the morning express found the entire Maddox family, except Irene Maddox, gathered on the platform of the quaint little station.

'What do you suppose has given them this sudden impulse to go in to town?' whispered Kennedy to Hastings.

The lawyer shrugged. 'I shouldn't be surprised if they were getting back into their normal state after the first shock,' he replied dryly. 'I think they are all going to consult their various attorneys—Shelby probably will see Harvey, and Mrs Walcott and her husband will see Duncan Bruce.'

As we waited for the train I realised why it was that Westport was popular. The little town was not only within fair access to the city, but it was far enough away to be beyond the city's blight. Going back and forth was so easy that each of the contending parties was able to take it as a matter of course that he should go to New York.

The crowning surprise came, however, just a moment before the express swung around the curve. The cream-coloured speedster swung up to the platform, turned, and backed in with the other cars. No one could miss it. The beautiful Paquita jumped airily out, more baffling than ever in her artificiality.

As I watched her my former impression was confirmed that the notoriety which she courted was paradoxically her 'cover.' She seemed to seek the limelight. In so doing did she hope to divert attention from what was really going on back-stage? It would have been a bold stroke. I expressed my idea to Kennedy. He smiled, but not with his usual indulgence. Was it his own idea, too?

Nothing occurred during the ride in to town in the chair-car, except that each was still furtively watching the other and all were watching Paquita. Paquita was trying desperately to attract the notice of Shelby. The young man seemed greatly embarrassed. As he sat beside his sister I saw that Frances Walcott was keenly appreciative of the efforts of the little dancer.

Once I excused myself on the pretext that I wanted another

morning paper, and walked forward into the smoking-car. It was as I had suspected. Sanchez was there.

'I think we had better split our forces,' planned Kennedy, when I reported to him what I had seen. 'Sanchez, I suppose, will trail along after Paquita. In that case, Walter, I shall leave them to you. I want to handle Shelby myself. Meet me at the laboratory and then we can go down to your office, Mr Hastings. And, by the way, if you will take a hint from me, sir, you will be careful what you do and what you say at your office. I think you'll understand when I see you there again.'

The astonished look on Hastings's face was quite worth study. It was as though someone had told him to guard his thoughts. The very possibility that there could be a 'leak,' which was evidently the way in which he interpreted Kennedy's cryptic remark, had never seemed to occur to him, so sure was he about those whom he employed.

Nothing more was said about the matter, however, and as our train rolled through the under-river tube into the station the various groups began to break up as we had expected.

With a parting word from Kennedy I wormed my way through the crowd in the direction of the cab-stand and was already in a cab and halfway up the ramp to the street when, looking back through the little glass window, I saw, as I had expected, Paquita trip gaily up to the same starter and enter another. On the avenue a stop gave me ample time to tip my driver and instruct him to follow the cab that was coming up back of us. Then by settling back from the windows I was able to let Paquita's cab pass and pick her up again without her knowing that she was being trailed. Without looking back, I knew that Sanchez had tried to follow, but it was not until we had gone several blocks and made a sudden turn into Broadway that I realised, on looking cautiously around, that somehow he had missed out. Perhaps there had not been another cab on the instant. Anyhow, I was not myself followed.

On up-town Paquita's cab proceeded, until finally it stopped before a building which I knew to be full of theatrical agencies and offices. I could not, of course, follow her into the office into which she went, but I managed to find out that she had gone to the office that had recently been opened by a company that proposed to put on a new feature in the fall known as La Danza Mexicana. It seemed like a perfectly legitimate business trip, yet according to my idea Paquita was merely using her notoriety to attract those whom she might use for her own purposes. What interested me was whether it was purely money or a deeper motive that actuated her.

From the office of her agent she hurried over to Fifth Avenue, and there she made several lengthy stops at fashionable costumers, milliners, and other dealers and designers of chic wearing apparel. In all this there seemed to be nothing to take exception to and I became weary of the pursuit. It was not her legitimate theatrical career that interested me.

However, so it went until the lunch hour arrived. Quite demurely and properly she stopped at a well-known tea-room where tired shoppers refreshed themselves. I swore softly under my breath. I could not well follow her in, for a man is a marked card in a tea-room. To go in was like shouting in her ear that I was watching her.

Therefore, I stayed outside and, instead of lunching, watched the passing crowd of smart shoppers while the clock on the taximeter mounted steadily.

I had fidgeted in my cab for perhaps half an hour when I became aware that mine was not the only cab that was waiting in the neighbourhood. In these shadowing jobs one has to keep his eyes glued on the door through which the 'subject' must exit, for it is unbelievable how easily a person, even when not aware of being watched, may slip out into a crowd and disappear. Consequently I had not paid much attention to my surroundings.

But once when I leaned forward to speak to my driver, who by this time was fully convinced that I was crazy, I happened to glance across the street. At the window of another cab I saw a familiar face. Sanchez had lost Paquita at the station, but by some process of reason had picked her up again at the tea-room. I was determined more than ever now to hang on to both of them.

Luncheon over, Paquita finally emerged, still alone. What business she may have transacted over the telephone during her various stops I do not know. What I wanted was for her to feel perfectly free, in the hope that she might do something. Yet she had not given me the satisfaction of meeting a single person whom she should not have met.

Again her cab started on its round, but this time it rolled back into the theatre district.

My driver almost jolted me from the seat as he stopped once. I looked ahead. Paquita's cab had pulled up before the office of a well-known music publisher and she was getting out.

To my surprise, however, instead of entering she deliberately turned and walked back in the direction of my cab. I sank farther back into its shallow recesses, trusting that she would not glance my way.

A dainty creation of headgear intruded itself through the open window of my cab.

'You have been following me all day, Mr Jameson,' purred Paquita in her sweetest tone, as her baffling brown eyes searched my face and enjoyed the discomfiture I could not hide. 'I know it—have known it all the time. There's another cab, too, back of you. I've been going about my own business—haven't I?— making arrangements for my new show this fall. You haven't anything—except a bill, have you? Neither has the man in the other cab. Now I'm going to go right on. You are welcome to follow.'

Before I could reply she had swept disdainfully back and had entered the building. Chagrined though I was at the way she had led the chase, I determined to stick to her, nevertheless.

In the publishing house she remained an uncommonly long

time, but when at last she came out I saw that she gave a little petulant glance first to see whether I was still there.

Her cab shot away, but my man was alert and we trailed along down the avenue. Twice, now, I saw her looking back at me. That, at least, was some encouragement. Perhaps vexation might impel her to do something.

As we came to a tangle of cars crossing Longacre Square, Paquita leaned forward through the front window of her taxicab and deliberately turned the wheel that the driver was steering. The unexpected interference caused him to stop suddenly.

As my driver pulled up, there came a crash and a smashing of glass behind me. His pulling up had fortunately thrown me forward. The car in which Sanchez was riding had crashed into mine, and only my being thrown forward prevented me from receiving the shattered glass.

Instantly the traffic policeman was beside us and a crowd began to collect. Before I knew it Paquita in her taxi was off and there was no possibility of following.

Where she was going I could not now find out. Perhaps there was, as Burke suspected, a gang, and she had all day been seeking to get to their rendezvous. As I watched the officer and the crowd blankly, I had but one satisfaction. At least Sanchez could not follow, either.

Quickly I gave the policeman my name as a witness, glanced at the 'clock,' and paid my taxicab bill. Sanchez saw what I did and that it was no use for him to try to get away. He paid his own bill and deliberately turned away, on foot, and walked down Seventh Avenue.

A few feet behind I followed.

He paid no attention to me, but kept on down-town, until at last I realised that we had come to the neighbourhood of the railroad terminal.

At the station he turned, and I knew that he had decided to take the early train back to Westport. Still following, I went through all the motions of having also decided to take the train myself. I let Sanchez go through the gate, then at the last moment retreated and walked over to the telegraph office as the gate banged shut.

I would not have missed the appointment with Kennedy and Hastings for anything, and the train, except for one stop, was an express to Westport. A wire to Riley out there would prevent Sanchez from getting away from sight, even if he should decide to get off at the only other stop.

What the little dancer was up to was just as mysterious as ever.

CHAPTER X

THE DETECTAPHONE DETECTOR

KENNEDY was waiting impatiently for me at the laboratory and enjoyed a quiet laugh at my expense when I told him of my fiasco in untangling the secret of Paquita.

'Is there any news?' I asked, hastily endeavouring to change the subject.

'Yes,' he replied, glancing at his watch. 'Irene Maddox and Winifred have come in to town on a later train. As nearly as I can make out they've joined forces. They have a common hatred of Paquita, whatever else they may lack.'

'How do you know they are here?' I queried.

'They have called me up and made an appointment to meet me at the laboratory. They ought to be here any minute, now. I'm glad you came. I shouldn't like to meet them alone. I'd rather have someone as a witness. It's strange that they should be seeking to have me work for them,' considered Kennedy.

'What do you mean?' I asked. 'Hastings sought you out first. It may be quite natural that Irene Maddox should consult the detective retained by her former husband's lawyer in such a case. Have any of the others been after you?'

'Yes,' he replied thoughtfully. 'After I left you this morning I had a most peculiar experience. Shelby Maddox is either the most artless or else the most artful of all of them.'

'How is that?' I inquired.

'Just as I said,' repeated Kennedy. 'Shelby hurried into one of those slot-machine telephone booths in the station and I slipped into the next one. Instead of calling up, I put my ear to the wall and listened. There wasn't anything much to what he said. It was merely a call to his lawyer, Harvey, telling him that he was on his way down-town. The strange thing came afterward. By that time the station was cleared of those who had come on the train. Shelby happened to glance into the other booth as he left his own and saw me in the act of making a fake telephone call. Instead of going away, he waited. When I came out, he looked about quickly to see if we were alone, then took my arm and hurried me into another part of the station. I didn't know what was coming, but I was hardly prepared for what he said.'

'And that was?' I asked eagerly.

'That I work for him, too, in the case,' exclaimed Kennedy, to my utter surprise.

'Work for him?' I repeated. 'Was it a stall?'

Kennedy shook his head doubtfully. 'I'm not prepared to say. It was either clever or simple. He even asked me to go down-town with him and see Harvey.'

'And you went?'

'Certainly. But I can't say I learned anything new. I haven't quite decided whether it was because they knew too much or too little.'

'Are you going to do it? What did you tell him?'

'I told him quite frankly that as long as I had come into the case as I was—without mentioning any names or facts—the best I could do was to see that he got a square deal.'

'Did that satisfy him?'

'Not much. But it was all that I would say. At least it gave me a chance to study him at close range.'

'What did you think of him?'

'Shelby Maddox is nobody's fool,' replied Kennedy slowly. 'I may not know his story yet, but I have begun to get his number.'

'How about Harvey?'

'A very clever lawyer. Shelby will keep out of a great deal of trouble if he takes Harvey's advice.'

The sound of footsteps down the hall outside interrupted

us, and an instant later the laboratory door opened. Irene Maddox entered first and for a moment Winifred stood in the doorway, rather timidly, as though not yet quite convinced that she was right in coming to Kennedy.

Kennedy advanced to greet them, but still Winifred did not seem to be thoroughly reassured that the visit was just the proper thing. She looked about curiously at the instruments and exhibits which Kennedy had collected in his long warfare of science against crime, and it was evident that she would a great deal rather have had this a social visit than one in connection with the case. I guessed that it was Irene Maddox who had urged her on.

'I—we've come to see you about that woman, Paquita,' began Mrs Maddox, almost before she had settled herself in one of our easy-chairs, which Craig had installed to promote confidences on the part of his clients.

Mrs Maddox's voice was trembling slightly with emotion and Winifred's quick glance at Kennedy indicated that Paquita had furnished the leverage by which Mrs Maddox had persuaded Winifred to accompany her.

'Yes,' encouraged Kennedy, 'we have been watching the young lady—and others—with some interest. Do you know anything about her that you think we ought to know?'

'Know anything?' repeated Mrs Maddox bitterly. 'I ought to know that woman.'

Her feelings were easily understood, although as far as I could see that did us very little good in getting at the real mystery that surrounded the little dancer.

'You must have noticed,' went on Mrs Maddox, nervously, 'how she is hanging around out there. For weeks and months I have been watching that woman. Sometimes I think they are all in league against me—the lawyers, the detectives, everybody.'

Kennedy was about to say something, then checked himself. How could we know but that this was merely an attempt to find out just how much it was we knew? I longed to ask about

Sanchez, yet felt that it would be better not to disclose how much—or rather how little—we actually had discovered.

'Why,' she continued, 'it even seems as if her hostility was levelled against Winifred, too.'

Winifred said nothing, though it was evident that she was consumed with curiosity to find out what hold, if any, Paquita had on Shelby.

'Then you really do not know who or what Paquita is?' asked Kennedy directly.

'I know that she is an adventuress,' asserted Mrs Maddox. 'Mr Hastings has always professed to know nothing of her. At least so he has said. Even when I have watched her I must admit I have found out only what she was doing at that time. But my intuition tells me that there is something more. Oh, Professor Kennedy, is there no such thing as *justice* in this world? Must that woman continue to flaunt herself brazenly before me? Cannot you *do* something?'

'You may depend on it,' assured Kennedy. 'I shall make my investigation—arrive at the truth. Even my own client cannot prevent me from doing that. And if I find that an injustice is being done, you may be sure that I will do my best to set it straight. More than that I could not say even to Shelby Maddox this morning when he asked me to take up the case for him.'

Both women glanced quickly at Kennedy. The mention of Shelby's name came, quite apparently, as a surprise to them. Winifred seemed rather more reticent now than ever before. It was evident that Irene Maddox had not succeeded in what she had intended. Yet she did not betray her disappointment.

'Thank you,' she said, rising. 'Then I may expect you to help me—I mean us?'

'In every way in my power,' promised Kennedy, accompanying them to the door.

Kennedy looked after them as the door closed. 'I wonder what that visit was for,' he considered as their footsteps died away.

Having no answer for the query, I attempted none.

'What has Burke been doing?' I inquired, suddenly recollecting the Secret Service man. 'Have you heard anything from him today since we came to the city?'

'Yes,' he replied, opening a cabinet. 'Burke has undertaken some work along another line in tracing out the telautomaton robbery and what may have become of that model. I haven't heard from him and I don't imagine that anything will develop right away in that direction.'

'What is that?' I inquired, watching Craig as he took from one cabinet an apparatus which appeared to consist of two coils, or rather sets of wires, placed on the ends of a magnet bar. He began to adjust the thing, and I saw from the care with which he was working that it must be an instrument of some delicacy.

'Just an instrument that may enable me to discover how that attack was made on you last night,' Kennedy answered perfunctorily, forgetting even my question as he worked over the thing.

For several minutes I watched him, wondering at the strange turn of events that had sent both Shelby and Winifred secretly to Kennedy.

'By the way,' exclaimed Craig, suddenly looking at his watch, 'if we are to meet Hastings and accomplish anything we had better be on our way down there.'

In the Subway Kennedy relapsed into a brown study of the events of the day, only breaking away from his reverie as, above the rattle and bang of the train, he tapped the package he was carrying.

'I was just thinking of that garage incident of yours last night,' he remarked. 'What struck you as being peculiar about it?'

'The whole thing,' I replied, smiling weakly. 'I leaned into trouble—and got it.'

'Just so,' he returned. 'Well, do you realise that the only mention we made of the garage was when we were talking in Hastings's office? Think it over.'

He relapsed again into his study and nothing more was said until we arrived at Wall Street.

Hastings was waiting for us, nervously pacing the floor. Evidently the warning Kennedy had given had impressed him. He had been so afraid of even his own shadow that he had scarcely transacted any business at all that day.

'Kennedy, I'm glad to see you,' he greeted. 'What has happened today? What's that?'

'Nothing much,' returned Craig vaguely, although his face was not at all vague, for he had placed his finger on his lips and was most vigorously pantomiming caution.

Carefully he unwrapped the paper about the coils I had seen. Then he set the instrument on Hastings's desk, unscrewed an electric-light bulb from its socket and attached a wire to the socket. After a final careful adjustment he placed something to his ear and began walking quietly about the room, a tense, abstracted, far-away look on his face, as now and then he paused and listened, holding the free end of the apparatus near the wall, or a piece of furniture, wherever he chanced to be.

What he was looking for neither of us could guess, but his caution had been emphatic enough to halt any question we might have.

Over and over he passed the free end of the apparatus along wall and floor. At each stop he seemed to be considering something carefully, then with a negative nod to himself went on.

This had been going on for some fifteen minutes, when he stopped in the corner back of a coat-tree. He looked about as he pulled the thing from his ear, saw a heavy pair of shears on Hastings's desk, and seized them.

Deliberately he dug into the plaster of the wall, while Hastings and I bent over anxiously.

He had not gone half an inch before he began to scrape very carefully, as though he were afraid of hurting something alive.

I looked. There on the wall, back of the plaster, hung a little tell-tale black disc. I recognised it the instant I saw it and turned quickly just in time to prevent a question from Hastings.

Someone had been using the detectaphone against us!

Though not a word was said, I realised vaguely what Kennedy later explained. He had suspected it and had made use of a method of finding pipes and metals electrically, when concealed in walls under plaster and paper.

It was a special application of the well-known induction balance principle. One set of coils on the magnet bar received an alternating or vibrating current The other was connected with a little sensitive telephone. Craig had first established a balance so that there was no sound in the telephone. When the device came near metal piping the balance was destroyed and a sound was heard in the telephone. He had located all the water, steam, and other pipes, the wires from the telephone, the messenger-call box, and other things. There still remained one other pair of wires unaccounted for. The balance had located their existence and exact position. Clever though the installation of the little mechanical eavesdropper had been as an aid to crime, Craig's detectaphone detector had uncovered it!

Impulsively I seized at the devilish little black disc that had forewarned someone and had nearly cost me my life. I started to yank at it. The wires yielded their slack, but before I could give them a final pull Kennedy grasped my hand.

Without a word he wrote on a pad on the desk:

'Leave it there. They don't know we've found it. We can use it against them!'

CHAPTER XI

THE FRAME-UP

HASTILY Craig wrote on the paper, while Hastings and I read in silence:

'We'll lay a trap by a fake conversation about the garage.'

Neither of us spoke a word, waiting for our cue from him.

'Well,' he said, in a rather loud tone, as though he had just come into the office, 'one thing that we must do is to find out whether there was a car that came into the city from Westport that night—and perhaps went back there. There's a clue in that garage, Walter. Someone is making that a headquarters. But we can't do anything tonight—not after your experience. No, we'll have to wait until daylight tomorrow and then we'll make a thorough search.'

'You won't get me here again alone at night,' I put in, and my tone was rather convincing after my experience.

'I'm sure there's something there, all right,' added Hastings, following the lead, although he seemed to have only the most indefinite notion of where it took him.

'Indeed there is,' agreed Kennedy quickly.

'Personally, I think that Mito knows more than he should about the whole business,' I added. 'The Jap is a mystery to me.'

'And Sanchez, too,' put in Hastings, evidently thinking of how he seemed always to be crossing our path.

'Yes, that's the place to look into, all right,' concluded Craig, beckoning us to leave the room and the conversation.

'If that doesn't sink into somebody's mind,' he chuckled, when we were outside, 'I shall be surprised. We must get back to Westport before it is too late.'

'Why didn't you follow the wire down and find out where it ended?' I asked, as we left Hastings's office. 'You might have—'

'Surprised a stenographer at the other end taking notes,' he interrupted. 'We can do that any time. What I wanted was to plant something that would make the real criminal act and throw him off his guard. We'll have to stop again at the laboratory. There is something there I must take out with me. That will give us just time to catch the late afternoon express if we hurry.'

While Hastings and I waited outside Kennedy went in and soon returned with the instrument he sought. Even yet, Hastings could not resist the impulse to gaze about nervously, recalling the shot that had been fired at him on the occasion of his first visit. Nothing happened this time, however, and we made the train by a matter of seconds.

Frances Maddox and her husband were the only persons on the express whom we knew. The others seemed to have returned already. I saw that we would have to rely on Riley and the Secret Service men to get anything that might have happened in the meanwhile. Once or twice I caught the eye of Mrs Walcott furtively gazing in Kennedy's direction, and I fancied she was a trifle nervous. Walcott himself read a magazine stolidly, as though declining to get excited and I wondered, from his manner, whether the affair and the constant feud in the family into which he had married might not be getting on his nerves. They did not talk much, nor did we, and it was with a sense of relief that we all arrived finally at Westport.

'Well,' I remarked, aside to Kennedy, as we three piled into the little 'flivver' that did public hack duty at the station, 'I wonder what we shall run into now.'

'Things ought to develop fast, I should say,' he returned. 'I think we've laid a good foundation.'

Without even looking about or inquiring for Burke or Riley,

Kennedy rather ostentatiously went directly to the hotel office on our arrival at the Harbour House.

'Our rooms are at the north side of the hotel,' he began. 'I wonder if there are any vacant on the bay side?'

The clerk turned to look at his list and I took the opportunity to pluck at Kennedy's sleeve.

'Why don't you get rooms in the rear?' I whispered. 'That's the side on which the garage is.'

Kennedy nodded hastily to me to be silent and a moment later the clerk turned.

'I can fix you up on the bay side,' he reported, indicating a suite on a printed floor-plan.

'Very fine,' agreed Craig. 'If you will send a porter I will have our baggage transferred immediately.'

As we left the desk Kennedy whispered his explanation. 'Don't you understand? We'll be observed. Everything we do is watched, I am convinced. Just think it over. Selecting a room like this will disarm suspicion.'

In the lobby of the hotel Riley was waiting for us anxiously.

'Where's Mr Burke?' asked Kennedy. 'Hasn't he returned?'

'No, sir. And not a word from him yet. I don't know where he can be. But we are handling the case at this end very well alone. I got your wire,' he nodded to me. 'We haven't missed Sanchez since he got back.'

'Then he didn't make any attempt to get away,' I remarked, gratified that I had lost nothing by not following him on the earlier train. 'Is Paquita back?'

'Yes; she came on the train just before yours.'

'What has she done—anything?'

Riley shook his head in perplexity.

'If it didn't sound ridiculous,' he replied slowly, 'I would say that that fellow Sanchez was on the trail of Paquita more than we are.'

'How's that?'

'Why, he follows her about like a dog. While we're watching her he seems to be watching us.'

'Perhaps he's part of her gang—her bodyguard, if there is such a thing as a gang,' I remarked.

'Well, he acts very strangely,' returned Riley doubtfully. 'I'm not the only one who has noticed it.'

'Who else has?' demanded Kennedy quickly.

'Mrs Maddox, for one. She went up to the city later—oh, you know? Miss Walcott went with her. You know that, too? They returned on the train with Paquita.'

'What has Mrs Maddox done since she came back?' inquired Craig.

'It wasn't half an hour before they returned that Paquita came downstairs,' replied the Secret Service man. 'As usual Sanchez was waiting, in the background, of course. As luck would have it, just as she passed out of the door Mrs Maddox happened along. She saw Sanchez following Paquita—you remember she had already paid him off for the shadowing he had done for her. I don't know what it was, but she went right up to him. Oh, she was some mad!'

'What was it all about?' asked Craig, interested.

'I didn't hear it all. But I did hear her accuse him of being in with Paquita even at the time he was supposed to be shadowing her for Mrs Maddox. He didn't answer directly. "Did I ever make a false report about her?" he asked Mrs Maddox. She fairly spluttered, but she didn't say that he had. "You're working for her—you're working for somebody. You're all against *me!*" she cried. Sanchez never turned a hair. Either he's a fool or else he's perfectly sure of his ground, as far as that end of it went.'

'I suppose he might have double-crossed her and still made honest reports to her,' considered Kennedy; 'that is, if he made the same reports to someone else who was interested, I mean.'

Riley nodded, though it was evident the remark conveyed no more idea to him than it did to me.

'Shelby Maddox has returned, too,' added Riley. 'I found out that he sent that Jap, Mito, with a note to Paquita. I don't know what it was, but I have a man out trying to get a line on it.'

'Mito,' repeated Kennedy, as though the Japanese suggested merely by his name a theory on which his mind was working.

There seemed to be nothing that could be done just now but to wait, and we decided to take the opportunity to get a late dinner. Winifred Walcott and Mrs Maddox had already dined, but Frances Walcott and her husband were at their table. They seemed to be hurrying to finish and we did the same—not because they did, but because we had work to do.

Dinner over, Hastings excused himself from us, saying that he had some letters to write, and Kennedy made no objection. I think he was rather pleased than otherwise to have the opportunity to get away.

Outside we met Riley again, this time with one of his operatives.

'What's the matter?' inquired Kennedy.

'Matter enough,' returned Riley, much exercised. 'You know I told you that Shelby had come ashore from the *Sybarite* with Mito? Well, we've been following them both pretty closely. I think I told you of his sending a note to Paquita. Both Shelby and Mito have been acting suspiciously. I had this man detailed to watch Shelby. That confounded Jap is always in the way, though. Tell Mr Kennedy what happened,' he directed.

The operative rubbed his back ruefully. 'I was following Mr Maddox down to the beach,' he began. 'It was rather dark and I tried to keep in the shadow. Mr Maddox never would have known that he was being followed. All of a sudden, from behind, comes that Jap. Before I knew it he had me—like this.'

The man illustrated his remark by lunging forward at Kennedy and seizing both his hands. He stuck his crooked knee upward and started to fall back, just catching himself before he quite lost his balance.

'Over he went backwards, like a tumbler,' went on the man, 'threw me clean over his head. If it had been on a stone walk or there had been a wall there, it would have broken my head.'

'Jiu-jitsu!' exclaimed Kennedy.

'I wonder why Mito was so anxious to cover his master?' considered Riley. 'He must have had some reason—either of his own or orders from Maddox. Anyhow, they both of them managed to get away, clean.'

Riley looked from Craig to me in chagrin.

'Quite possibly orders,' put in the man, 'although it's not beyond him even to be double-crossing Mr Maddox, at that.'

'Well, try to pick them up again,' directed Kennedy, turning to me. 'I've some rather important business just now. If Mr Burke comes back, let me know at once.'

'You bet I'll try to pick them up again,' promised the Secret Service man, viciously, as we left him and went to our room.

There Craig quickly unwrapped one of the two packages which he had brought from the laboratory while I watched him curiously but did not interrupt him, since he seemed to be in a great hurry.

As I watched Kennedy placed on a table what looked like a miniature telephone receiver.

Next he opened the window and looked out to make sure that there was no one below. Satisfied, he returned to the table again and took up a pair of wires which he attached to some small dry cells from the package.

Then he took the free ends of the wires and carefully let them fall out of the window until they reached down to the ground. Leaning far out, he so disposed the wires under the window that they fell to one side of the windows of the rooms below us and would not be noticed running up the side wall of the hotel, at least not in the twilight. Then he took the other package from the table and was ready to return downstairs.

We had scarcely reached the lobby again when we ran into Hastings, alone and apparently searching for us.

'Is there anything new?' inquired Kennedy eagerly.

Hastings seemed to be in doubt. 'None of the Maddox family are about,' he began. 'I thought it might be strange and was looking for you. Where do you suppose they all can be? I haven't seen either Paquita or Sanchez. But I just saw Winifred alone.'

'What was she doing? Where is she?' demanded Kennedy.

Hastings shook his head. 'I don't know. I was really looking for Shelby. I think she was going toward the Casino. Have you heard anything?'

'Not a thing,' returned Kennedy brusquely. 'You will pardon me, I have a very important matter in hand just now. I'll let you know the moment I hear anything.'

Kennedy hurried from the Lodge toward the Casino, leaving Hastings standing in the hotel, amazed.

'Nothing new!' he almost snorted as he suddenly paused where he could see the Casino. 'Yet Hastings sees Winifred going out in a hurry, evidently bent on something. If he was so confounded eager to find Shelby, why didn't it occur to him to stick about and follow Winifred?'

It was quite dark by this time and almost impossible to see anyone in the shadows unless very close. Kennedy and I took a few turns about the Casino and along some of the gravel paths, but could find no trace of any of those whom we were watching.

'I oughtn't to let anything interfere with this "plant" I am laying,' he fretted. 'Riley and the rest ought to be able to cover the case for a time. Anyhow, I must take a chance.'

He turned and for several minutes we waited, as if to make perfectly sure that we were not being watched or followed.

Finally he worked his way by a round-about path from the Casino, turned away from the Lodge into another path, and at last we found ourselves emerging from a little hedge of dwarf poplars just back of the little garage, which had evidently been his objective point.

Mindful of my own experience there, I looked about in some

trepidation. I had no intention of running again into the same trap that had nearly finished me before. Nor had Kennedy.

Cautiously, in the darkness, he entered. This time it was deserted. No asphyxiating gun greeted us. He looked about, then went to work immediately.

Back of the tool-box in a far corner he bent down and unwrapped the other package which he had been carrying. As nearly as I could make it out in the darkness, there were two rods that looked as though they might be electric-light carbons, fixed horizontally in a wooden support, with a spindle-shaped bit of carbon between the two ends of the rods, the points of the spindles resting in hollows in the two rods. To binding screws on the free ends of the carbon rods he attached wires, and led them out through a window, just above.

'We don't want to stay here a minute longer than necessary,' he said, rising hurriedly. 'Come—I must take up those wires outside and carry them around the wing of the Harbour House, where our room is.'

Without a word we went out. A keen glance about revealed no one looking, and trusting that we were right, Kennedy picked up the wires and we drove back into the shadow of the grove from which we came.

Carefully as he could, so that no one would trip on them and rip them out, Kennedy laid the wires along the ground, made the connection with those he had dropped from the window, and then, retracing our steps, managed to come into the hotel from the opposite side from the garage and the other wing from our room.

'Just had a wire from Mr Burke,' announced Riley, who had been looking all over for us, a fact that gave Craig some satisfaction, for it showed that we had covered ourselves pretty well. 'He's coming up from the city and I imagine he has dug up something pretty good. That's not what I wanted to tell you, though. You remember I said Shelby Maddox had sent Mito with a note to Paquita?'

Kennedy nodded. No encouragement was necessary for Riley to continue his whispered report.

'Well, Shelby just met her on the beach.'

'Met Paquita?' I exclaimed, in surprise at Shelby's secret meeting after his public ignoring of the little adventuress.

'On the beach alone,' reiterated Riley, pleased at retailing even this apparent bit of scandal.

'What then?' demanded Craig.

'They strolled off down the shore together.'

'Have you followed them?'

'Yes, confound it, but it's low tide and following them is difficult, without their knowing it. I told the men to do the best they could, though—short of getting into another fight. Mito may be about, and, anyhow, Shelby might give a very good account of himself.'

'You're not sure of Mito, then?'

'No. No one saw him again after he threw my operative. He may have disappeared. However, I took no chance that Shelby was alone.'

For a moment Kennedy seemed to consider the surprising turn that Shelby's secret meeting with the little dancer might give to the affair.

'Walter,' he said at last, turning to me significantly, 'would you like to take a stroll down to the dock? This matter begins to look interesting.'

We left Riley, after cautioning him to make sure that Burke saw us the moment he arrived, and again made our way quietly from the Lodge toward the Casino, in which we now could hear the orchestra.

A glance was sufficient to reveal that none of those whom he sought were there, and Kennedy continued down the bank toward the shore and the Harbour House dock.

CHAPTER XII

THE EAVESDROPPERS

IT was a clear, warm night, but with no moon. From the Casino the lights shone out over the dark water, illuminating here and seeming to deepen the already dark shadows there.

A flight of steps ran down to the dock from the dance pavilion, but, instead of taking this natural way, Kennedy plunged into the deeper shadow of a path that wound around the slight bluff and came out on the beach level, below the dock. From the path we could still hear the sounds of gaiety in the Casino.

We were about to emerge on the beach, not far from the spiling on which the dock platform rested, when I felt Kennedy's hand on my elbow. I drew back into the hidden pathway with him and looked in the direction he indicated.

There, in a little summer-house above us, at the shore end of the dock, I could just distinguish the figures of two women, sitting in the shadow and looking out intently over the strip of beach and the waves of the rising tide that were lapping up on it. It was apparent that they were waiting for someone.

I turned and strained my eyes to catch a glimpse down the beach, but in the blackness could make out nothing. A look of inquiry toward Kennedy elicited nothing but a further caution to be silent. Apparently he was determined to play the eaves-dropper on the two above us.

They had been talking in a low tone when we approached and we must have missed the first remark. The answer was clear enough, however.

'I tell you, Winifred, I saw them together,' we heard one voice in the summer-house say.

Instantly I recognised it as that of Irene Maddox. It needed no clairvoyancy to tell precisely of whom she was talking. I wondered whether she was trying to vent her grudge against Paquita at the expense of Shelby and Winifred. At least I could fancy how Shelby would bless his sister-in-law as a trouble-maker, if he knew.

'I can't believe that you are right,' returned the other voice, and it was plainly that of Winifred.

There was a quiver of emotion in it, as though Winifred were striving hard to convince herself that that something she had heard was not true.

'I can't help it,' replied Mrs Maddox. 'That is what I used to think—once—that it couldn't be so. But you do not know that woman—nor men, either.'

She made the last remark with unconcealed bitterness. I could not help feeling sorry for her in the misfortune in which her own life with Maddox had ended. Yet it did not seem right that she should poison all romance. Still, I reflected, what, after all, did I really know, and why should I rise to the defence of Shelby? Better, far, that Winifred should learn now than to learn when it was too late.

'I have been watching her,' pursued Irene. 'I found that I could not trust any man where that woman was concerned. I wish I had never trusted any.'

'I cannot believe that Shelby would deliberately deceive me,' persisted Winifred.

Irene Maddox laughed hollowly. 'Yet you know what we discovered this afternoon,' she pressed. 'Why, I cannot even be sure that that detective, Kennedy, may not be working against me. And as for that lawyer of my husband's, Hastings, I don't know whether I detest him more than I fear him. Let me warn you to be careful of him, too. Remember, I have been observing for a long time. I don't trust him, or any other lawyer. You never can tell how far they may be concerned in anything.'

There was a peculiar piquancy to the innuendo. Evidently

Irene Maddox suspected Hastings of much. And again I was forced to ask myself, what did I really so far know?

I fancied I could detect that the poor woman had reached a point where she was suspicious of everybody and everything, not an unnatural situation, I knew, with a woman in her marital predicament.

'What has Mr Hastings done?' inquired Winifred.

'Done?' repeated Mrs Maddox. 'What has he left undone? Why, he shielded Marshall in everything, whenever I mentioned to him this Paquita woman—said it was not his business what his client's private life was unless he was directed to interest himself in it by his client himself. He was merely an attorney, retained for certain specific purposes. Beyond that he was supposed to know nothing. Oh, my dear, you have much to learn about the wonderful freemasonry that exists among men in matters such as this.'

I caught Kennedy's quizzical smile. We were having a most telling example of freemasonry among women, into which Irene was initiating a neophyte. I felt sure that Winifred would be much happier if she had been left alone, and events might have a chance to explain themselves without being misinterpreted—a situation from which most of the troubles both in fact and in fiction arise. In her watching of her errant husband, Irene had expected everyone immediately to fall in line and aid her— forgetting the very human failing that most people possess of objecting to play the role of informer.

'What fools men are!' soliloquised Irene Maddox a moment later, as though coming to the point of her previous random remarks. 'Just take that little dancer. What do they see in her? Not brains, surely. As for me, I don't think she has even beauty. And yet, look at them! She has only to appear up there in the Casino at this very moment to be the most popular person on the floor, while other girls go begging for partners.'

I could feel Winifred bridling at the challenge in the remark. She had tasted popularity herself. Was she to admit defeat at the hands of the little adventuress? Criticise as one might, there was still a fascination about the mystery of Paquita.

One could feel the coolness that had suddenly risen in the summer-house—as if a mist from the water had thrown it about. Nor did the implication of the silence escape Irene Maddox.

'You will pardon me, my dear,' she said, rising. 'I know how thankless such a job is. Perhaps I had better not be seen with you. Yes, I am sure of it. I think I had better return to the hotel.'

For a moment Winifred hesitated, as if in doubt whether to go, too, or to stay.

Finally it seemed as if she decided to stay. I do not know which course would have been better for Winifred—to accompany the elder woman and imbibe more of the enforced cynicism, or to remain, brooding over the suspicions which had been injected into her mind. At any rate, Winifred decided to stay, and made no move either to detain or accompany the other.

Irene Maddox arose and left Winifred alone. If she had been watching Paquita there was no further need. Winifred would watch now quite as closely.

As her footsteps died away, instead of remaining near the dock Kennedy turned and, keeping back in the shadows where we could not be seen by the silent watcher in the summer-house, we went along down the shore.

In the shelter of a long line of bath-houses that belonged to the hotel we paused. There was no one in bathing at this hour, and we sat down and waited.

'What did you make of that conversation?' I whispered cautiously, lowering my voice so that we might not be eavesdropped upon in turn.

'Not strange that Mrs Maddox hates the little dancer,' replied Craig sententiously. 'It's quite evident Riley was right and that Shelby must be with her. I wonder whether they will return this way or on the land? It's worth taking a chance. Let's stay awhile, anyway.'

He lapsed into silence, as though trying to motivate the actors in the little drama which was unfolding.

It was not long before, down the beach, we saw a man and a woman coming toward us rapidly. Kennedy and I drew back farther, and as we did so I saw that the figure above us in the summer-house had moved away from the edge so as to be less conspicuous.

The crackle of some dry sea-grass back of the bathhouse startled us, but we did not move. It was one of the Secret Service men. There was no reason why we should conceal from him that we were on a similar quest. Yet Kennedy evidently considered it better that nothing should happen to put anyone on guard. We scarcely breathed. He passed, however, without seeing us, and we flattered ourselves that we were well hidden.

A few minutes later the couple approached. It was unmistakably Shelby Maddox and Paquita.

'It's no use,' we heard Shelby say, as they passed directly beside the bath-houses. 'Even down here on the beach they are watching. Still, I have had a chance to say some of the things I wanted to say. From now on—we are strangers—you understand?'

It was not said as brutally as it sounds on paper. Rather it gave the impression, from Shelby's tone, that they had never been much more.

For a moment Paquita said nothing. Then suddenly she burst forth with a little bitter laugh.

'It takes two to be strangers. We shall see!'

Without another word she turned, as though in a fit of pique and anger, and ran up the flight of steps from the bath-houses to the Casino, passing within five feet of us, without seeing us.

'We shall see,' she muttered under her breath; 'we shall see!'

In surprise Shelby took a step or two after her, then paused.

'The deuce take her,' he swore under his breath, then strode on in the direction of the steps to the dock and the summer-house.

He had scarcely gained the level when the figure in the summer-house emerged from the gloom.

'Well, Shelby—a tryst with the other charmer, was it?'

'Winifred!'

Miss Walcott laughed sarcastically. 'Is that all that your fine speeches mean, Shelby?' she said reproachfully. 'At the Lodge you scarcely bow to her; then you meet her secretly on the beach.'

'Winifred—let me explain,' he hastened. 'You do not understand. She is nothing to me—never has been. I am not like Marshall was. When she came down here the other night she may have thought she could play with me as she had with him. I met her—as I have scores of others. They have always been all the same to me—until that night when I met you. Since then—have I even looked at her—at anyone else?'

'Another pretty speech,' cut in Winifred icily. 'But would you have met her now, if you had known that you would be watched?'

'I should have met her in the lobby of the hotel, if that had been the only way,' he returned boldly. 'But it was not. I do not understand the woman. Sometimes I fear that she has fallen in love with me—as much as her kind can fall in love. I sent for her, yes, myself. I wanted to tell her bluntly that there could never be anything between us, that we could not—now—continue even the acquaintance.'

'But you knew her before—in the city, Shelby,' persisted Winifred. 'Besides, was it necessary to take her arm, to talk so earnestly with her? I saw you when you started.'

'I had to be courteous to her,' defended Shelby, then stopped, as though realising too late that it was not defence he should attempt, but rather confession of something that did not exist and a prayer of forgiveness for nothing.

'I did not believe what I heard,' said Winifred coldly. 'I was foolish enough to listen to you, not to others. It is what I see.'

'To others?' he asked, quickly. 'Who—what have they told you about me? Tell me.'

'No—it was in confidence. I cannot tell you who or what. No, not another word of that. You have opened my eyes yourself. You have only yourself to thank. Take your little Mexican dancer—let us see what she does to you!'

Winifred Walcott had moved away toward the steps up to the Casino.

'Please!' implored Shelby. 'Why, I sent for her only to tell her that she must keep away. Winifred!'

Winifred had turned and was running up the steps. Instead of waiting, as he had done with Paquita, Shelby took the steps two at a time. A moment later he was by her side.

We could not hear what he said as he reached her, but she took no pains to modulate her own voice.

'No—no!' she exclaimed angrily, choking back a sob. 'No—leave me. Don't speak to me. Take your little dancer, I say!'

A moment later she had come into the circle of light from the Casino. Pursuit meant only a scene.

At the float at the other end of the pier bobbed one of the tenders of the *Sybarite*. Shelby turned deliberately and called, and a moment later his man ran up the dock.

'I'm not going to go out to the yacht tonight,' he ordered. 'I shall sleep at the Lodge. Tell Mito, and come ashore with my things.'

Then he turned, avoiding the Casino, and walked slowly up to the Harbour House, as we followed at a distance.

I wondered if he might be planning something.

CHAPTER XIII

THE SERPENT'S TOOTH

WE were approaching the hotel when we met Riley's operative with whom we had been talking shortly before. He was looking about as though in doubt what to do next.

'So you managed to pick them up again on the beach?' greeted Kennedy.

'Yes,' he replied in surprise. 'How did you know?'

'We were back of the bath-houses as they came along. You passed within a few feet of us.'

The detective stared blankly as Kennedy laughed.

'What happened?'

'Nothing very much. I missed them at first, because of the delay of that fellow, Mito. But I reasoned that they must have strolled down the beach, though I didn't know how far. I took a chance and made a short cut overland. Fortunately I caught up with them just as they were about to turn back. I was a little careful, I suppose—after what happened.'

He hesitated a bit apologetically, then went on: 'I couldn't hear much of what they said. Queer fellow, that Shelby. First he sends to meet the girl, then they quarrel nearly all the time they are together.'

'What did the quarrel seem to be about?' demanded Kennedy. 'Couldn't you get any of it?'

'Oh, yes, I caught enough of it,' returned the operative confidently. 'I can't repeat exactly what was said, for it came to me only in snatches. They seemed to be arguing about something. Once he accused her of having been the ruin of his brother. She did not answer at first—just laughed sarcastically. But Shelby wasn't content with that. Finally she turned on him.

"'You say that I ruined Marshall Maddox," she cried. "His wife says I ruined him. Oh, Shelby, Shelby, he wasn't a man who had reached the age of discretion, I suppose—was he? Oh, it's always I who do things—never anybody else."'

'Yes,' prompted Kennedy. 'What else did she say?'

'She was bitter—angry. She stopped short. "Shelby Maddox," she cried, "you had better be careful. There is as much crime and hate and jealousy in every one of you as there is in Sing Sing. I tell you, be careful. I haven't told all I know—yet. But I will say that wherever your house of hate goes and whomever it touches, it corrupts. Be careful how you touch me!" Say, but Paquita was mad! That was when they turned back. I guess Shelby sort of realised that it was no use. They turned so suddenly that they almost caught me listening.'

'Anything else?' inquired Kennedy. 'What did Shelby have to say about himself? Do you think he's tangled up with her in any way?'

'I can't tell. Most of what they said was spoken so low that it was impossible for me to hear even a word. I think both of them realised that they were being watched and listened to. It was only once in a while when their feelings got the better of them that they raised their voices, and then they pretty soon caught themselves and remembered.'

'Then it was no lover's meeting?' I asked.

'Hardly,' returned the detective, with a growl. 'And yet she did not seem to be half as angry at Shelby as she did at the others. In fact, I think that a word from him would have smoothed out everything. But he wouldn't say it. She tried hard to get him, too. That little dancer is playing a game—take it from me. And she's artful, too. I wouldn't want to be up against her—no, sir.'

There was something incongruous about the very idea of this bull-necked flatty and the dainty little adventuress—as though the hippopotamus might fear the peacock. I would have laughed had the business itself not been so important. What was her game? In fact, what was Shelby's game? Each seemed to be playing a part.

'How about Mito?' I asked. 'Have you seen him again since you were jiu-jitsued?'

The detective shook his head. 'No,' he returned, reminiscently. 'He seems to have disappeared altogether. Believe me, I have been keeping an eye peeled for him. That Jap is a suspicious character. And it's just when you can't put your fingers on him that he is plotting some deviltry, depend on it.'

We left the Secret Service operative and continued toward the hotel. In the lobby Kennedy and I looked about eagerly in the hope of finding Winifred, but she was nowhere to be seen.

Our search was partly rewarded, however. At the end of the porch, in the shadow, we did find Frances Walcott and Irene Maddox. It was evident that they had seriously disagreed over something, and it did not require much guessing to conclude that it had to do with Winifred. Though Frances Walcott was really a Maddox and Irene Maddox was not, one would have scarcely guessed it. The stamp of the house of hate was on both.

Just a fragment of the conversation floated over to us, but it was enough.

'Very well, then,' exclaimed Mrs Maddox. 'Let them go their own way. You are like all the rest—you seem to think that a Maddox can do no wrong. I was only trying to warn Winifred, as I wish someone had warned me.'

The answer was lost, but Mrs Walcott's reply was evidently a sharp one, for the two parted in unconcealed anger and suspicion. Everywhere the case seemed to drag its slimy trail over all.

Look about as we might, there was no sign of Paquita. Nor was our friend Sanchez about, either. We seemed to have lost them, or else, like Mito, they were undercover.

'I think,' decided Kennedy, 'that I'll just drop into our rooms,

Walter. I haven't much hope that we'll find anything yet, but it will be just as well to be on the watch.'

Accordingly, we mounted by a rear staircase to our floor, and for a moment Kennedy busied himself adjusting the apparatus.

'A bit early, I think,' he remarked finally. 'There are too many people about to expect anything yet. We may as well go downstairs again. Perhaps Burke may return and I'm rather anxious to know what it is he has been after.'

For a moment, as we retraced our steps downstairs, I attempted, briefly, a résumé of the case so far, beginning with the death of Maddox, and down to the attack on Hastings and then on myself. As I viewed the chief actors and their motives, I found that they fell into two groups. By the death of Maddox, Shelby might profit, as might his sister, Frances. On the other hand were to be considered the motives of jealousy and revenge, such as might actuate Irene Maddox and Paquita. Then, too, there was always the possibility of something deeper lying back of it all, as Burke had hinted—an international complication over the telautomaton, the wonderful war engine which was soon likely to be the most valuable piece of property controlled by the family. Into such calculations even Mito, and perhaps Sanchez, might fit, as indeed might any of the others.

It was indeed a perplexing case, and I knew that Kennedy himself had not yet begun to get at the bottom of it, for the simple reason that when in doubt Kennedy would never talk. His silence was eloquent of the mystery that shrouded the curious sequence of events. At a loss for a means by which to piece together the real underlying story, I could do nothing but follow Kennedy blindly, trusting in his strange ability to arrive at the truth.

'One thing is certain,' remarked Kennedy, evidently sensing that I was trying my utmost to arrive at some reasonable explanation of the events, 'and that is that this hotel is a very jungle of gossip—sharper than a serpent's tooth. In my opinion, none of us will be safe until the fangs of this creature, whoever it may be, are drawn. However, we'll never arrive anywhere by trying merely to reason it out. This is a case that needs more facts— facts—facts.'

Following out his own line of thought, Craig decided to return downstairs to the seat of operations, perhaps in the hope of running across Hastings, who might have something to add. Hastings was not about, either. We were entirely thrown upon our own resources. If we were ever to discover the truth, we knew that it would be by our own work, not by the assistance of any of them.

Attempts to locate Hastings quickly demonstrated that we could not depend on him. Having worked secretly, there seemed to be little else to do now but to come out into the open and play the game manfully.

'What was the matter?' inquired Riley, as Kennedy and I sauntered into the lobby of the Harbour House in such a way that we would appear not to be following anybody.

'Why?' asked Kennedy.

'First it was Paquita,' continued Riley. 'She bounced into the hotel, her face flushed and her eyes flashing. She was as mad as a hornet at something. Sanchez met her. Why, I thought she'd bite his head off! And he, poor shrimp, took it as meekly as if he were the rug under her feet. I don't know what she said, but she went directly to her room. He has been about, somewhere. I don't see him now. I guess he thought she was too worked up to stay up there. But I haven't seen her come down.'

'Shelby must have been telling her some plain truth,' said Craig laconically.

'Shelby?' echoed Riley. 'Why, it wasn't five minutes afterward that Winifred Walcott came through, as pale as a ghost. She passed Irene Maddox, but they scarcely spoke. Looked as if she had been crying. What's the matter with them? Are they a bunch of nuts?'

Kennedy smiled. Evidently Riley was unacquainted with the softer side of life.

'Where's Shelby?' inquired Craig. 'Have you seen him—or Mito?'

'Down in the café, the last I saw him,' replied Riley. 'Shelby's another nut. You know how much he loves the rest. Well, he came in all excited, too. And what does he do? Sees Johnson Walcott reading a paper, grabs him by the arm as though he was a long lost friend, and drags him down to the café. Say, I'll be dippy, too, if this keeps on. They can't even remember their own feuds!'

Kennedy glanced at me with an amused significance. I gathered that he meant to hint that Shelby was stopping at nothing to secure the aid of Johnson Walcott in smoothing affairs over with his sister, Winifred. Just how Walcott himself would look on such a match I had no idea and was rather glad when Kennedy suggested that we adjourn to the café ourselves to look them over.

In a leather-cushioned booth were Shelby and Walcott, Shelby doing most of the talking, while Walcott listened keenly. We could not very well deliberately take the next booth, but we did manage to find a corner where they were not likely to notice us.

We had not been there long before Mito came in, carrying a grip in which were the clothes and linen his master had ordered ashore. Shelby directed him where to take the things, and as the Jap stood there I saw that Walcott was watching him closely. Not once did Mito look at him, yet one could not help feeling that the Oriental knew that he was watched and that Walcott was absorbing something from Shelby.

Mito bowed as he received his orders. No sooner had he turned than I saw Walcott shoot a glance at Shelby. If I had been a lip-reader I might have been more certain of the words framed by his lips. As it was, I was ready to swear that Walcott asked, 'Do you trust that fellow?' Shelby's answer I could not guess, but his face showed no anxiety, and it seemed as though he passed off the remark lightly.

Though the others had not seen us, Mito spied us with his beady eyes, though he did not turn his head to do so. At the door he almost ran into Sanchez, who was engrossed in watching Shelby. Neither said a word, but the quick scowl of Sanchez spoke a volume. He hated Shelby and everything pertaining to him.

Whatever it was that Shelby and Walcott were discussing, it was apparent that Walcott was not at all enthusiastic. He did not betray any feeling in the matter other than coldness.

'It wouldn't surprise me if they were discussing Winifred,' concluded Kennedy. 'If that is what it's about, it doesn't look as though Johnson Walcott had any overburdening desire to have Shelby as a brother-in-law.'

In spite of Walcott's coldness Shelby continued talking earnestly, but it seemed to have no effect. Walcott's reticence seemed to exasperate Shelby, who with difficulty restrained his own feelings. I fancied that, had it not been for Winifred, Shelby's temper would have got the better of him.

When finally Walcott rose and with a polite excuse started to move away, it was apparent that Shelby was intensely resentful. However, he said nothing, nor did he even attempt to follow Walcott out of the café.

'Evidently he has made little progress in patching up the tiff with Winifred,' concluded Craig, as we, too, rose and sauntered out into the main part of the hotel.

CHAPTER XIV

THE GEOPHONE

WE had no more than reached the lobby of the hotel again when we found Hastings seeking us. Evidently he had sensed that Kennedy was vexed at him for letting Winifred pass without finding out what was her mission.

'This time, at least, I think I have something to tell you,' he hastened, drawing us aside.

'What is it about?' encouraged Kennedy eagerly.

'Paquita,' he replied, scanning our faces. 'She has returned to the hotel.'

Kennedy's countenance betrayed some disappointment, for we already knew that.

'I saw Frances and Irene together, too,' went on Hastings.

Again Kennedy could not conceal his disappointment, for it was all an old story to us. Hastings was not to be gainsaid, however.

'Well, after Frances left Irene Maddox,' he continued, 'I saw that she was wrought up and nervous. So I watched her. She sought out Paquita.'

He drew back, gratified at the flash of interest that Craig instantly betrayed.

'Indeed?' asked Craig. 'What took place?'

'I could not hear it all,' continued the lawyer. 'But it seemed as though Frances was pleading with Paquita for something. I heard the names of both Shelby and Winifred mentioned. Paquita seemed quite haughty. Whatever it was that Frances was after, I am quite sure that she was not successful.'

I could see that Kennedy was actively trying to piece together the fragmentary information that we had gained during the evening.

What it all meant I could not fathom. But we knew enough to be quite sure that something important was afoot. First, Shelby had sent for Paquita and had his supposedly secret interview, of which we had learned enough to know that he had sought to influence the little dancer to let him alone. The meeting of Winifred and Irene we knew, as well as the meeting of Irene and Frances. It seemed that Frances Walcott had an interest in the events much more than we had expected, for, failing to obtain any satisfaction from Irene, she had even swallowed her pride and sought out Paquita.

What did it mean? Was Frances really trying to play the match-maker? Was it for her brother, Shelby, that she showed the concern, or was it for her sister-in-law, Winifred? There was a positive motive in the fact that a marriage between the two might more closely protect her own interests.

'They were talking,' pursued Hastings, 'when I saw her husband, Johnson, coming from the café. I think Paquita must have seen him first, for she cut the interview short very curtly and left her, though not before Johnson saw them together. He came over to his wife and I think he was a trifle angry at what he had seen. At any rate, it seemed that she was endeavouring to explain something to him and that he did not in the least approve.'

'Could you hear anything?' queried Kennedy.

'Not a thing, except that there seems to be something about which the Walcotts do not quite agree.'

I wondered whether Johnson Walcott's dissatisfaction had been more at finding his wife talking with Paquita than at the romance between Shelby and his own sister. In the café he had seemed to be far from delighted over the affair. Frances, on the other hand, bore every evidence of wishing to promote the match. It was a strange romance that we were watching.

'Was there anything else?' asked Kennedy.

'No,' replied Hastings. 'They walked away, still talking earnestly, and I think they have gone to their rooms.'

'Winifred was not about?'

'No. I saw Shelby, finally, though. But he seemed to be pre-occupied and didn't give me a chance to speak to him.'

'Where is he?'

'In the café, I suppose.'

Riley's approach at that moment served to introduce a new element into the situation.

'You saw Mito again?' asked Kennedy.

The Secret Service man nodded. 'Saw him take his master's things into the café, then to his room. After that he managed to slip away again. He seems to have something on his mind. I don't know what it is. We had a glimpse of Sanchez. He is about, but is keeping very low.'

'What has he been doing?'

'Nothing in the open, as far as I know,' returned Riley. 'He may be planning something. I don't like him any more than my man likes Mito. These Japs and wops are deep ones.'

Kennedy smiled, but said nothing. To Riley any foreigner was a suspicious character, if for no other reason than that he could not understand him.

'Any word from Mr Burke?' I reiterated.

Riley nodded. 'Yes, he will be here soon, now, I think.'

'Nothing else on Mito or Sanchez?' resumed Kennedy.

Riley negatived. 'Trouble with them is they know I'm watching them,' he explained. 'And when a man knows he is being watched it's easy for him. There's only one way to get him and that is to stick so close that it means a fight. We've had one and I hate to take the responsibility of another without orders from Mr Burke. Another fight with Mito might not turn out so luckily, either. Besides, I don't know that we want it to come to a fight—yet. Sanchez looks as though he might give an account of himself. These dark fellows are all knife-men, you know. I decided that it was best to pick up what we could without making a scene.'

Kennedy shrugged. There seemed to be nothing to criticise,

though it was a shame that circumstances were such that we were compelled to be content with fragments at a time when we needed every scrap of information.

'It's getting late,' he abserved, glancing at his watch. 'I think we might leave the field to Riley to cover, Walter, while we retire to our rooms. Goodnight, Mr Hastings. You'll tell Mr Burke to wake us, no matter what time he comes in?' he added, turning to Riley.

The Secret Service man agreed, and together Kennedy and I went back to our suite a second time. I was glad enough to go, too, for I wanted to see what the instrument was which he had installed in the garage.

As we entered, I could not help thinking of Winifred's action and why she had cut Shelby off so shortly. Was it a case of intuition, or was it merely what often passes for intuition—the capacity for making hasty and incorrect judgments on slender grounds?

What, too, was Mito? Was it he who had committed the murder of Marshall Maddox? Had he stolen the telautomaton plans? I wondered whether, after all, he might not be in the service of some foreign government, perhaps even be a spy.

With scarcely a word, Kennedy had taken his position at the table on which he had placed the peculiar miniature transmitter, holding it to his ear and listening intently.

'Is anyone talking there?' I asked, supposing that it was some special form of the detectaphone which he was using.

'I don't expect that there'll be any talking,' he replied. 'In fact, there may be only one person, for all I know, and he certainly won't talk to himself.'

A knock at our door cut short further inquiry. I opened it cautiously and was greeted by the cheery voice of Burke, who had come in on the last train.

'I think I've earned a rest tonight,' he remarked, dropping down into the easiest chair he could find. 'I'm tired, but at least I have some satisfaction for the day's work.'

'What have you found?' asked Kennedy eagerly, remembering that Burke had devoted himself first of all to tracing what had become of the deadly wireless destroyer itself.

'For one thing,' replied Burke slowly, 'I'm convinced, as far as I can be regarding something I don't actually know, that the telautomaton model is out here at Westport—at least not far away.'

'What makes you think so?' I asked quickly.

'That clue of the car waiting near the office interests me,' went on Burke slowly. 'I wasn't able to get anything out of the rookie on the beat. But I went on the supposition that somewhere between here and New York I might find a clue. And I have found several clues from constables and special officers in towns between Westport and the city. A car answering the description was seen at several points, and the time matches up. So I think it is safe to conclude that we are on the right track. The model is out here—somewhere—I am sure.'

'Have you made any progress in running down your band of foreign criminals?' asked Kennedy.

'No trace so far,' returned Burke, still cheerfully, 'except that it is entirely likely that Mito, or Paquita, or that fellow Sanchez may be the outside workers. Of course they would cover up their connection pretty closely. We can't expect to beat the most clever minds of the Continent as easy as we would a gang of sneak-thieves. Riley tells me you have been in the city most of the day. Have you uncovered anything?'

Briefly Kennedy outlined what had happened, coming down to the events of the evening down on the beach.

Another knock on the door, and Riley entered.

'You didn't come down, so I knew that Mr Kennedy and Mr Jameson were awake. You don't mind my coming in?'

'Not a bit,' returned Kennedy. 'We were just going over what I had gathered today. I was telling about that meeting between Frances and Irene Maddox.'

Riley's face assumed the same look of perplexity as it had

when we left him, nonplussed by the queer actions of the Maddox family.

'You saw it,' demanded Burke. 'What do you make of it?'

'I don't know,' confessed Riley. 'Maybe it means something, maybe not. I think it does. There's some kind of difference between those two women. I can't make it out. They seemed to be so friendly at first. Why, they even tell me Mrs Walcott backed Mrs Maddox in her fight with Mr Maddox over that Paquita. But now it's different, and it's growing worse.'

'Natural enough,' commented Burke. 'If Marshall Maddox was separated from his wife, don't you see he would have destroyed his will in her favour. If he was intestate, as it is most likely, then the other heirs—his brother and sister—stand to gain. There were no children. Mrs Maddox has her interest in a third. They can't take that away from her. But no doubt it makes her feel as if she had been done out of something, to see the others get what might have been hers under different circumstances.'

'That's it, I guess,' considered Riley. 'I've heard her say that she thought now that Paquita was put up to winning Marshall Maddox away from her, so that the others would benefit.'

'Pretty deep,' pondered Burke. 'but not impossible.'

'If she thinks that way,' I interposed, 'it might account for her attitude toward Winifred. She might be just jealous enough not to want her to come into not only Shelby's share, but part of the remainder.

'On the other hand,' I reconsidered, remembering my first theory, 'Mrs Maddox with her third interest is much better off than she was on what had been allowed her during the life of Marshall Maddox.'

'Shelby Maddox profits by it, any way you look at it,' observed Burke, following out our general review of possible motives. 'Where is he now?'

'Gone up to his room, I suppppose,' replied Riley.

'And Mito?'

'In the servants' quarters—unless he manages to slip out and get into some more deviltry.'

'Confound it, Riley,' broke in Burke, 'you've got to trail these people better! What's the matter? Haven't you enough men to—'

"Sh!' cautioned Craig from his place at the instrument on the table, his face showing intense attention to something.

'What's that?' asked Burke.

Kennedy was busy for the moment and did not answer. But a minute or so later he replied.

'A geophone, designed originally to record earth tremors, microseisms, small-amplitude earth shakings. It is really a microphone, he simplest form of telephone, applied to the earth—hence its name. Any high-school student in physics could make one. All that is necessary is to place that simple apparatus, which Mr Jameson saw, on the ground anywhere and attach it to a microphone receiver at the other end of the wire. You can hear an earthquake, or a big gun, or someone walking about. Hallo!—here's our friend again.'

Craig was again listening intently. What the most sensitive mechanical eavesdropper could not overhear this little geophone was now transmitting to him.

'Someone is in that garage,' he reported to us. 'Those are his footsteps. Our frame-up is working. He never would have gone there unless he thought we were not only going to go there tomorrow ourselves, but were out of sight now, too. By George!—there's another—there are two of them!'

I listened a moment myself, with Kennedy. The diaphragm vibrated terrifically. Then, suddenly, all was still.

What was going on?

Kennedy dropped the receiver on the table regardless of what might happen to its delicate adjustment, jumped up, and dashed out into the hall. Downstairs he went, not waiting for an elevator, for it was only three flights.

We followed madly, past the amazed night clerk, and out the back door of the hotel.

As we entered the garage, in the fitful light we could see a dark mass on the floor. Craig flashed his electric bull's eye. In the circle of light we saw that it was a man. Craig turned the form over.

It was Mito—dead!

CHAPTER XV

In utter bewilderment we looked at one another. Evidently Mito had entered, had been surprised by someone, and in a fight had been overpowered and killed.

Quickly I tried to reason it out. Plainly, even if the Jap had been the murderer of Marshall Maddox for the plans, he could not have been the thief of the telautomaton model in New York. Yet he must have known something about it all. Had we begun to get too close to Mito for someone's comfort?

Where was the annihilator which was to revolutionise warfare and industry? In whose hands were the secrets of the 'patent of death?' Who was the master criminal back of it all?

Mito's lips were sealed, at least.

It needed only a cursory examination of the body to determine how he had met his death. His face was drawn, as though he had seen the blow descending and was powerless to avoid it. On his skull was a deep gash, made by some heavy implement. The weapon, too, was lying there—Burke discovered it—a broken leaf of an automobile spring, used by someone to force tyres over rims. There was no art, no science, no finesse about the murder. It was just plain, brutal force.

If a bomb had been dropped among us, however, we could not have been more stunned than by the murder of Mito.

Burke and Riley were plainly at a loss, but I did not mind that. It was the look on Kennedy's face that worried me. He did not say much, but it was plain that he was thinking much.

'Just a brutal murder,' he remarked at length, after he had

surveyed the garage and finally come back to Mito himself again. 'There doesn't seem to be a clue. If it were odd, like the murder of Marshall Maddox, then there'd be more to work on. But it isn't. No, it's the harder just because of its simplicity. And it puts us just that much further back, because one whom we thought might lead us to the person higher up has been removed in the most primitive and, after all, most startling fashion.'

'I'll wager that fellow Sanchez could tell something about this if we could only get at him right,' put in Burke, to whom Kennedy had delegated the removal of Mito's body.

Kennedy said nothing, but it surely had begun to look as though he might be acting for Paquita in some capacity. Was she, in turn, acting for a desperate band of crooks? I felt that if we could break down Sanchez we might reach her.

Burke barked his orders to Riley and the rest. 'You fellows have been marking time too long. Get out and find that man Sanchez.'

His men knew better than to question or defend. Action was the only thing that satisfied Burke. They took the orders on the jump and hurriedly organised themselves into a searching party, though what it was that was tangible that they had on Sanchez, supposing that they got him, it was hard to see. As thoroughly as they could the men under Burke and Riley covered the hotel, the Casino, the grounds, and finally turned their attention to the town.

Kennedy and I took up the search together, beginning at the hotel. Hunting through the corridors and other rooms brought no trace of the man we sought. He was not registered at the Harbour House, and though the clerk and some of the attendants knew him, they professed to be able to tell nothing. Nor was there any trace of Paquita.

Meanwhile Burke and Riley had spread a general alarm through the town, although I am sure that many of those whom they enlisted as searchers had not the slightest idea who Sanchez was or even what he looked like. The search was rapidly resolving itself into an aimless wandering about in the hope of running across this elusive individual. There seemed to be no particular way of tracing the man. The farther they got away from the hotel, however, the more convinced did it seem to make Kennedy to stick about the Lodge and Casino, if for no other reason than to keep an eye on any possible moves of the Maddoxes and Walcotts.

We were standing not far from the garage, back of the hotel, when from a second-story window, around the corner, issued a series of screams for help in a woman's voice. We dashed into the hotel, following the shouts of alarm inside and upstairs.

'It's Winifred Walcott's room,' answered one of the boys as we breathlessly questioned him.

As we approached the room on the second floor we came upon the maid, one or two guests, and several servants.

'Miss Winifred—she's gone, carried off!' blurted out the maid, catching sight of Kennedy.

She gestured wildly about. The outer sitting-room of the suite was in great disorder. The window, low and leading out on the roof of the hotel porch, was wide open. Some chairs were overturned and the portières between the living-room and the bedroom were torn from their fastenings, and gone.

'Tell me what happened?' demanded Kennedy.

The maid was almost too excited to talk coherently.

'In the room—Miss Winifred was pacing up and down—nervous—I don't know what it was about, sir,' she managed to blurt out. 'I was in the next room, preparing some tea over an electric heater.'

'Yes, yes,' urged Kennedy impatiently. 'But what happened?'

'The window, sir, from the porch roof—opened—a man must have entered.'

'Did you see a man?'

'No, sir, but I heard a scream from Miss Winifred, as though something had been held over her mouth. No, I didn't see anyone. By the time I got in here I saw no one.'

Kennedy had stepped over by the door and was examining the torn hangings, hastily trying to reconstruct what had happened.

'Apparently the intruder, whoever it was, seized her from behind,' he concluded hastily, 'wrapped the portières over her head, and jerked her backward. The rush of the abductor must have torn them from their fastenings. Besides, they were a good muffler for her cries. The kidnapper must have carried her off, with them wrapped about her head, to prevent her screams from being heard again.'

He leaped out on the roof and I quickly followed. 'It would be quite possible,' he pointed out, approaching the far end, 'at this point for anyone to have gained entrance from the lower porch and to lift a girl like Winifred down from the roof to the ground.'

The slope of the land at this point was such that the second-floor level was not many feet above the ground level of the hillside.

I looked at Kennedy, at a loss to know what to do. Almost under our eyes, while everyone was looking for something else, Winifred had been spirited off. Why—and by whom?

Craig turned to the night clerk, who had been among the first to arrive and had followed us out on the porch roof.

'Has anyone any bloodhounds about here?' he asked quickly.

'Yes, sir—in the cottage back of the hotel there is a dog-fancier. He has a couple.'

'You know him?'

'Well.'

'Then you can borrow them?'

'Surely,' returned the clerk.

'Get them,' ordered Kennedy, waving away a group who had come up on the ground just below us. 'And hurry, before the scent gets cold.'

The clerk nodded and disappeared on the run.

Down below the crowd kept collecting.

'Keep them back,' ordered Kennedy, 'until the bloodhounds get here. See—there are marks in the grass that show that someone has been here—and—look—on this bush a torn corner of the portière.'

A moment later two men from the hotel stables appeared, with the dogs tugging on leash.

Quickly Kennedy gave them the scent before the trail of the footprints and the dragging portière had been destroyed by the curious.

They were off, tugging at the leash, Kennedy with one and I with the other. Burke and Riley had come up by this time, post-haste from their search for Sanchez, and joined us.

Away across the lawn, through the shrubbery, the trail led us, over a fence until farther along through a break in the hedge we came upon the road. Together we four hastened out over the highway.

'There's one thing in our favour,' panted Kennedy. 'No car was used—at least not yet. And if one or even two are carrying her, we can go a great deal faster than they can.'

My dog, which seemed to be the more active of the two, was outrunning the other, and, not through any desire on my part, but through his sheer tugging at the leash, he kept me a few paces ahead of the rest.

The road which had been taken by the kidnappers bent around the head of the harbour, branching off at a little country store, closed since early in the evening. No help was to be expected there, and we followed the road which ran down through a neck of land that led to the harbour opposite Westport.

So accustomed had I become to the steady tug of the dog on his leash, that, as we passed a little brook, where it seemed the abductor had paused, I was surprised to feel his pull on my hand suddenly relax.

THE ADVENTURESS   123

Before I knew it the dog had stopped. He uttered a peculiar wheeze—half sneeze, half gasp. Before I realised what it could be about he rolled over, as though he had been shot. It was not that he had lost the scent. Again and again, as he lay for the few seconds, gasping, he tried to pick up the trail.

As I watched him in utter astonishment I noticed a peculiar, subtle odour, with just the faintest suggestion of peach pits.

Kennedy, with more presence of mind than I had shown, drew up sharply on the leash of his dog, some feet behind me.

'Here, Burke,' he cried. 'Hold him—well away. Don't let him break loose.'

As Craig advanced toward me he stopped and picked up something that his foot had kicked in the dust. He advanced, holding away from him what looked like a small glass vial, while with his other hand he fumbled a small pocket flash-light.

'Whoever he was,' he exclaimed excitedly, 'the fellow is clever. Read the label.'

I did and drew back, with a hasty glance at my hound, which already lay dead at my feet.

The vial was labelled, 'PRUSSIC ACID—POISON.'

'Winifred!' I exclaimed, voicing the first fear that flashed through my mind.

'I think she is all right,' reassured Craig. 'If the abductor had wanted to kill her he would have had plenty of chances before this. No, I can imagine him stopping a second to wet a hand-kerchief in the brook and bind it over his nose as he opened the bottle and smeared the deadly fluid over the soles of his shoes, casting the empty bottle back of him. Certainly a clever ruse.'

Together we had retreated from the danger zone toward Burke and Riley, who were agape with astonishment as they learned of the unheard-of discovery we had made.

We looked at one another in blank astonishment and fear. Would the abductor get away, after all?

'A vexatious delay,' interrupted Kennedy calmly, 'But I doubt if they counted on our having another dog. The stuff must have worn off their shoes rapidly as they hurried on. Here, Burke, let me have the hound, now. It may take me some time, but I am sure that I can overcome this obstacle.'

While we waited, Craig cut a wide circle off the road, with the dog whining at having lost the scent. For some minutes down the road he let him run pretty free, trying to pick up the scent again at some point well past that at which we had found the deadliest of acids, where a dirt road debouched from the macadam.

'Come on!' he shouted at last, as a deep bay from the dog announced that he was off again and now running silent, since he had found the trail.

We made splendid progress now, and, by hasty calculation of the time, which must have been brief before the alarm was given, we concluded that we were without a doubt rapidly gaining on the abductor.

It was growing darker and darker as we went out of the lights of the main road into a deeper recess of the woods. Our little pocket flash-lights were too puny for such work.

Just then along the dirt road back of us came tearing a car. As it pulled up the driver flashed his spot-light ahead and it cut through the blackness like a bull's-eye.

'I heard you had gone this way,' shouted a voice from the darkness. 'Here, let me drive behind and light you ahead.'

In the shaft of light we could see a single figure of a man, staggering along with some heavy burden in his arms, and behind, several hundred yards away, Kennedy swiftly following with the hound.

As the light played on them, the figure seemed to realise that escape was now hopeless, unless he dropped his burden.

He paused just an instant, as though calculating something desperate. Just then I raised my gun and fired. I had no hope of hitting him in the fitful light and at the distance. But at least the shot had its effect.

He dropped Winifred and bolted.

At that moment the car came abreast of me. I turned quickly. The man in the car with the spot-light was Sanchez!

We had all come up with Kennedy now, the car stopping on the road with its lights playing full on the group.

Slowly now Winifred, who had fainted, revived. As she opened her eyes she seemed in a daze. Beyond what we already knew of her exciting adventure, she could tell nothing. Sanchez offered to drive her back to the hotel.

It was the first time he had spoken, and I wondered what Burke, fire-eater that he was, would do.

For a moment he hesitated, then strode up to the sallow-faced man deliberately.

'This thing has gone too far,' he ground out. 'Has all this been staged so that you could play the hero?'

Sanchez flared. For a moment I thought that there would be a fight. But he seemed to consider.

With a shrug, he replied quietly, 'I am at your service, if I can be of assistance to the young lady.'

The man was baffling. There was nothing for Burke to do but to hide his exasperation and take advantage of the offer.

To me, the sudden appearance of Sanchez was most mystifying. Had he in reality been on his way to overtake his own agent, when he had, fortunately for himself, overtaken us? Or were we all wrong and was Sanchez innocent? No one said a word as we made our quick return to the hotel.

Winifred was, by this time, herself and able to return to her room, which was now guarded from below. Neither she nor any of the rest of us could offer any explanation of the sudden attack or its purpose.

It had been a night of terror and we were about ready to drop from sheer exhaustion. Besides, it was too late now to do anything more. Kennedy and I decided to retire, leaving the

Secret Service operatives to watch for any further suspicious move on the part of anyone, especially those who, to all appearances, at least, seemed to be safely asleep at the Lodge.

CHAPTER XVI

THE INVISIBLE INK

WE were awakened very early by the violent ringing of our room telephone. Kennedy was at the receiver almost before I realised what was going on.

'Have you a machine to follow her?' I heard him ask hurriedly, then add: 'All right. I'll leave the trailing to you. Don't let her get away. We will go to the city on the train and then you can communicate with me at Mr Hastings's office. I'll go there.'

'Who was it?' I asked as Craig hung up. 'What has happened?'

'Paquita has tried to steal a march on us, I imagine,' he replied, beginning to dress hastily. 'Riley must have been up all night—or at least very early. He saw her come downstairs—it's scarcely five o'clock now—and a moment later her car pulled up. She's off, apparently by the road to New York. It's strange, too. Except that she got off so early, she made very little effort at concealment. You would think she must have known that she would be seen. I wonder if she wanted us to know it, or was just taking a chance at getting away while we were napping?'

'Is Riley following her?' I asked.

'Yes. As soon as he saw her speedster at the door he went out by another door and around to the garage. It just happened that the night man was there and Riley wheedled him into letting him have a car. It isn't as fast as Paquita's, but then it isn't always the fast car that gets away with it between here and New York. Sometimes, if you know how to drive and where the bad spots in the road are, you can make up what you lack in speed.'

Kennedy had pulled a timetable out of his pocket and was hurriedly consulting it.

'The service is very poor at this hour,' he remarked. 'It will be an hour before we can get the next train. We've missed the first by a few minutes.'

'What do you suppose she's up to now?' I speculated.

Kennedy shrugged silently.

We had finished dressing and for the moment there seemed to be nothing to do but wait.

'By George!' Craig exclaimed suddenly, starting for the door. 'Just the chance! Hardly anybody is about. We can get into her room while she is gone. Come on!'

Paquita's room, or rather suite, was on the floor above and in a tower at the corner. It was difficult to get into, but from a porch at the end of the hall we found that it was possible to step on a ledge and, at some risk, reach one window. Kennedy did not hesitate, and I followed.

As was to be supposed, the room was topsy-turvy, showing that she had been at some pains to get away early and quick.

We began a systematic search, pawing with unhallowed fingers all the dainty articles of feminine finery which might conceal some bit of evidence that might assist us.

'Pretty clever,' scowled Kennedy, as drawer after drawer, trunk after trunk, closet after closet, yielded nothing. 'She must have destroyed everything.'

He paused by a dainty little wicker writing-desk, which was scrupulously clean. Even the blotters were clean, as though she had feared someone might, by taking her hand-mirror, even read what she blotted.

The scrap-basket had a pile of waste in it, including a couple of evening papers. However, I turned it over and examined it while Craig watched.

As I did so I fairly pounced on a sheet of paper crumpled into a ball, and eagerly straightened it out flat on the table.

'Humph!' I ejaculated in disgust. 'Blank! Might have known she wouldn't leave anything in writing around, I suppose.'

I was about to throw it back when Kennedy took it from me.

He held it up to the light. It was still just a crumpled sheet of white paper. He looked about. On a dressing-table stood an electric curling-iron. He heated it and passed it over the paper until it curled with the heat. Still it was just a blank sheet of paper.

Was he pursuing a will-o'-the-wisp?

For a moment he regarded it thoughtfully. 'If I were in the laboratory,' he ruminated, 'I could tell pretty quick whether—Wait!—that's foolish. She hasn't any laboratory here. Walter, fill that basin with warm water.'

In the bottom of the basin Craig laid the sheet of paper and we bent over it.

'Nothing doing,' I remarked, disappointed.

'Why not?' he returned eagerly, turning the wet paper. 'We had it wrong side up!'

There, before our eyes, under the water, characters of some sort were appearing.

'You can make a perfectly good sympathetic ink from linseed oil, liquor of ammonia, and any of several other ingredients,' he said, watching with me. 'When writing with it dries it is invisible. Only water will bring it out. Then when it dries it is invisible again. Look.'

I did, but could not yet make out what it was, except that it seemed to be a hodge-podge of figures:

25153333151454324543441215251535443333¹552
543442254533442431521521243324432323154215

'It's a cipher!' I exclaimed with that usual acumen that made Kennedy smile indulgently.

'Quite right,' he agreed, studying the peculiar scrawl of the figures. 'But if are going to get to New York at anything like the time she does, we must get that train. I can't stop to decipher it now. We'll have plenty of time later in the morning. There's no use staying here, with the bird flown from the cage. I wonder whether Hastings is up yet.'

The lawyer, who was not as young as he used to be, was not awake, and it took some pounding on his door to wake him. As he opened it sleepily he was prepared to give someone a piece of his mind, until he saw that it was Kennedy and myself.

'Hallo!' he suppressed a surly growl. 'What's the trouble?'

Quickly Craig told him of the strange departure of Paquita.

'Up to something again,' muttered Hastings, finding someone at least on whom he could vent his spleen, although by this time he was fully awake. 'But, man, I can't get away for that early train!'

'Oh, that's all right,' reassured Kennedy. 'I think it will be enough if you come down on the express. But I wanted to tell you that when Riley called up and said he was off after Paquita, I could not think of a place in the city that was more central than your office and I took the liberty of telling him to call me up there, without thinking how early it would be.'

'I'll let you have the key,' returned Hastings, taking one from a ring. 'I'll join you as soon as I can get away.'

'Just what I wanted,' commented Kennedy, as we left the lawyer and hurried down to the dining-room for the few remaining minutes before the hotel 'bus left for the station. 'Besides, I wanted to get there when no one was around, so that I could have a chance to look at that confounded detectaphone again. Whoever it was who installed it was clever.'

'Might not that be the purpose of Paquita's trip to New York?' I queried.

'I was thinking of that. Between us, Riley and ourselves ought to be able to find that out.'

There was just time for a hasty bite of breakfast and we went into the dining-room, where Burke was evidently looking for us, for he came over and sat down. No one else was about and he felt free to talk.

'If you're going,' he decided, after telling us of Riley's report to him also of Paquita, 'I think I had better stay. We ought not to let any of them remain here unobserved—not after last night,' he added.

'Quite right,' agreed Kennedy. 'Have you heard anything more about the attack on Winifred?'

Burke negatived. He was still sore at Sanchez, who seemed to have come out of the affair with credit. I fancied that if ever the sallow-faced man ran afoul of Burke it would go hard with him.

'I didn't get that business straight last night,' mused the detective. 'Why should anyone have wanted to kidnap Winifred? It couldn't have been to hurt her—for there was plenty of opportunity to do that. It must have been to hold her somewhere and force someone to do something. What do you think of that, Kennedy?'

'Your reasoning is very logical,' agreed Craig. 'There is only one thing missing—who was it and what was it for?'

'Pretty large questions,' agreed Burke, good-humouredly now. 'There must have been some big reason for it. Well, I hope this trip of Paquita's proves to be the key to something. I almost wish I had told Riley to stay. I'd like to go with you.'

'No,' reassured Craig. 'It's better that you should be here. We must not leave any loopholes. You'll communicate with me if anything happens?'

Burke nodded and glanced hastily at his watch as a hint to us to hurry. With a parting assurance from him, we made the dash for the train in the hotel 'bus.

The crisp morning air as we spun up to the station was a tonic to Kennedy. He seemed to enjoy the excitement of the chase keenly and I must admit that I, too, felt the pleasing uncertainty of our errand.

I had found by this time that there was an entirely different crowd that regularly took each train. None of those whom we had seen the previous day on the express were on this train, although I felt sure that some of them at least would take their regular trip to the city later, especially Shelby. Whatever happened, at least we were ahead of them, although I doubted whether we would be ahead of Paquita unless she had some trouble on the road.

Nothing was to be gained by the study of the other passengers, and there was not even a chair car on the accommodation. The papers had not arrived from New York in spite of the fact that Westport was not very far out, and the time consumed in stopping at every station on the road seemed to hang heavy.

Kennedy, however, was never at a loss for something to do. We had no more than settled ourselves in the smoker with its seats of hot, dirty, worn, antiquated railroad plush, when he pulled from his pocket a copy he had made of the figures that had appeared on the wet paper.

In a moment he was deeply engaged in a study of them, trying all manner of tricks, combining them, adding them, setting figures opposite the letters of the alphabet, everything that could occur to him on the spur of the moment, although I knew that he had worked out a scientific manner of reading any cipher. Still, his system of deciphering would take time, and in the brief interval of the railroad journey it was his intention to see whether he might not save the labour and perhaps stumble on some simple key.

Evidently the cipher was not so simple. One after another he used up sheets from his loose-leaf note-book, tearing up the scrawls and throwing them out of the window, but never seeming to become discouraged or to lose his temper at each fresh failure.

'I can't say I'm making much progress,' he admitted finally, closing his note-book and taking from his wallet carefully the original crumpled sheet I had found in the scrap-basket. 'There's just one thing I'd like to try—not to decipher it, for that will take time, I see—but to see if there is anything else that I missed as I looked at it so hastily up there in that room.'

At the ice-water cooler, which never had any ice in it, nor cups about it, he held the sheet of paper for a moment under the tepid running water. Since he had first wet it, it had dried out and the figures were again invisible. Then he returned to our seat and soon was deep in the study of the original this time.

'I can say one thing,' he remarked, folding the cipher carefully so as not to tear the weakened fibres, as we rolled into the New York terminus, 'the person who wrote that thing is a crook—has the instincts of a spy and traitor.'

'How do you know that?' I inquired.

'How?' he repeated quietly, glancing up sharply from a final look at the thing. 'Did you ever hear of the science of graphology—the study of character in handwriting? Much the same thing applies to figures. It's all there in the way those figures are made, just as plain as the nose on your face, even if the meaning of the cipher is still hidden. We have a crook to deal with, and a very clever one, too, even if we don't know yet who it is. It's possible to hide a good deal, but not everything—not everything.'

From the station Kennedy and I went immediately down to the office of Hastings. It was still very early and few offices were occupied. Kennedy opened the door and, as I anticipated, went directly to the spot in the office where he had unearthed, or rather unwalled, the detectaphone transmitter.

There was not a chance that anyone would be listening at the other end, yet he proceeded cautiously. The transmitter had been placed close to the plaster which had not been disturbed in Hastings's office. So efficient was the little machine that even the plaster did not prevent sound waves from affecting its sensitive diaphragm.

'But how could it have been put in place?' I asked as Kennedy explored the hole he had made in the wall.

'That's new plaster back there,' he pointed out, peering in. 'Someone must have had access on a pretence to the next office and placed the transmitter that way, plastering up the wall again and painting it over. You see, Hastings wouldn't know about that.'

'Still,' I objected, 'anyone going in and out of the next office would be likely to be seen. Who has the office?'

'It's no use to look,' replied Kennedy, as I started for the hall. 'They are as ignorant as we are. See—the wire doesn't go there. It goes horizontally to that box or casing in the corner which carries steam-pipes. Then it goes down. It's not likely it goes down very many floors. Let's see what's under us.'

The office beneath bore on its doors the name of a well-known brokerage firm. There was no reason to suspect them, and Kennedy and I walked down another floor. There, in a little office, directly under that occupied by Hastings, gilt letters announced simply 'Public Stenographer Exchange.' Without a doubt that was the other end of the eavesdropper.

'There's no one in yet, sir,' informed a cleaning woman who happened to see us trying the door.

Kennedy was ready with a story. 'That's too bad,' he hastened, with a glance at his watch. 'They want to sublet it to me and I'd like to look at it before I decide on another office at nine o'clock.'

'I can let you see it,' hinted the woman, rattling a string of keys.

'Can you?' encouraged Kennedy, slipping a silver coin into her hand. 'Thank you. It will save me another trip.'

She opened the door and we saw at once why Kennedy's chance story had seemed so plausible. Whatever furniture had been there had been moved out, except a single plain chair and a very small table. But on the table stood a box, the receiving end of the detectaphone. It was the eavesdropper's station, all right.

The woman left us a moment and we made the best of the opportunity. Not even a scrap of paper had been left. Except for what greeted us on our first entrance, there was nothing.

Who had rented the place? Who had listened in, had heard and anticipated even our careful frame-up?

Could it have been that this was the objective of the hasty

visit of Paquita, that it had been she who was so eager to destroy the evidence of the eavesdropping on Hastings?

It was galling to have to stand here in inaction at a time when we felt that we might be learning much if we had only so much as a hint where else to look.

'The easiest way of finding out is to watch,' concluded Kennedy. 'We can't just stand about in the hall. That in itself will look suspicious. You wait here a few minutes while I see if I can find the agent of the building.'

Around a bend in the hall I waited, trying to seem interested more in some other office down the hall No one appeared, however, looking for any of the offices and it was only a few minutes before Kennedy returned.

'I found him,' he announced. 'Of course he could tell me next to nothing. It was as I had supposed, just someone who was an emissary of our criminal. I doubt if it would do us much good to catch the person now, anyway. Still, it's worth while taking a chance on. A girl who said she was a typewriter and stenographer hired the place, and paid for it in cash in advance. I managed to persuade the agent to let me have the key to this vacant office opposite. We can watch better from that.'

We let ourselves into the opposite office, which was bare, and I could see that I was in for a tiresome wait.

No one had arrived yet in Hastings's office and Kennedy was eager to receive some word from Riley as well as watch the eavesdropping plant. Accordingly, he left me to watch while he returned to the lawyer's office.

Every footfall in the hall raised my hopes, only to dash them again as the newcomer entered some other office than the one I was watching.

CHAPTER XVII

THE CIPHER LETTER

IRKSOME though it was to be compelled to do fruitless watching in a vacant office, there was nothing to do but stick at it. What Paquita might be up to was a mystery, but I knew that until we heard from Riley we could have only the most slender chance to locate her in the big city.

It was perhaps half an hour later when, to my relief, Kennedy returned, bringing with him a strange man. I looked at him inquiringly.

'You're just wasting time here, Walter,' Craig explained. 'I've got one of the Secret Service men here in the city to relieve you of your job. But I very much suspect that, after what happened last night, whoever had that place across the hall is through and would rather lose the detectaphone receiver than risk being caught.'

'Have you had any word from Riley?'

'Not a word. I'm getting anxious,' he replied, turning to the new man and instructing him what to do.

Kennedy was eager to get back, in case there might be a hasty call about Paquita. I could see, too, that he was convinced that we were baffled, at least as far as discovering who had been using the detectaphone was concerned.

We returned quickly to Hastings's office, which was still deserted, and there, as we waited nervously, Kennedy drew forth the cipher and began to study it again, but this time on an entirely different line, following his own scientific principles, which he had laid down after investigating the work of other expert decipherers.

My hopes rose momentarily when we heard footsteps in the

hall and the door was burst open. It was, however, merely a messenger boy.

'Telegram for Mr Kennedy,' he shouted, penetrating even the sacred inner office of Hastings.

Craig tore open the yellow envelope, read the message, and tossed it over to me. It was from Burke at Westport.

'Wireless operators at Seaville Station,' it read, 'report strange interference. May be in reference to telautomaton. Will keep you advised if anything happens.'

The possibility of a new twist to events was very fascinating, though I did not understand it. I was just about to question Kennedy about the telautomaton when the door opened again. This time it was Hastings himself.

'Has there been any word?' he asked eagerly.

'Nothing so far,' replied Craig. 'You came on the express, I suppose?'

'Yes,' he replied, his face wearing a puzzled expression. 'I don't quite understand what is going on.'

'What in particular?' queried Craig, seeing that there was something on Hastings's mind.

'Why, Shelby, of course,' he answered. 'Some change has taken place in him. He's not like the Shelby I used to know. Yesterday he came into town. He was on the train again today. I wasn't the only one who noticed it. Johnson Walcott was on the train, too. He noticed it—called my attention to it, as a matter of fact. I saw some of the younger men, too. Shelby as a regular commuter is a joke to them. But it's more than a joke, I'm thinking. Shelby never came near Wall Street—or Broad Street—before. But now they tell me he seems to be taking an active interest in the Maddox Munitions stock on the curb. I don't understand it.'

'Could he be trying to put through some deal?' I inquired hastily. 'Perhaps he's trying to get the control his brother would have had.'

'I don't doubt that he has some such scheme,' agreed

Hastings. 'But—well, what do you say, Kennedy? Doesn't it look suspicious, so soon afterward? It may be real ambition, now. He may have changed. But—'

Hastings's 'but' meant volumes.

Just then the telephone rang and the lawyer answered it, handing the instrument over to Kennedy.

We listened eagerly. It was the first long-delayed report of Paquita from Riley, and as Kennedy pursued the one-sided conversation that we heard I gathered that, far from clearing up things, the actions of Paquita had further muddled them.

Hastings glanced at me and shook his head sagely, whispering, 'That's a clever and a dangerous woman: When she looks most innocent is the time to be wary.'

I tried to pay no attention to his banal remarks, but still was unable to follow, from what I heard, the course of the report from Riley.

Finally it seemed as if Kennedy were cut off in the middle of a remark or that Riley had hung up suddenly. Kennedy jiggled the hook but was unable to get anyone back again, though Central tried for some time.

'What was it?' I asked, keenly interested.

'I'm afraid she's putting one over on us again,' commented Kennedy as he hung up the receiver.

'How's that?' I asked.

'Why, it's evidently a purposeless visit to the city, as nearly as I can make it out. Riley followed her in—had no difficulty. In fact, he thinks that she knew she was being followed before they reached the turnpike from Westport.'

'Where did she go after she got here?' I asked, hoping that at last there was some clue that might lead to the 'gang' which Burke suspected, but which I was almost tempted to believe was mythical.

'Just stopped at her city apartment,' returned Craig. 'There wasn't any telephone handy and Riley was afraid to leave her for fear she might come out and get away before he could get

back. It was very early. When it came time for the offices to
open she made a call at her theatrical agents again. After that
she came down-town. She wasn't far away from us here. This
will interest you, Mr Hastings.'

Hastings needed no prompting. He was already interested.

'Riley found her talking to a clerk in a brokerage house—
Dexter and Co. You know them?'

'Slightly. I wonder what that can mean.'

'Perhaps something to do with Shelby—at least Riley thinks
so. It was while she was talking to the clerk that he got his first
chance to telephone me. What cut him short was that he could
see from the telephone booth that she was starting away. He
had to go, but he did get time to say that he had just seen
Shelby Maddox enter the same building, though Shelby didn't
see Paquita.'

'Did she see him?'

'I suppose so. That must have been why she went away so
quickly. I suppose she didn't want to be seen.'

'What can that girl be up to now?' considered Hastings. 'You
may just rest assured that it is something devilish.'

'Any word from Sanchez?' I asked, remembering my own
experience the time I had tried to trail Paquita.

'Nothing so far,' replied Kennedy. 'Riley was looking for
him, but hasn't seen a trace of him. Except for the visit down-
town, Paquita seems to be just going about as though giving
Riley something to do. He thinks it's mighty strange she
doesn't try to throw him off. Really, she seems to want to be
shadowed.'

'How can that be?'

Kennedy shrugged. 'I don't know. Riley promised to call up
the next chance he got.'

'Why not go over to Dexter's?' suggested Hastings.

'She can't be there,' returned Kennedy. 'If she was, Riley
would have had a chance to make a second call. Therefore I
reason that she must have gone away after she had seen the

clerk and when Shelby appeared. I think I'll stay here awhile, until I hear again—especially as I have nowhere else to go,' he decided, pulling out the cipher from his pocket again. 'We may hear some more about Shelby and his schemes.'

Kennedy had now fallen into an earnest study of the peculiar cryptogram which we had discovered.

'I suppose you've noticed that there's no figure above five in it,' he remarked to me, looking up for an instant from several sheets of paper which he was covering with a hopeless jam of figures and letters.

'I had not,' I confessed. 'What of it?'

'Well, I've tried the numbers in all sorts of combinations and permutations. They don't work. Let me see. Suppose we take them in pairs.'

For several moments he continued to figure and his face became continuously brighter.

'There are six pairs of 33's,' he remarked, almost to himself. 'Now, it's well known that the letter "e" is the most commonly used letter. That's the starting point usually in working out a cipher. Wait—there are eight "15's"—that must be "e." Yes, the chances are all for it. Now what letter is 33, if any?'

He appeared to be in a dream as he recalled from his studies of cryptograms what were the probabilities of the occurrence of the particular letters. Suddenly he exclaimed,—

'Perhaps it's "n"—let's see.'

Hastily he wrote down some letters and numbers in the following order:—'25enne1454.'

He looked at it for a moment, and then his face registered the dawn of an idea.

'By George!' he exclaimed, 'we don't have to go any further! I have it. It's my own name—Kennedy. Let me see how that works. I believe it's the system we call—'

Kennedy was again interrupted by the entrance of the messenger-boy with another telegram. He tore it open and, as I expected, it was a second message from Burke.

'Seaville Station has reported interference to Government. Just received orders Washington to take up investigation. Not wireless messages that interfere. Some mystery. When can you come out?'

Kennedy read and re-read the message. To neither Hastings nor myself did it convey any idea upon which we could build. But to Kennedy, seemingly, it suggested a thousand and one things.

It was evident that the appeal from Burke had moved Kennedy very much. Paquita had lured us into town, but I cannot say that it was giving us much to show for our pains.

'What do you suppose that message can mean?' I questioned. 'What does Burke mean about the telautomaton?'

'I can't say at this distance. There must be more to it than he has put into the telegram. But at least it is possible that the men at the station have stumbled over some attempt to use the wireless in testing out the little model. It's pretty hard to tell. Really, I wish I was out there. A clue like this interests me much more than our little adventuress.'

Kennedy had scarcely laid down the message from Burke when the telephone tinkled again. He seized the receiver expectantly. By his excitement I could see that it was Riley again.

'Yes, Riley,' we heard him answer. 'Where are you now?'

The conversation was rapid-fire. As Kennedy hung up his face showed considerable interest.

'That woman is just making sport of Riley,' exclaimed Kennedy hotly, facing us in perplexity.

'Why, what is she doing?'

'Seems to be aimlessly driving about the city. I'll bet she is just laughing at him. I wonder what the game may be?'

'Where is she now?'

'Up-town again. I suppose that we could jump up there and probably catch Riley somewhere, by keeping in touch with this office, if both of us kept calling up here. But what good it would do I can't see. I'm disappointed. This thing has degenerated into a wild-goose chase.'

His eye fell on the telegram from Burke, and I knew that the two things had placed Kennedy in a dilemma. If he might have been in two places at once, he would have been satisfied. Should he drop everything and go to Burke or should he wait for Riley?

'We'll let the cipher decide,' concluded Kennedy, turning to the scribbled papers before him.

'What is the cipher system?' I asked mechanically, my head rather in a whirl at the fast-crowding events.

'Don't you understand?' he cried, almost gleefully, working at the solution of the secret writing. 'I've got it! How stupid of me before not to think of it. Why, it's the old chequerboard cipher again!'

Quickly he drew on paper a series of five squares horizontally and five vertically and filled them in with the letters of the alphabet, placing I and J in the same square, thus using twenty-five squares. Over the top he wrote the numbers to 5 and down the side he did the same, as follows:

	1	2	3	4	5
1	A	B	C	D	E
2	F	G	H	IJ	K
3	L	M	N	O	P
4	Q	R	S	T	U
5	V	W	X	Y	Z

'Do you see?' he cried eagerly. 'The letter "e" is in the first row, the fifth letter—15. The letter "n" is the third letter in the third row—33. Why, it's simple!'

It might have been simple to him now, but to Hastings and myself, as Kennedy figured the thing out, it was little short of marvellous. For all we could have done it, I suppose the blank scrap of paper would still have been a hidden book.

We were crowded about Kennedy, eagerly watching what his deciphering might yield, when the office-boy announced, 'Mr Shelby Maddox to see you, Mr Hastings.'

Kennedy quickly covered the papers on which he was writing with some others on the desk, just as Shelby entered.

'Is Kennedy here?' cried Shelby. 'Oh—I thought maybe you might be. They told me that you'd gone early to the city.'

Our greeting was none too cordial, but Shelby either did not notice it or affected not to do so.

'I wanted to ask you about that kidnapping,' he explained. 'You see, I wasn't about when they found Mito, and it wasn't until later that I heard of it and the attempt on Winifred. What do you suppose, Mr Kennedy, was the reason? Who could have wanted to carry her off?'

Kennedy shrugged. 'So far I haven't been able to give a final explanation,' he remarked keenly.

'Then the kidnappers got away clean?' asked Shelby.

'It was very clever,' temporised Kennedy, 'but I would hardly say that there is no clue.'

Shelby eyed Craig keenly, as though he would have liked to read his mind. But Kennedy's face did not betray whether it was much or little that he knew.

'Well,' added Shelby, 'all I've got to say is that someone is going to get into trouble if anything happens to that girl.'

I was listening attentively. Was this a bluff, or not? From the expression on Hastings's face one would have said that he was convinced it must have been Shelby himself who kidnapped her. I wondered whether it was wholly interest in Winifred that prompted Shelby's visit and inquiry.

'At any rate,' he went on, 'you'll all be watching now against a repetition of such a thing, won't you? I don't need to remind you, Kennedy, of your promise when I talked to you before?'

Craig nodded. 'I'll give you a square deal, Mr Maddox,' returned Craig. 'Of course I can't work for two people at once. But I shall do nothing for any client that I am not convinced is perfectly right. You need not fear for Miss Walcott as long as I can protect her.'

Maddox seemed to be relieved, although he had found nothing that pointed to the origin of the attack. Or was it because of that?

He glanced at his watch uneasily. 'You'll pardon me,' he said, rising. 'I had a few minutes and I thought I'd drop in and see you. I must keep an appointment. Thank you for what you have said about Winifred.'

As he withdrew I shot a hasty glance at Craig. Should I follow him? Kennedy negatived.

Apparently not even the intrusion of Shelby had got out of his mind either the dilemma we were in or the hidden message that he seemed on the point of reading.

'An engagement,' commented Hastings incredulously. 'Since when has Shelby had important engagements? More than likely it is something to do with this Paquita woman.'

There was no mistaking the opinion that Hastings had of the youngest scion of the house of Maddox. Nor was it unjustified. Shelby's escapades had been notorious, although I had always noticed that, in the aftermath of the stories, Shelby was quite as much, if not more, sinned against than sinning. Young men of his stamp are subject to many more temptations than some of the rest of us. If Shelby were coming through all right, I reflected, so much the greater credit for him.

Kennedy either shared my own feelings toward Shelby or had decided that he was not at present worth considering to the delay of something more important.

I looked over his shoulder, fascinated, as he fell to work again immediately on the cipher with the same zest which he had displayed before Shelby's interruption.

Rapidly Kennedy translated the figures into letters and, as each word was set down on paper, became more and more excited.

Finally he leaped up and seized his hat.

'Confound her!' he exclaimed, 'that explains it all! Look!'
Hastings and I read what he had written:

'KENNEDY MUST BE KEPT IN NEW YORK UNTIL
WE FINISH HERE.'

CHAPTER XVIII

THE RADIO DETECTIVE

HERE, it seemed, was a new danger. Was it to be taken as a proof of Burke's theory that someone, perhaps a gang, was back of Paquita! I was almost inclined to Hastings's opinion, for the moment. What was the reason that Shelby had been so interested in Kennedy as to seek him out even in the office of the lawyer of his brother who hated him?

I could evolve no answer in my own inner consciousness for the questions. As far as I could see we were still fighting in the dark, and fighting an unknown.

Kennedy quickly chose one horn of the dilemma that had been presented to him. Both the wording of the cipher and Burke's enigmatic message regarding the wireless which came so close on its heels quite decided him to hurry back to Westport—that is, if one might so call travelling on midday trains that lounged along from station to station.

We left Hastings in a high state of excitement. Some pressing business prevented his immediate return to Westport, and Kennedy was evidently rather pleased than otherwise, for he did not urge him to go.

'There's just one thing that I must stop for, and we shall have plenty of time, if we don't waste it,' he planned. 'I must go to the laboratory. There's some stuff there I want to take out if, as I foresee, we are to have to deal with wireless in some way. Besides, I may need some expert assistance and I want to arrange with one of the graduate students at the university, if I can.'

In the laboratory he found what he wanted and began gathering it into bundles, packing up some head telephone receivers, coils of wire, and other apparatus, some of which was very cumbersome. The last he placed in a pile by itself.

The door opened and a young man entered.

'Oh, Watkins,' Craig directed, as I recognised one of the students who had attended his courses, 'there's a lot of apparatus I would like you take out to Westport for me.'

They talked briefly in a wireless jargon which I did not understand, and the student agreed to carry the stuff out on a late train, meeting us at the Harbour House. At the last moment Kennedy was off for the railroad station. It was making close connections, but we succeeded.

The ride out was nerve-racking to us under the circumstances. We had taken the bait so temptingly displayed by Paquita and had gone to New York. Now we could not get back fast enough. We had not been in the city long, it is true. But had it been too long? What had happened out in the town we were anxious to learn. I felt sure that in our absence some of the Maddoxes might well have attempted something which our presence would have restrained.

Burke met us at the station with a car, so sure was he that Kennedy would return immediately on receipt of his second message, and it was evident that he felt a great sense of relief at regaining Kennedy's help.

As we spun along down from the station Kennedy hastened to tell Burke what had happened, first about Paquita as Riley had reported, then his deciphering of the cipher message, our failure to discover anything in the scantily furnished office at the other end of the detectaphone wire, Shelby's visit, and the whole peculiar train of circumstances.

Instead of going directly to the Harbour House Burke drove us around by the hotel dock, where we saw that there was a stranger in a power boat apparently waiting for him.

Kennedy was just finishing his recital of our unsatisfactory experience as we approached.

'Perhaps it all has something to do with what I wired you

about,' returned Burke, thoughtfully. 'This new affair is some-thing that I know you'll be interested in. You see, among my other jobs for the Government, I'm what you might call a radio-detective, I guess. You know that there are laws aimed against these amateur wireless operators, I suppose?'

Kennedy nodded, and Burke went on, 'Well, whenever regular operators find anything illegal going on in the air, they notify the Government, and so the thing is passed along for me to take up. Heaven knows I don't know much about wireless. But that doesn't matter. They don't want a wireless man so much as they do a detective to ferret out from the operator's evidence who can be violating the law of the air, and where. So that is how I happened to get hold of this evidence which, I think, may prove valuable to us.'

As we pulled up near the hotel dock Burke beckoned to the strange man who had been waiting for him.

'Let me introduce you to Steel, whom they have sent to me on that matter I told you about.'

Kennedy and I shook hands with the man, who glanced out over the harbour as he explained briefly 'I'm an operator over there at the Seaville Station, which you can see on the point.'

We also gazed out over the water. The powerful station which he indicated was on a spit of sand perhaps two miles distant and stood out sharply against the horizon, with its tall steel masts and cluster of little houses below, in which the operators and the plant were.

'It's a wonderful station,' Steel remarked, noticing that we were looking at it also. 'We'd be glad to have you over there, Mr Kennedy. Perhaps you could help us.'

'How's that?' asked Craig keenly.

'Why,' explained the operator, with a sort of reflective growl, 'for the past day or so, now and then, when we least expect it, our apparatus has been put out of business. It's only temporary. But it looks as though there was too much interference. It isn't static. It's almost as though someone was jamming the air. And we don't know of anyone around here that's capable of doing it. None of us can explain it, but there are some powerful impulses in the air. I can't make it out.'

Kennedy's eye rested on the graceful white hull of the *Sybarite* as she lay still at anchor off the Harbour House. I had not noticed, although Kennedy had, that the yacht was equipped with wireless.

'It's not likely that it is anyone on the *Sybarite* who is responsible?' he considered tentatively.

The operator shook his head. 'No, the apparatus isn't strong enough. We would be more likely to put them out of business.'

Burke turned the car around and drove up to the Harbour House. Kennedy jumped out of the car and carried part of the stuff he had brought from the laboratory, while I took the rest, followed by Burke and Steel.

'When I got your message, Burke,' he said, 'I thought that there might be something going on such as you've told me. So I came out prepared. I've got some more apparatus coming, too, in case we don't get what we want with this. Will you see if we can get permission to go up on the roof—and do it without attracting attention, too?'

Burke quickly made the arrangements and we quietly went upstairs by a back way, finally coming out on a flat portion of the Lodge roof.

From one of the packages Kennedy took some wire and hastily and ingeniously strung it so that in a short time it was quite evident that he was improvising the aerial of a wireless outfit of some sort. Finally, when he had finished, he led the proper wires down over the edge of the roof.

'One of these,' he said, preparing to leave the roof, 'I want to carry down to the ground, the other to our own room.'

We went down again by the back stairs and outside, where Kennedy picked up the wire that hung down to the earth.

Having completed this part of his preparations, Kennedy entered the Harbour House and we followed.

We were passing through the corridor when a page stepped up to Kennedy. 'I beg your pardon, sir,' he announced, 'but there is a lady in the parlour who would like to speak to you and Mr Jameson, sir.'

Kennedy excused himself from Burke and Steel, and together we went in the direction of the parlour, eager to discover who it was that sent for us.

To my surprise, it was Winifred Walcott whom we saw sitting all alone.

'How are you after your thrilling experience last night?' inquired Kennedy. 'It was so early this morning when we left that we really could not disturb anyone to find out. I trust that you are feeling better?'

'Yes—better,' she repeated, her eyes with an absent look, as though she was not thinking of how she felt. 'I wanted to thank you ever so much for what you did. Without you, who knows what might have happened to me or where I should be now?'

There was genuine feeling in her words now, as she went on, 'Professor Kennedy, after what has happened I am afraid that I shall have to appeal to you for protection. I have thought about it all a great deal, and still there is no explanation of the strange events of last night.'

'You have no idea who it was who carried you off?'

She shook her head. 'You may not believe it, but I have not. All I remember was being seized from behind and before I knew it I was half choked, half smothered. That thing wrapped about my head kept me from seeing or crying out until it was too late. Even then I could not see. There is only one thing I can say I really know, and that is that whoever it was that carried me off, it was someone of great strength. You see, I am no light-weight and pretty strong. Yet I never had a chance until you and Mr Jameson and the rest came up back of me. Oh, I am so sorry I came to your laboratory that day with her!'

Winifred paused. It was evident that she was in a very nervous and high-strung state, and naturally so. The one thing that seemed uppermost in her mind was that she had listened to the biased interpretations of Irene Maddox. The dénouement had proved how wrong they had been, at least in their suggested characterisation of Kennedy. And she hastened to apologise.

'Not a word about that,' insisted Kennedy. 'There was no reason why you should not have come to see me on any errand and with anybody.'

'Just the same, I'm sorry.'

'Has anything more happened today?' queried Kennedy, changing the subject deftly.

'N-no, nothing in particular. I have been thinking mostly of what it all was about last night. Someone wanted to hold me—but didn't want to hurt me. Who could it be? Why?'

'That is exactly what I am trying to find out,' assured Craig. 'We went into the city on what looked as though it might prove to be a very promising clue, but nothing came of it. However, it is only a short while, now, and we shall soon have something to report, I am convinced.'

'Did you see—Mr Maddox?' she asked, hesitatingly, and I knew that the mention of Shelby's name had cost her some effort, after the serious tiff of the evening before. 'He was very solicitous, sent up word, and some flowers, but could not miss the express, he wrote on account of an important engagement.'

'Yes, we saw him for just a minute—down in Wall Street. I believe he has taken some interest in business lately and has spent much time at the office of his brokers down-town.'

The look of relief that passed over her face could not easily be concealed. It was evident that she knew of the sudden early departure of Paquita and, like Hastings, in her suspicions, had been afraid that there might be some connection with Shelby. Kennedy did not say anything about the appearance of Paquita in Wall Street; and, on reflection, I reasoned that he was right, for it could have no effect except to arouse unjust suspicions.

Winifred said nothing for a few moments. I wondered what was passing in her mind. Was she sorry that she had not taken

Shelby at his word the night before? At any rate she said nothing, nor should I have expected her to admit anything to us.

'What do your brother and sister-in-law think?' asked Kennedy, at length.

'Johnson promised to get a detective himself if there was anything new on which to base suspicions,' she replied. 'He seemed rather vexed at me that I could tell no more, said that no detective could be expected to catch anyone on my hazy description—which, I suppose, is true.'

'And Mrs Maddox?'

'Oh, she seems to think—well, it's pretty hard to tell what poor Irene thinks from one moment to another. She says it's what I might expect for being mixed up with the Maddoxes. I can't see what that has to do with it, though. I'm not mixed up with them, even if Johnson is.'

There was a naïveté about the remark that was not lost on Kennedy. Winifred was still mistress of her own heart, at least so she would have us think. Her solicitude about Shelby and the careful way in which she refused to let us see that it went too far would have indicated otherwise. She was really afraid of herself.

'There has been absolutely nothing suspicious since this morning?' reiterated Kennedy, hoping that she might recall something, no matter how trivial, that might point the way further ahead.

'Nothing,' she repeated. 'I didn't come down from my room until pretty late. Everybody had left for the city by that time. I did see that gentleman who brought us back in his car, though.'

'Oh, Sanchez?' interrogated Craig, his attention aroused in an instant. 'What of him? Did he do or say anything?'

'Nothing except that he inquired very particularly how I was and whether I had found out anything—nothing more than common politeness might suggest.'

As for me, I felt sure, now, that there was something much deeper than courtesy in the inquiry of Sanchez.

'I don't suppose you noticed anything about him?' asked Craig.

'Nothing except that he avoided Irene Maddox when he saw her coming toward me. I think I can guess why.'

She nodded knowingly to Kennedy.

'Did he seem to be interested in Paquita's absence?' pursued Kennedy.

'I can't say,' strove Winifred to remember. 'I did see him talking to some of the boys about the hotel—that is all.'

'And where did he go?'

'Drove off in his car. It was about the middle of the morning. I haven't seen him about since then.'

Winifred seemed quite reassured by the few words with Kennedy, and with a parting assurance of protection Kennedy and I excused ourselves.

We rejoined Burke and Steel in the lobby, where Burke was nervously pacing up and down, for precious minutes were being wasted, he felt. And yet I could not see that he was able to make a move without the aid of Kennedy.

Like Burke, I, too, was eager to know what it was that Kennedy was planning to accomplish by the elaborate and secret preparations he was making. Accordingly, I was not sorry when he decided to go immediately up to our rooms.

Naturally, I was keenly interested in what Kennedy was doing in establishing his own little wireless plant, but the operator, Steel, looked at it in increasing wonder as Craig laid out the apparatus in the room.

'It's not exactly like anything that I've ever seen before,' Steel remarked finally. 'What do you expect to do with it, sir?'

Kennedy smiled. 'I don't believe you ever did see one of these sets, although you may have heard of them,' he explained, not pausing in his work of installing it. 'It is an apparatus only lately devised for use by the United States Government to detect illegalities in the air in wireless, whether they are committed by amateurs or not.'

As we watched in silence, Kennedy went on explaining. 'You know that wireless apparatus is divided into three parts—the source of power, whether battery or dynamo; the making and sending of wireless waves, including the key, spark condenser, and tuning oil; and the receiving apparatus, head telephones, antennæ, ground and detector.'

Kennedy was talking to us rather than the operator, but now he turned to him and remarked, 'It's a very compact system, with facilities for a quick change from one wave-length to another. I suppose you've noticed it—spark gap, quenched type—break system relay, and all the rest. You understand, I can hear any interference while I'm transmitting. Take the transformation—by a single throw of this six-point switch. It tunes the oscillating and open circuits to resonance. It's very clever and, best of all, efficient.'

His wireless installed and adjusted, Kennedy clapped the ear-pieces on and tuned it up. Not only he, but the wireless operator tried it, rapidly changing the wave-lengths, as the system admitted, in the hope of discovering something. Whatever it was that had caused the trouble at the Seaville Station, it was not working now. They seemed able to discover nothing.

This had been going on for some time when our telephone rang and Burke jumped to answer it.

'That's one of my men,' he exclaimed with a gesture that indicated he had forgotten something. 'I meant to tell you that they were holding a funeral service for Marshall Maddox, and this apparatus of yours clean knocked it out of my head. Hallo! . . . Yes, I remember. Wait.' Burke put his hand over the transmitter and looked at us. 'Do you want to go?' he asked.

'I think I would like to see them together again,' Craig replied, after a moment's consideration.

'All right,' returned Burke, removing his hand. 'We'll be down in a minute.'

Kennedy took from another package what looked like an

arrangement containing a phonograph cylinder, and attached it, through a proper contrivance, to his receiving apparatus.

'Now I think we can safely leave this thing,' bustled Kennedy, eager to get back in touch with things at Westport.

The wireless operator, Steel, glanced at his watch. 'I'm due back at Seaville soon to do my trick. Is there anything else I can tell you or do for you?'

Kennedy thanked him. 'Not just at the moment,' he returned. 'We shall have to wait now until something happens. Perhaps you are right. I think the best thing you can do is to return to Seaville and keep your eyes and ears open. If there is anything at all that comes up that seems to lead to our wireless jammer, I wish you would let me know.'

Steel was only too glad to promise and, a moment later, left us to return to the wireless station.

CHAPTER XIX

THE WIRELESS WIRETAPPER

A FEW moments later we went downstairs again and Burke drove us in his car up to the town, where, in the main street, was a little chapel whose bell was now tolling slowly and mournfully.

As his car drew up at the end of the long line down the street, I saw why Kennedy had decided to break into the time so sorely needed in our own investigation of the case. It seemed as though everyone must be at the funeral, even the reporters from New York. Kennedy and I managed to avoid them, but their presence testified to the wide interest that the case had aroused throughout the country.

'Rather a telling object-lesson in the business that the Maddoxes are in,' commented Kennedy as we walked the rest of the way to the shrubbery-surrounded chapel. 'If there is such a thing as retributive justice, this is the result of the business of making a profit out of mere instruments to kill.'

I fancied that there was more than coincidence behind the reasoning. The Maddoxes had been so long engaged in making munitions, devoid of any feeling of patriotism, had amassed such an immense fortune out of which the curse had been taken by no philanthropy, that it must undoubtedly be a true philosophy which traced from their very business and consequent character the evils and tragedies that followed in the wake of the Maddox millions. I reflected that even over the telautomaton, the destroyer itself, there had been no thought of public service in the family, but merely the chance to extort more gain from the frailties and sufferings of humanity. And now this was the end of one arch-extortioner.

There seemed to be something hollow in the funeral of Marshall Maddox. It took me some time to explain it to myself. It was not because we were there, outsiders, and in our capacity of observers, in fact almost spies, although that may have had something to do with the impression it made on me.

The little chapel was crowded, but with the curious who had heard vague rumours about the death. As I looked at the real mourners I fancied that my impression must be due to them, that somehow this was a mockery of mourning.

I could not imagine that Irene Maddox was overwhelmed by grief after what had occurred to her. As for the gay little Paquita, she was, of course, not there at all, and her presence would only have sounded a new note of hollowness. I had not seen her manifest any deep sign of grief. At present, I supposed, she was still in New York, going about her own or some unknown business as unconcerned as if nothing had happened.

Shelby Maddox had come up from whatever business he was engaged in in New York just in time for the service. Once or twice I thought he showed real grief, as though the death of his brother brought back to his recollection other and better days. Yet I could not help wondering whether even his emotions might not be affectation for our benefit, for the tragedy seemed not to have deterred him from doing pretty much as he might have done anyhow.

I looked about for Winifred Walcott. Evidently the strain of events had been too much for her. She was not there, but her brother was there with his wife, who was next to her own brother, Shelby.

The service was short and formal, and I shall not dwell on it, for, after all, nothing occurred during it which changed our attitude toward any of those present.

For a brief moment at the close the family were together, and I felt that Shelby was the most human of them all, at least. Mrs Walcott and her husband were the first to leave, and I could not help comparing it with a previous occasion, when they had taken Irene Maddox in their car. A little later Shelby appeared with his sister-in-law, leaving her only when some of her own family, who had come to Westport evidently to be with her, appeared.

Instead of going to the Lodge he walked slowly down to the pier and jumped into one of his tenders that was waiting to take him out to the *Sybarite,* alone. Now and then I had seen him glance sharply about, but it was not at us that he was looking. He seemed rather to be hoping that he might chance to meet Winifred Walcott. I think she was much more on his mind at present than even his brother.

Johnson Walcott and his wife passed us in their car and we could see them stop at the Harbour House porte-cochère. Frances Walcott alighted and, after a moment talking together, Johnson drove away alone, swinging around into the road to the city.

Our friends of the Secret Service seemed to be about everywhere, but unobtrusively, observing. There was much that was interesting to observe but nothing that pointed the way to the solution of the mystery. The funeral over; it was again the old Maddox house of hate, each member going his own way. It was as though an armistice had been declared, and now the truce was over. I felt that we might now expect war again, to the last dollar. It was not to be expected that any of them would allow the other to control without a fight, nor relinquish any claim that was not fully compensated.

One bright spot only shone out in the drab of the situation. So far the dead hand of the Maddox millions had not stretched out and fallen on the lovely and pure personality of Winifred Walcott. The more I thought of it the more I had come to fear that these hates and jealousies and bitter rivalries might engulf her as they had many others.

Had that been the trouble with Irene Maddox? Had she been once even as Winifred now was? Had she been drawn into this maelstrom of money? I dreaded the thought of the possible outcome of the romance of Shelby Maddox and Winifred. Would it, too, blast another life—or might it be that by some miracle Winifred might take out the curse that hung over the blood-money of the Maddoxes? Never before had our responsibility in the case, far beyond the mere unravelling of the mystery, presented itself to me so forcibly as it did now, after the solemn and sobering influence of the last rites of the murdered head of the house.

We came along past the carriage entrance to the Lodge again. Beside the door were piled several large packages, and the uniformed boy who presided over that entrance of the Lodge was evidently much worried over them. Burke had left us on the way up, and as we turned the boy at the door caught sight of Kennedy and hurried over to us.

'The young man said these were for you, sir,' he announced, indicating the packages, undecided whether to play for a tip or to ask to have them taken away.

'Oh, yes,' recognised Kennedy, as Watkins, who had brought them down, appeared. 'Some stuff I had brought from the city. Will you help me down to the dock with them?'

The boy was more than willing. Not only were the packages to be taken away from his door, but Kennedy had crossed his palm with a coin. With Watkins he carried the things down.

Kennedy had no intention at present, evidently, of using the material which had come from New York, but left it in the summer-house in charge of the student.

We were about to turn back to the Casino and the Lodge, when Craig caught my eye and nodded in the direction of the beach. There I could see the solitary figure of a girl coming slowly along. It was Winifred Walcott. I watched her. Evidently she had been out for a walk alone.

Now and then she gave a quick glance across the water and I soon realised that it was at the *Sybarite* she looked. Shelby had long since reached the yacht, but apparently she had seen his tender dashing out there. I could not help but think of the stroll that Shelby had taken with Paquita the night before down the beach in the same direction. Was Winifred thinking of it, too, and was she sorry that she had dismissed him without accepting his explanation at its face value?

'That shows what a great part chance plays in our lives,' mused Kennedy to me, as we watched her. 'They're thinking of each other. If Shelby had been a few minutes later, or she had been a few minutes earlier, they would have met. I suppose they are both too proud to go to each other now.

'You're not contemplating being a matchmaker?' I hazarded.

'On the contrary,' he smiled, 'I think we shall gain more by letting events take their natural course. No, chance must bring them together again.'

Miss Walcott had seen us by this time, and seemed to realise that we were talking about her, for she quickened her pace and, instead of coming up to the summer-house, left the beach by another flight of steps, though not so far away that we could not see a faint flush on her cheeks as she purposely avoided us.

We, too, went toward the Lodge, but did not overtake her.

On the veranda of the Lodge, waiting for us, was Riley, just returned from the city.

'Where is Paquita?' inquired Kennedy. 'Tell me what has happened?'

'Nothing much,' returned Riley, chagrined. 'I stuck to her pretty closely. She's back, you know.'

'I think I have an idea of what it was all about,' ventured Kennedy.

Riley nodded. 'Mr Burke has told me something of the cipher message to her, sir. I think you are right. She must have tried to divert our attention.

'How does she seem?' inquired Kennedy.

Riley chuckled. 'I think she's terribly miffed,' he replied. 'She acts to me as though she was disappointed in us—in you particularly. You don't follow her about New York. I don't think she quite understands what happened. You don't play according to Hoyle.'

'What did she do after that last telephone call?'

'Nothing—absolutely nothing. Oh, it was a plant, all right. She came back in the car, after awhile. We passed the church while the funeral was going on. She never even looked. Say, what has become of Sanchez?'

Kennedy retailed what Winifred had said about the sallow-faced man and his solicitude.

'I'll wager he'll be along soon, now,' asserted Riley, with professional assurance. 'I just saw Irene Maddox, after she came back from the funeral. She seems to be rather out of it, doesn't she? Since her own folks arrived the Maddoxes and the Walcotts seem to feel that they have no further responsibility.'

Kennedy smiled at the garrulity of the detective. 'What made you connect Sanchez and Irene Maddox?' he asked. 'Don't you think she is really through with him?'

'I guess she is,' returned Riley. 'But I can't say the same of him. If I could only get at the true relation of that fellow with Paquita I'd be a good deal happier. Mrs Maddox may have hired him to shadow her, but, if you want to know what I think, it is that that Mex, or whatever he is, has actually fallen in love with the girl.'

'Another love affair?' I queried sarcastically. 'Then all I've got to say is that they're well matched.'

'All right,' defended Riley, rather hotly. 'But we know that he double-crossed Mrs Maddox, don't we? Well, then, if he's working for anybody else now, what reason have you to suppose that he won't double cross them too? Mr Burke thinks there may be a gang of them. All right. What's to prevent this Sanchez from being stuck on her in that case? There are all sorts in the under-world, and there's no telling what a woman or a man may do.'

'But look at the way she acts toward Shelby Maddox,' I urged. 'If ever there was a woman who threw herself at a man, that's a case of it.'

'Part of the game, part of the game,' returned Riley.

'What game?' interrupted Kennedy, who had been listening to us in amused silence.

Riley was not ready with an answer on the spur of the moment, and, as it was not my contention, I did not attempt it.

'Well,' finished the Secret Service man as he left us, 'I'm going to look about, just the same, and you can take it from me that this thing will never be cleared up until we explain that fellow Sanchez.'

Kennedy said nothing as Riley walked away, but I fancied that underneath he concurred largely with the operative.

We were about to leave the veranda when Burke rejoined us, his face indicating that some new problem had come up.

'I wonder what Shelby Maddox can be up to,' he began, as though appealing for aid. 'I was using the telephone, and while I waited for my number I got to talking with the little girl at the switchboard. She tells me that in the last day or two, while Shelby has been out here, he has been talking a great deal over the wire with New York and has placed some large orders through different brokers for Maddox Munitions stock.'

It was an important piece of news. I recalled Hastings's wonder at Shelby's trips into the city and our own discovery that he had been visiting a broker, coupled with the presence of Paquita down-town in the same building.

'Maddox Munitions isn't so low that it's a good buy,' considered Burke, 'unless there's some scheme to manipulate it up. It had a little slump when Marshall Maddox died, but recovered. What its future will be without him no one can say. There's no reason why it shouldn't decline—but it hasn't done so.'

'Perhaps that's the game,' I suggested. 'Maybe Shelby is holding the market up. Someone must be supporting it. Why, if it weren't for some support, I'll wager the stock would have broken worse than it did, and it wouldn't have recovered.'

Kennedy nodded, not so much in approval of the explanation as at the line of thought that the idea suggested.

'Do you suppose,' speculated Burke, 'that there can be some manipulation of Maddox Munitions going on undercover? What can be Shelby's purpose in all this? Perhaps we're mistaken in that young man, and he's a great deal deeper than any of us give him credit for being. Would it be impossible that he might be planning to get the control from the others?'

It was an explanation that could not be easily put aside. Only death had wrested the control from the elder brother. Who was there to take his place? Had Shelby undergone a transformation almost overnight? Or—more horrible thought—had the whole affair been preconceived from the conference on the yacht and the murder to the manipulation of the market?

What with both Riley and Burke theorising on the case, I could see that Kennedy was growing a bit impatient. Though he formed many of them, theories never appealed to Kennedy as long as one little fact might knock out the prettiest deduction.

'We've been away from our room a long time,' he interjected, as though remembering what we had originally started to do. 'Something must have happened by this time or we'll never get anything. Let's go up there and see whether our wireless wiretapper has caught anything yet.'

Scarcely past the door Kennedy nudged me, a signal to be on guard. I looked cautiously about. Sitting in the lobby where she could see everybody who came and went was Paquita. She saw us approaching, but made no effort to avoid us. In fact, I felt sure that it was we for whom she was looking. If it was, Kennedy did not give her any satisfaction by letting her know that we even noticed it. We passed by, still chatting, though careful to say nothing that could not safely be over-heard, and entered the elevator. As the door clanged shut Paquita flashed a chagrined glance at us. It said as plainly as words that she wanted to focus our attention on herself instead of something else.

Up in the room Kennedy fairly ripped the wax cylinder from his wireless machine and jammed it into what looked like a miniature phonograph.

'A recording device invented by Marconi,' he explained, as a succession of strange sounds issued from the reproducer.

I could make nothing out of it, but Kennedy seemed quite excited and elated.

'It's not a wireless message at all,' he exclaimed.

'Then what is it?' I inquired.

He listened a moment more, then burst out, 'No, not a message. That's just wireless power itself. And it seems to come from the water side, too.'

He relapsed into silence, leaving us only to speculate.

What possible object could there be in the use of wireless power solely? Why did it come from the water? Was there a boat hanging about, perhaps flying the burgee of some well-known club, yet in reality to be used for some criminal purpose?

CHAPTER XX

THE SPEED DEMON

THERE seemed to be no use in staying longer in our room observing the behaviour of the wireless detector, when the very neighbourhood still bristled with mystery and perhaps danger.

Accordingly, we went downstairs again with Burke, just in time to meet Hastings, who had come down on the late afternoon train from the city.

'Has anything happened since we left?' inquired Kennedy of the lawyer, before he could begin to quiz us.

'Very little,' he replied. 'The man was still watching that little office where the detectaphone wire led, when I left. Not a soul has been near it. I think you can assume that it has been left abandoned.'

'I thought as much,' agreed Craig. 'Have you heard anything more about the activity of Shelby? He was here at the funeral this afternoon. He's out on the *Sybarite* now, and has been very quiet, at least down here.'

'I've been making some inquiries,' replied Hastings slowly. 'As nearly as any of the brokers I know can tell, I should say that Shelby must be doing something. There have been several large blocks of stock unloaded and they have all been taken up. In spite of it the price has been maintained. But it's all underground. I haven't decided which side Shelby is on, bear or bull. He never was on either side before, so I don't know what he is up to. You can reason it out either way—and, after all, it is a matter of fact, not reason.'

'It won't take long to find that out tomorrow, if we want to,' remarked Kennedy. 'The trouble today was that there were more pressing things that had to be done.'

We had scarcely finished outlining to Hastings what we had discovered at Westport when Riley edged up to report to Burke.

'Miss Walcott's acting very strangely, sir,' he ventured. 'You'd think she hadn't a friend in the world.'

'How's that?' cut in Kennedy.

'I saw her coming up from the beach a while ago alone,' replied Riley. 'First she passed Mrs Maddox and they scarcely spoke, then later I saw her do the same thing with Mrs Walcott. They've been that way, now, for some time.'

'Where is she—in her room?' asked Burke.

Riley nodded. 'Yes.'

'I can't see any reason why she should stay here, if she feels this way about it,' put in Hastings testily. 'She doesn't belong to the family.'

Kennedy glanced covertly at me. I fancied I understood what was in his mind. Winifred Walcott probably would not have admitted, even to herself, why she stayed.

'That little dancer and Miss Walcott are as friendly as Kilkenny cats, too,' added Riley, with a left-handed attempt at humour.

'You have an X-ray eye,' commented Craig, with veiled sarcasm, which quite amused me, for the detective actually took it literally and thanked him. 'Paquita is still about, then?'

'Yes, sir. Right after you went upstairs she had her car brought around and started out for a spin—down the shore road. But she must have seen that one of our men was following, for she turned up country and was back again in half an hour. If she intended to do anything, she must have been scared off. She's upstairs now, dressing for dinner, I suppose. I've got her checkmated. She can't move without my knowing it—and she knows it.'

'Down the shore road,' repeated Kennedy, reflectively. 'I wonder what she could have wanted down there. The wireless impulses came from the water side. Walter, would you mind going down on the dock and telling that young man of mine he had better get a bite to eat right away and that then he can begin getting the stuff unpacked and set up!'

While Watkins took a hasty dinner at the Lodge, I relieved him of watching the packages he had brought. It was a tiresome wait, for I longed to be with Kennedy.

One thing, however, broke the monotony. Once when I looked up I caught sight of a launch putting out from the *Sybarite* and feathering over the choppy waves in the direction of the dock. As it came closer I saw that it contained Shelby Maddox, still alone. He came ashore and, as he walked up the dock, saw me and nodded absently. Evidently he was thinking of something else.

I was glad to rejoin Kennedy a few minutes later when Watkins returned and began to unwrap the packages, as Craig had ordered. Fortunately for the sake of my curiosity, nothing had occurred during my absence, except that Craig and Burke had seen Shelby enter, although he had done nothing.

It was the dinner hour and the guests were beginning to enter the dining-room. Shelby had already done so, selecting a table where he was in sight of that usually occupied by the Walcotts. Their table seemed deserted tonight. Johnson Walcott was not yet back, and Irene Maddox now sat at another table, with those of her family who had come to be with her at the funeral. Winifred did not come down to dinner at all, which seemed to vex Shelby, for it looked as though she were avoiding him. The only person at the table was Frances Walcott.

Convinced that no one else was coming in, Shelby glumly hurried through his meal, and finally, unable to stand it any longer, rose, and on the way out stopped to talk with his sister.

What was said we could not guess. But it was more like a parley during an armistice than a talk between brother and sister, and it did not seem to do Shelby much good.

Finally he drifted out aimlessly into the lobby again. As he stood undecided, we caught a glimpse of the petite figure of

Paquita flitting from an alcove in his direction. Before he could avoid her she spoke to him.

However unwelcome the meeting might have been to Shelby—and his face showed plainly that it was so—there could be no doubt of Paquita's eagerness to see him. As I looked at her I could only wonder at the strangeness of life. She whom men had pursued and had found elusive, even when they thought they had her captured, was now herself in the anomalous role of pursuer. And the man whom she pursued cared no more for her than she for those who pursued her. Nay more, he was openly, hopelessly in love with another woman, in every respect the antithesis of herself. Much as I disliked Paquita's type, though realising her fascination as a study, I could not help seeing the potential tragedy and pathos of the situation.

She did not accuse or upbraid. On the contrary, she was using every art of which she was a past mistress to fascinate and attract. I did not need prompting from Kennedy to see the strange romance of the situation. The little dancer was subtly matching all the charm and all the knowledge of men and the world which she possessed against the appeal that Winifred had made to a hitherto latent side of Shelby's nature. The struggle between the two women was no less enthralling than the unravelling of the mystery of Marshall Maddox's death.

'By Heaven!' I heard Kennedy mutter under his breath, as we watched Paquita and Shelby, 'I wonder whether it is right to let events take their course. Yes—it must be. If he cannot go through it now, he'll never be able to. Yes, Shelby Maddox must fight that out for himself. He shall not ruin the life of Winifred Walcott.'

His remark set me thinking of the responsibility Craig had thrust on him. It was far more than merely running down the murderer of Marshall Maddox, now.

Shelby himself evidently appreciated what faced him. I could see that he was talking very bluntly and pointedly to her, almost rudely. Now and then she flashed a glance at him which, with her flushed face and the emotion expressed in her very being, could not have failed only three days ago. Shelby seemed to feel it, and took refuge in what looked to be an almost harshness of manner with her.

Kennedy jogged my arm and I followed his eyes. In the alcove from which she had come I was not surprised to see Sanchez, standing and looking at them. His dark eyes seemed riveted on the man as though he hated him with a supernal hate. What would he himself not have given to be where Shelby was? I wondered whether his blinded eyes saw the truth about Shelby's position. I doubted it, for it was with difficulty that he restrained himself. Black and ominous were the looks that he darted at the younger man. Indeed, I did not envy him.

As I turned to say something to Kennedy I saw that Sanchez and ourselves were not the only ones interested. Frances Maddox had just come out of the dining-room, had seen her brother and Paquita, and had drawn back into the shadow of a doorway leading to the porch, where she could see them better without being seen by them. Yet she betrayed nothing of her feelings toward either.

Meanwhile Shelby had been getting more and more vehement as he talked. I could not hear, but it was quite evident now that he was repeating and enforcing the remarks he had made to Paquita the night before during their secret stroll down the beach. And she, instead of getting angry, as he no doubt hoped she would, was keeping her temper and her control of herself in a most dangerous manner.

There was so much to think about that it was not until now that I noticed that the face we had seen in the alcove was gone. Sanchez had disappeared. Had the thing been too much for him? Was it that he could not trust himself to stay? At any rate, he was gone.

Just then Shelby turned on his heel, almost brutally, and deliberately walked away. It was as though he felt it his only escape from temptation.

Paquita took an involuntary step after him, then stopped short. I followed her quick glance to see what it might be that had deterred her. She had caught sight of Frances Walcott, whose interest had betrayed her into letting the light stream through the doorway on her face. Instantly Paquita covered the vexation that was on her face. Least of all would she let this man's sister see it. Consummate actress that she was, she turned and walked across the lobby, and a moment later was in gay conversation with another of her numerous admirers. But it did not take an eye more trained than mine to see the gaiety was forced, the animation of quite a different character from that she had showed to Shelby.

'Of one thing we can be sure,' remarked Craig. 'Miss Walcott will hear all about this. I hope she hears the truth. I'm almost tempted to tell her myself.' He paused, debating. 'No,' he decided finally, 'the time hasn't come yet.'

Shelby had retreated to the porch, where now he was pacing up and down, alone. As he came past the door his abstracted glance fell with a start on his sister. He drew himself together and spoke to her. Evidently he was debating whether she had seen anything, and, if so, how much and how she had interpreted it. At any rate, he was at pains to speak now, hoping that she might carry a message which he dared not send. What was going on in their minds I could not guess, but to outward appearance they were more like brother and sister than I had seen them ever before.

They parted finally and Shelby continued his measured tread about the porch, as though trying to make up his mind on a course of action. For about a quarter of an hour he walked, then, his face set in determined lines, entered the Lodge and went deliberately over to a florist's stand. There, oblivious to anything else, he selected the handsomest bunch of violets on the stand. He was about to drop his card into their fragrant and reconciling depths when he paused, replaced the card in his case, and directed the man to deliver them anonymously. There was no need for us to inquire where they were sent.

Still oblivious to the gay life of the Lodge and Casino, he strode out into the night and down to the dock, paying no attention to Craig's student as he passed. He stepped into the tender which was still waiting and we saw him head straight for the *Sybarite*. Ten minutes later the lights in the main saloon flashed up. Shelby was evidently at work over some problem, wrestling it out himself. Was it his relations with Winifred or his stock-market schemes—or both?

'Well, I've been looking all over for you. Where have you been?' sounded Burke's voice back of us, as Kennedy and I were silently looking out over the dark waters at the yacht.

Without waiting for us to reply Burke hurried on. 'You remember that operator, Steel, that was here from Seaville?'

'Yes,' encouraged Kennedy. 'What of him?'

'He went back to the station and has done his trick. He has just crossed over again with a message to me. That wireless power, whatever it is, is jamming the air again. I thought you'd like to know of it.'

For just a second Kennedy looked at Burke in silence, then without further inquiry turned and almost ran down the length of the dock to the float at the end.

There Watkins had already set up on the float a large affair which looked for all the world like a mortar. We watched as Craig fussed with it to make sure that everything was all right. Meanwhile the student continued adjusting something else that had been let down over the edge of the float into the water. It seemed to be a peculiar disc, heavy, and suspended by a stout wire which allowed it to be submerged eight or ten feet.

'What's this thing?' inquired Burke, looking at the mortar over which Craig was bending. 'Fireworks, or are you going to bombard somebody?'

'It's a light-weight rocket mortar,' explained Kennedy,

ramming something into it. 'You'll see in a moment. Stand back, all of you—off the float—on the dock.'

Suddenly there came a deep detonation from the mortar and a rocket shot out and up in a long, low parabola. Kennedy rushed forward, and another detonation sent a second far out in a different angle.

'What is it?' gasped Burke, in amazement.

'Look!' called Kennedy, elated.

Another instant, and from every quarter of the harbour there seemed to rise, as if from the waves, huge balls of fire, a brilliant and luminous series of flames literally from the water itself. It was a moonless night but these fires seemed literally to roll back the Cimmerian darkness.

'A recent invention,' explained Craig, 'light-bombs, for use at night against torpedo-boat and aeroplane attacks.'

'Light-bombs!' Burke repeated.

'Yes, made of phosphide of calcium. The mortar hurls them out, and they are so constructed that they float after a short plunge in the water. You see, the action of the salt water automatically ignites them merely by contact and the chemical action of the phosphide and the salt water keeps them phosphorescing for several minutes.'

As he talked he shot off some more.

'Kennedy, you're a genius,' gasped Burke. 'You're always ready for anything.'

The sight before us was indeed a beautiful pyrotechnic display. The bombs lighted up the shores and the low-lying hills, making everything stand forth and cast long spectral shadows. Cottages hidden among trees or in coves along the wide sweep of the shore line stood out as if in an unearthly flare.

What people on the shore thought we had no time even to wonder. They crowded out on the porches, in consternation. The music at the Casino stopped. No one had ever seen anything like it before. It was fire on water!

As yet none of us had even an inkling of what it was that Kennedy expected to discover. But every craft in the harbour now stood out distinct—in the glare of a miniature sun. We could see that, naturally, excitement on the boats was greater than it was on shore, for they were closer to the flares and therefore it seemed more amazing.

Craig was scanning the water carefully, seeking any sign of something suspicious.

'There it is!' he exclaimed, bending forward and pointing.

We strained our eyes. A mile or two out I could distinguish a power-boat of good size, moving swiftly away, as though trying to round the shelter of a point of land, out of the light. With a glass someone made out a stubby wireless mast on her.

Kennedy's surmise when we had first studied the wireless interference had proved correct.

Sure enough, in the blackness of the night, there was a fast express cruiser, of the new scout type, not large, almost possible for one man to control, the latest thing in small power-boats and a perfect demon for speed!

Was that the source of the strange wireless impulses? Whose was it, and why was it there?

CHAPTER XXI

THE SUBMARINE EAR

Almost before we knew it the speed demon had disappeared beyond the circle of the flares.

'Suspiciously near the *Sybarite*,' remarked Kennedy, under his breath, watching the scout cruiser to the last moment as she ran away.

I wondered whether he meant that the swift little motor-boat might have some connection with Shelby Maddox and his new activities, but I said nothing, for Kennedy's attention was riveted on the wake left by the boat. I looked, too, and could have sworn that there was something moving in the opposite direction to that taken by the boat. What could it be?

On the end of the deck was an incandescent lamp. Craig unscrewed the bulb and inserted another connection in the bulb socket, an insulated cable that led down to the apparatus on the float over which his assistant was still working.

By this time quite a crowd had collected on the dock, and on the float, watching us.

'Burke,' ordered Kennedy, 'will you and Jameson make the people stand back? We can't do anything with so many around.'

As we pressed the newcomers back I saw that among them was Paquita. Though I looked, I could not discover Sanchez, but thought nothing of it, for there were so many about that it would have been hard to find any particular person.

'If you will please stand back,' I implored, trying to keep the curious from almost swamping the float 'you will be able to see what is going on just as well and, besides, it will be a great deal safer—providing there is an explosion,' I added as a happy

174

afterthought, although I had almost as vague an idea what Kennedy was up to as any of them.

The words had the effect I intended. The crowd gave way, not only willing, but almost in panic.

As they pressed back, however, Paquita pressed forward until she was standing beside me.

'Is—Mr Maddox—out there?' she asked, pointing out at the *Sybarite* anxiously.

'Why?' I demanded, hoping in her anxiety to catch her off guard.

She shot a quick glance at me. There was no denying that the woman was clever and quick of perception.

'Oh, I just wondered,' she murmured. 'I wanted to see him, so much—that is all. And it's very urgent.'

She glanced about, as though hoping to discover some means of communicating with the yacht, even of getting out to it. But there did not seem to be any offered.

I determined to watch her, and for that reason did not insist that she get back as far as the rest of the crowd. All the time I saw that she was looking constantly out at the *Sybarite*. Did she know something about Shelby Maddox that we did not know? I wondered if, indeed, there might be some valid reason why she should get out there. What did she suspect?

Again she came forward, inquiring whether there was not some way of communicating with the *Sybarite*, and again, when I tried to question her, she refused to give me any satisfaction. However, I could not help noticing that in spite of the cold manner in which Shelby had treated her, she seemed now to be actuated more by the most intense fear for him than by any malice against him.

What it meant I had the greatest curiosity to know, especially when I noticed that Paquita was glancing nervously about as though in great fear that someone might be present and see her. Nor did she seem to be deterred from showing her feelings by the fact that she knew that I, Kennedy's closest friend, was watching and would undoubtedly report to him. It was as though she had abandoned discretion and cast fear to the winds.

As the minutes passed and nothing happened, Paquita became a trifle calmer and managed to take refuge in the crowd.

I took the opportunity again to run my eye over them. Nowhere in the crowd could I discover Winifred, or, in fact, any of the Maddox family. They seemed to be studiously avoiding appearance in public just now, and I could not blame them, for in a summer colony like that at Westport facts never troubled gossipers.

'What do you suppose Kennedy is afraid of?' whispered Hastings in my ear nervously. 'Your friend is positively uncanny, and I can almost feel that he fears something.'

'I'm sure I don't know,' I confessed, 'but I've seen enough of him to be sure that no one is going to catch him napping. Here's Riley. Perhaps he has some news.'

The Secret Service operative had shouldered his way through the throng, looking for Burke, who was right behind me.

'What's the matter?' demanded his chief.

'There's another message, by telephone from the Seaville Station,' Riley reported. 'They say they are having the same trouble again—only more of it.'

'That operator, Steel, came back again,' considered Burke. 'Where is he?'

'As soon as I got the message, I hunted him up and took the liberty of sending him up to Mr Kennedy's room to look at that arrangement there. I couldn't make anything out of it myself, I knew, and I thought that he could.'

'Did he?' inquired Burke.

'Yes. Of course he hadn't seen it work before. But I told him as nearly as I could what you had told me, and it didn't take him very long to catch on to the thing. After that he said that what was being recorded now must be just the same as it had been before when Mr Kennedy was there—not messages, but just impulses.'

'Where is he—down here?'

'No, I left him up there. I thought it might be best to have someone there. Did you want to speak to him? There's a telephone down here in the boat-house up to the switchboard at the Lodge.'

Riley jerked his thumb back over his shoulder at a little shelter built on the end of the dock.

'N-no,' considered Burke. 'I wouldn't know what to tell him.'

'But I think you ought to tell Kennedy that,' I interrupted. 'He might know what to do.'

Together Riley and I walked across the float to where Craig was at work, and briefly I told him what had happened.

He looked grave, but did not pause in his adjustment of the machine, whatever it was.

'That's all right,' he approved. 'Yes, get the operator on the wire. Tell him to stay up there. And—yes—tell him to detach that phonograph recording device and go back to straight wireless. He might try to wake up the operator on the *Sybarite*, if he can. I guess he must know the call. Have him do that and then have that telephone girl keep the line clear and connected from the boat-house up to my room. I want to keep in touch with Steel.'

Riley and I pushed through the crowd and finally managed to deliver Kennedy's message, in spite of the excitement at the Lodge; which had extended by this time to the switchboard operator. I left Riley in the boat-house to hold the wire up to our room, and rejoined Burke and Hastings on the float.

Kennedy had been working with redoubled energy, now that the light-bombs had gone out after serving their purpose. We stood apart now as he made a final inspection of the apparatus which he and his assistant had installed.

Finally Craig pressed down a key which seemed to close a circuit including the connection in the electric-light socket and the arrangement that had been let over the edge of the float. Standing where we were we could feel a sort of dull metallic vibration under our feet, as it were.

'What are you doing?' inquired Hastings, looking curiously at a headgear which Kennedy had over his ears.

'It works!' exclaimed Craig, more to Watkins than to us.

'What does?' persisted Hastings.

'This Fessenden oscillator,' he cried, apparently for the first time recognising that Hastings had been addressing him.

'What is it?' we asked, crowding about. 'What does it do?'

'It's a system for the employment of sound for submarine signals,' he explained hurriedly. 'I am using it to detect moving objects in the water—under the water, perhaps. It's really a submarine ear.'

In our excitement we could only watch him in wonder.

'People don't realise the great advance that has been made in the use of water instead of air as a medium for transmitting sounds,' he continued, after a pause, during which he seemed to be listening, observing a stop watch, and figuring rapidly on a piece of paper all at once. 'I can't stop to explain this apparatus, but, roughly, it is composed of a ring magnet, a copper tube which lies in an air gap of a magnetic field, and a stationary central armature. The magnetic field is much stronger than that in an ordinary dynamo of this size.'

Again he listened, as he pressed the key, and we felt the peculiar vibration, while he figured on the paper.

'The copper tube,' he resumed mechanically to us, though his real attention was on something else, 'has an alternating current induced in it. It is attached to solid discs of steel, which in turn are attached to a steel diaphragm an inch thick. Surrounding the oscillator is a large water-tight drum.'

'Then it makes use of sound-waves in the water?' queried Hastings, almost incredulously.

'Exactly,' returned Craig. 'I use the same instrument for sending and receiving—only I'm not doing any real sending.

You see, like the ordinary electric motor, it is capable of acting as a generator, too, and a very efficient one. All I have to do is to throw a switch in one direction when I want to telegraph or telephone under water, and in the other direction when I want to listen.'

'Talking through water!' exclaimed Burke, awestruck by the very idea, as though it were scarcely believable.

'That's not exactly what I'm doing now,' returned Kennedy indulgently, 'although I could do it if there was anyone around this part of the country equipped to receive and reply. I rather suspect, though, that whoever it is is not only not equipped, but wouldn't want to reply, anyhow.'

'Then what are you doing?' asked Burke, rather mystified.

'Well, you see I can send out signals and listen for their reflection—really the echo under water. More than that, I can get the sounds direct from any source that is making them. If there was a big steamer out there I could hear her engines and propellers, even if I couldn't see her around the point. Light travels in straight lines, but you can get sounds around a corner, as it were.'

'Oh,' I exclaimed, 'I think I see. Even if that little scout cruiser did disappear around the point, you can still hear her through the water. Is that it?'

'Partly,' nodded Kennedy. 'You know, sound travels through water at a velocity of about four thousand feet a second. For instance, I find I can get an echo from somewhere practically instantaneously. That's the bottom of the bay—here. Another echo comes back to me in about a twentieth of a second. That, I take it, is reflected from the sea wall on the shore, back of us, at high tide. It must be roughly a hundred feet—you see, that corresponds. It is a matter of calculation.'

'Is that all?' I prompted, as he paused again.

'No, I've located the echo from the *Sybarite* and some others. But,' he added slowly, 'there's one I can't account for. There's a sound that is coming to me direct from somewhere. I can't just place it, for there isn't a moving craft visible and it doesn't give the same note as that little cruiser. It's sharper. Just now I tried to send out my own impulses in the hope of getting an echo from it, and I succeeded. The echo comes back to me in something more than five seconds. You see, that would make twenty thousand-odd feet. Half of that would be nearly two miles, and that roughly corresponds with the position where we saw the scout cruiser at first, before it fled. There's something out there.'

'Then I was right,' I exclaimed excitedly. 'I thought I saw something in the wake of the cruiser.'

Kennedy shook his head gravely. 'I'm afraid you were,' he muttered. 'There's something there, all right. That wireless operator is up in our room and you have a wire from the boat-house to him?'

'Yes,' I returned. 'Riley's holding it open.'

Anxiously Kennedy listened again in silence, as though to verify some growing suspicion. What was it he heard?

Quickly he pulled the headgear off and before I knew it had clapped it on my own head.

'Tell me what it sounds like,' he asked tensely.

I listened eagerly, though I was no electrical or mechanical engineer, and such things were usually to me a sealed book. Still, I was able to describe a peculiar metallic throbbing.

'Record the time for the echo from it,' ordered Kennedy, thrusting the stop watch into my hands. 'Press it the instant you hear the return sound after I push down the key. I want to be sure of it and eliminate my own personal equation from the calculation. Are you ready?'

I nodded and an instant later, as he noted the time, I heard through the oscillator the peculiar vibration I had felt when the key was depressed. On the *qui vive* I waited for the return echo. Sure enough, there it was and I mechanically registered it on the watch.

'Five and thirty-hundredths seconds,' muttered Kennedy. 'I

had five and thirty-five hundredths. It's coming nearer—you hear the sound direct again?'

I did, just a trifle more distinctly, and I said so.

Confirmed in his own judgment, Craig hastily turned to the student. 'Run up there to the boat-house,' he directed. 'Have Riley call that wireless operator on the telephone and tell him to get the *Sybarite* on the wireless—if he hasn't done it already. Then have him tell them not to try to move the yacht under any circumstances—but for God's sake to get off it themselves— as quick as they can!'

'What's the matter?' I asked breathlessly. 'What was that humming in the oscillator?'

'The wireless destroyer—the telautomaton model—has been launched full at the *Sybarite*,' Craig exclaimed. 'You remember it was large enough, even if it was only a model, to destroy a good-sized craft if it carried a charge of high explosive. It has been launched and is being directed from that fast cruiser back of the point.'

We looked at one another aghast. What could we do? There was a sickening feeling of helplessness in the face of this new terror of the seas.

'It—it has really been launched?' cried an agitated voice of a girl behind us.

Paquita had pushed her way altogether through the crowd while we were engrossed in listening through the submarine ear. She had heard what Kennedy had just said and now stood before us, staring wildly.

'Oh,' she cried, frantically clasping her hands, 'isn't there anything—anything that can stop it—that can save him?'

She was not acting now. There could be no doubt of the genuineness of her anxiety, nor of whom the 'him' meant. I wondered whether she might have been directly or indirectly responsible, whether she was not now repentant for whatever part she had played. At least she must be, as far as Shelby Maddox was involved. Then I recollected the black looks that

Sanchez had given Shelby earlier in the evening. Was jealousy playing a part as well as cupidity?

Kennedy had been busy, while the rest of us had been standing stunned. Suddenly another light-bomb ricocheted over the water.

'Keep on sending them, one by one,' he ordered the student, who had returned. 'We'll need all the light we can get.'

Over the shadowy waves we could now see the fine line of foam left by the destroyer as it shot ahead swiftly.

Events were now moving faster than I can tell them. Kennedy glanced about. On the opposite of the float someone of the visitors from the cottages to the dance at the Casino had left a trim hardwood speedboat. Without waiting to inquire whose it was, Craig leaped into it and spun the engine.

'The submarine ear has warned us,' he shouted, beckoning to Burke and myself. 'Even if we cannot save the yacht, we may save their lives! Come on!'

We were off in an instant and the race was on—one of the most exciting I have ever been in—a race between this speedy motor-boat and a telautomatic torpedo to see which might get to the yacht first. Though we knew that the telautomaton had had such a start before it was discovered that we could not beat it, still there was always the hope that its mechanism might slow down or break down.

Failing to get there first, there was always a chance of our being in at the rescue.

In the penetrating light of the flare-bombs, as we approached closer the spot in which Watkins was now dropping them regularly, we could see the telautomaton, speeding ahead on its mission of death, its wake like the path of a great man-eating fish. What would happen if it struck I could well imagine.

Each of us did what he could to speed the motor. For this was a race with the most terrible engine yet devised by American inventive genius.

CHAPTER XXII

THE TELAUTOMATON

Devilishly, while the light-bombs flared, the telautomaton sped relentlessly toward its mark.

We strained our eyes at the *Sybarite*. Would they never awake to their danger? Was the wireless operator asleep or off duty? Would our own operator be unable to warn them in time?

Then we looked back to the deadly new weapon of modern war science. Nothing now could stop it.

Kennedy was putting every inch of speed into the boat which he had commandeered.

'As a race it's hopeless,' he gritted, bending ahead over the wheel as if the boat were a thing that could be urged on. 'What they are doing is to use the Hertzian waves to actuate relays on the torpedo. The wireless carries impulses so tuned that they release power carried by the machine itself. The thing that has kept the telautomaton back while wireless telegraphy has gone ahead so fast is that in wireless we have been able to discard coherers and relays and use detectors and microphones in their places. But in telautomatics you have to keep the coherer. That has been the barrier. The coherer until recently has been spasmodic, until we got the mercury steel disc coherer—and now this one. See how she works—if only it could be working for us instead of against us!'

On sped the destroyer. It was now only a matter of seconds when it would be directed squarely at the yacht. In our excitement we shouted, forgetting that it was of no use, that they would neither hear nor, most likely, know what it was we meant.

Paquita's words rang in my ears. Was there nothing that could be done?

Just then we saw a sailor rush frantically and haul in a boat that was fastened to a boom extending from the yacht's side.

Then another and another ran toward the first. They had realised at last our warning was intended for them. The deck was now alive and faintly over the water we could hear them shouting in frantic excitement, as they worked to escape destruction coming at them now at express train speed.

Suddenly there came a spurt of water, a cloud of spray, like a geyser rising from the harbour. The *Sybarite* seemed to be lifted bodily out of the water and broken. Then she fell back and settled, bow foremost, heeling over, as she sank down to the mud and ooze of the bottom. The water closed over her and she was gone, nothing left but fragments of spars and woodwork which had been flung far and wide.

Through my mind ran the terrible details I had read of ships torpedoed without warning and the death and destruction of passengers. At least there were no women and children to add to this horror.

Kennedy slowed down his engine as we approached the floating wreckage, for there was not only the danger of our frail little craft hitting something and losing rudder or propeller, but we could not tell what moment we might run across some of those on the yacht, if any had survived.

Other boats had followed us by this time, and we bent all our energies to the search, for pursuit of the scout cruiser was useless. There was not a craft in the harbour capable of overtaking one of her type, even in daylight. At night she was doubly safe from pursuit.

There was only one thing that we might accomplish—rescue. Would we be in time, would we be able to find Shelby? As my mind worked automatically over the entire swift succession of events of the past few days I recalled every moment we had been observing him, every action. I actually hated myself now for the unspoken suspicion of him that I had entertained. I could see that, though Kennedy had been able to promise him nothing openly, he had in reality been working in Shelby's real interests.

There flashed through my mind a picture of Winifred. And at the same time the thought of what this all meant to her brought to me forcibly the events of the night before. One attack after another had been levelled against us, starting with the following and shooting at Hastings at our very laboratory door. Burke had been attacked. Then had come the attack on Kennedy, which had miscarried and struck me. Death had been levelled even at Mito, as though he had possessed some great secret. Next had come the attempted abduction of Winifred Walcott. And at last it had culminated in the most spectacular attack of all, on Shelby himself.

Try as I could by a process of elimination, I was unable to fix the guilt on anyone in particular, even yet. Fixing guilt, however, was not what was needed now.

We had come into the area of the floating debris, and the possibility of saving life was all that need concern us. In the darkness I could make out cries, but they were hard to locate.

We groped about, trying hard to cover as much area as possible, but at the same time fearful of defeating our own purposes by striking someone with bow or propeller of our speedboat. Every now and then a piece of the wreckage would float by and we would scan it anxiously in mingled fear and hope that it would assume a human form as it became more clearly outlined. Each time that we failed we resumed the search with desperate determination.

'Look!' cried Burke, pointing at a wooden skylight that seemed to have been lifted from the deck and cast out into the waves, the glass broken, but the frame nearly intact. 'What's that on it?'

Kennedy swung the boat to port and we came alongside the dark, bobbing object.

It was the body of a man.

With a boat-hook Craig hauled the thing nearer and we

leaned over the side and together pulled the limp form into our boat.

As we laid him on some cushions on the flooring, our boat drifted clear and swung around so that the flare shone in his face. He stirred and groaned, but did not relax the grip of his fingers still clenched after we had torn them loose from the skylight grating.

It was Shelby Maddox—terribly wounded, but alive.

Others of the crew were floating about, and we set to work to get them, now aided by the volunteer fleet that had followed us out. When it was all over we found that all had been accounted for so far, except the engineer and one sailor.

Just at present we had only one thought in mind. Shelby Maddox must be saved, and to be saved he must be rushed where there was medical assistance.

Shouting orders to those who had come up to continue the search, Kennedy headed back toward the town of Westport.

The nearest landing was the town dock at the foot of the main street, and toward this Craig steered.

There was no emergency hospital, but one of the bystanders volunteered to fetch a doctor, and it was not long before Shelby was receiving the attention he needed so badly.

He had been badly cut about the head by flying glass, and the explosion had injured him internally, how serious could not be determined, although two of his ribs had been broken. Only his iron will and athletic training had saved him, for he was weak, not only from loss of blood, but from water which he had been unable to avoid swallowing.

The doctor shook his head gravely over him, but something had to be done, even though it was painful to move him. He could not lie there in an open boat.

Kennedy settled the matter quickly. From a tenant who lived over a store near the waterfront he found where a delivery wagon could be borrowed. Using a pair of long oars and some canvas, we improvised a stretcher which we slung from the top of the wagon and so managed to transport Shelby to the Harbour House, avoiding the crowd of curious onlookers at the main entrance, and finally depositing him in the bed in the room which he usually occupied.

The pain from his wounds was intense, but he managed to keep up his nerve until we reached the hotel. Then he collapsed.

As we tried to help the doctor to bring him around I feared that the injury and the shock might have proved fatal.

'Pretty serious,' muttered the doctor, in answer to my anxious inquiry, 'but I think he'll pull through it. Call up Main 21. There's a trained nurse summering at the house. Get her down.'

I hastened to do so and had hardly finished when Kennedy came over to me.

'I think we ought to notify his sister,' he remarked. 'See if you can get Mrs Walcott on the house 'phone.'

I called, but the voice that answered was not that of Frances Walcott. It took me a few seconds before I realised that it was Winifred Walcott, and I covered up the transmitter as I turned to Kennedy to tell him and ask what he wanted me to do.

'Let me talk to her,' decided Craig. 'I think I won't let events take their course any longer. She can be the best nurse for Shelby—if she will.'

Craig had evidently prepared to break the news gently to her, but, as nearly as I could make out, it was not necessary. She had already heard what had happened.

'No,' I heard him say, 'as if in answer to an anxious question from her. 'He is seriously hurt, to be sure, but the doctor says that with proper nursing he will pull through.'

I did not hear the reply, of course, but I recognised the appeal hidden in Kennedy's answer, as he waited.

'Just a moment,' I heard him say next.

His forehead wrinkled as he listened to something, evidently trying to make it out. Then he said suddenly: 'I think I had better say no more over the telephone, Miss Walcott. Someone is listening to us.'

An angry look flashed over his face, but his voice showed no anger as he said goodbye and hung up.

'What was it?' I asked. 'What did she do?'

'It wasn't Miss Walcott,' he replied, scowling. 'You heard me say that someone was listening? Well, just as I said it there came a laugh over the wire from somewhere, and a voice cut in, "Yes, there is someone listening. You haven't caught me yet, Kennedy—and you won't." I said goodbye after that. Oh, have no fear about Miss Walcott.'

Kennedy was right. It seemed an incredibly short time when there came a light tap on the door and he sprang to open it.

'Can I—be of any assistance?' pleaded a softly tremulous voice. 'Perhaps I—could play at nursing?'

Kennedy glanced at the doctor and the figure lying so quietly on the bed, then at the girl, and decided. She had hesitated not a moment, when she had heard how close Shelby was to death, but had hurried to him. He opened the door and she entered softly, tip-toeing toward the bed.

It must have been by some telepathic influence that Shelby, who had a moment before been scarcely conscious, felt her presence. She had scarcely whispered a word to the doctor, as she bent over him, but he opened his eyes, caught just a glimpse of her face, and seemed to drink it in as his eyes rested on the bunch of flowers she was wearing—his flowers, which he had sent her.

He smiled faintly. Not even by a word or look was any reference made to their misunderstanding. It was a strange meeting, but it seemed that the very atmosphere had changed. Even the doctor noticed it. In spite of his pain, Shelby had brightened visibly.

'I don't think we need that nurse,' whispered the doctor to Kennedy, with an understanding glance. 'What was that you said about someone listening over the telephone? Who could it have been?'

The doctor said it in a low enough tone, but it seemed that

Maddox's senses must have been suddenly made more acute by the coming of Winifred.

He had reached out, weakly but unhesitatingly, and had placed his hand on hers as it rested on his pillows. At the mention of the telephone he turned toward us with an inquiring look. It seemed to recall to his mind something that had been on it before the accident.

'Someone—listening,' he repeated, more to himself than to us.

Winifred looked inquiringly at us, too, but said nothing.

Kennedy tried to pass the thing over, but the doctor's remark seemed to have started some train of thought in Shelby's mind, which could not be so easily stopped.

'Someone—pounding Maddox Munitions,' he murmured brokenly, as if feeling his way through a maze. 'Now I'm out— they'll succeed. What can I do? How can I hold up the market?'

He repeated the last two questions as though turning them over in his mind and finding no answer.

Evidently he was talking about his operations in the market which had been so puzzling to Hastings as well as ourselves. I was about to say something that would prompt him to go on with his revelation, when Kennedy's look halted me. Apparently he did not wish to interfere with the train of thought the doctor's remark had started, inasmuch as it had been started now.

'Someone—listening—over the telephone,' strove Shelby again. 'Yes—how can I do it? No more secrecy—laid up here— I'll have to use the telephone. Will those Broad Street brokers take orders over long distance? Everybody will know—what I'm doing. They'll delay—play me for a sucker. What am I to do?'

It was evident now what Shelby had been doing, at least in part. The tragedy to his brother had quite naturally depressed the stock of the company. Indeed, with Marshall Maddox, its moving spirit, gone, it was no wonder that many holders had begun to feel shaky. Once that feeling began to become general, the stock, which had had a meteoric rise lately along with other war stocks, would begin to sag and slump sadly. There was no telling where it would stop once the downward trend began.

As I looked at the young man I felt a new respect for him. Even though I had not a much clearer idea than at the start of how or by whom Marshall Maddox had been killed, still I do not think any of us had believed that Shelby was capable of seeing such a crisis so clearly and acting upon what he saw. Evidently it was in his blood, bred in the Maddox nature. He was a great deal more clever than any of us had suspected. Not only had he realised the judgment of outsiders about himself, but had taken advantage of it. In keeping the stock up, if it had been known that it was he who was doing it, it would not have counted for half what it did when the impression prevailed that the public was doing it, or even some hazy financial interest determined to maintain the price. Both possibilities had been discussed by the market sharps. It had never seemed to occur to them that Shelby Maddox might be using his personal fortune to bolster up what was now in greater measure his own company.

For a moment we looked blankly at Kennedy. Then Shelby began to talk again.

'Suppose the bear raid continues?' he murmured. 'I must meet it—I must!'

The doctor leaned over to Craig. 'He can't go on that way,' he whispered. 'It will use up his strength in worry.'

Kennedy was thinking about that, too, as he considered the very difficult situation the telautomaton attack had placed Shelby in. It was more than a guess that the attack had been carefully calculated. Someone else, perhaps some hidden group, was engaged in taking advantage of the death of Marshall Maddox in one way, Shelby in another.

As for Shelby, here he was, helpless, at the Harbour House. Surrounded by spies, as he seemed to be, what could he do?

Every message in and out of the hotel was most likely tapped. To use the telephone was like publishing abroad one's secrets.

Kennedy moved over quietly to the bedside, as Winifred looked appealingly at him, as much as to say, 'Isn't there something you can do to quiet him?'

He bent down and took Shelby's hand.

'Oh—it's you, Kennedy—is it?' wandered Shelby, not quite clear yet where he was, in the fantasy of impressions that crowded his mind since the accident. 'I asked you to work with me once. You said you would play fair.'

'I will,' repeated Kennedy, 'as far as the interests of my client go, I'll give you every assistance. But if you are to do anything at all tomorrow, you must rest tonight.'

'Have I—have I been talking?' queried Shelby, as though in doubt whether he had been thinking to himself or aloud.

Kennedy ignored the question. 'You need rest,' he said simply. 'Let the doctor fix you up now. In the morning—well, tomorrow will be another day.'

Shelby passed his hand wearily over his aching head. He was too weak to argue.

While the doctor prepared a mild opiate Kennedy and I quietly withdrew into the next room.

'Professor Kennedy, *won't* you help us?' pleaded Miss Walcott, who had followed. 'Surely something can be done.'

I could not help noticing that she said 'us,' not 'him.' As I watched her the scene on the float, hours before, flashed over me. There another woman, under quite different circumstances, had made the same appeal. Where did Paquita fit into the scheme of things? Two women had been striving over Shelby's life. Did one represent his better nature, the other his worse?

Kennedy looked frankly at Winifred Walcott.

'You will trust me?' he asked in a low tone.

'Yes,' she said, simply, meeting his eyes in turn.

'Then when the nurse arrives,' he directed, 'get some rest. I shall need you tomorrow.'

CHAPTER XXIII

THE CURB MARKET

'IT's impossible to trace all the telephone lines back,' considered Kennedy, thinking still of the eavesdropping, as we met Burke again downstairs. 'Perhaps if we begin at the other end, and follow the wires from the point where they enter the building to the switchboard, we may find something. If we don't, then we shall have to work harder, that's all.'

With the aid of Burke, who had ways of getting what he wanted from the management of anything, from a bank to a hotel, we succeeded in getting down into the cellar quietly.

Kennedy began by locating the point in the huge cellar of the Lodge where the wires of the two telephones, 100 and 101 Main, entered underground, that system having been adopted so as to avoid unsightly wires outside the hotel.

Carefully Craig began a systematic search as he followed the two lines to the point underneath the switchboard upstairs. So far nothing irregular had been apparent.

Craig looked up perplexed, and I feared that he was about to say that the search must be continued wherever the wires led through the house, a gigantic and almost impossible task.

Instead, he was looking at a little dark store-room that was near the point where we were standing. He walked over to it curiously and peered in. Then he struck a match. In the flickering light we could see a telephone receiver and a little switchboard standing beside it.

For a moment his hand hesitated on the receiver, as though he were afraid that by taking it off the hook it might call or alarm somebody. Finally he seemed to decide that unless something were risked nothing would be gained. He took the receiver deliberately and held it up to his ear.

'Do you hear anything?' I asked.

He shook his head as if to discourage conversation. Then he changed the plugs and listened again. Several times he repeated it. At last he kept the plugs in for some time, while we waited in the darkness, in silence.

'Evidently someone has tapped the regular telephone wires,' he said to us at length, 'and has run extensions to this little switchboard in the store-room, prepared to overhear almost anything that goes on over either set of wires that come in. And they have done more. They must have tampered with the switchboard upstairs. Just now I heard the girl call Shelby's room. The doctor answered. That trained nurse has arrived and Miss Walcott has gone to her room as she promised. We can't take the time to trace out how it is done, and besides it is too dark at night to do it, anyhow. Shelby was right.'

For a moment Kennedy tried to puzzle the thing out, as though determining what was the best course to pursue. Then he stooped down and began picking up even the burnt matches he had dropped.

'Don't disturb a thing,' he said to Burke. 'We must circumvent this scheme. Has the last train back to the city gone?'

Burke looked at his watch. 'Yes, unfortunately,' he nodded.

'Then I'll have to send someone back to the city to my laboratory by automobile,' continued Kennedy. 'I can't wait until morning, for we shall have to go to the city then. There's that student of mine—but he's pretty tired.'

'I can get a car and a fresh driver for him,' remarked Burke. 'Perhaps he could doze off during the ride. How would that do?'

'It will have to do,' decided Kennedy. 'Get the car.'

We went back upstairs by the way of the kitchen to avoid suspicion, and while Burke hunted up a car and driver Kennedy found Watkins and gave him detailed instructions about what he wanted.

'I calculate that it will take him at least four hours to go and get back,' remarked Kennedy, a few minutes later. 'There isn't anything we can do yet. I think we had better get a little rest, for I anticipate a strenuous time tomorrow.'

We passed through the lobby. There was Sanchez, talking to the night clerk.

'I was down on the dock in front of the Casino when the explosion came,' we could hear him telling the clerk. 'Yes, *sir*, it's a wonder any of them were saved.'

'What do you think of that?' queried Burke, in the elevator. 'A crude attempt at an alibi?'

Kennedy shrugged non-committally.

'I think I'll have Riley watch him until he goes to bed,' continued the Secret Service man. 'I can telephone down from the room. No one is listening now, at least.'

'By all means,' agreed Craig.

Tired though we were, I do not think we slept very much as we waited for the return of the car from New York. Still, we were at least resting, although to me the hours seemed to pass as a shifting phantasmagoria of fire-balls and explosions strangely blended with the faces of the two beautiful women who had become the chief actresses in the little drama. From one very realistic dream in which I saw Winifred, Paquita, Irene Maddox, and Frances Walcott all fantastically seated as telephone operators and furiously ringing Shelby's bell, I woke with a start to find that it was our own bell ringing and that Kennedy was answering it.

'The car is back from the city,' he said to me. 'You needn't get up. I can do this job alone.'

There was no sleep for me, however, I knew, and with a final yawn I pulled myself together and joined Craig and Burke in the hall as we went downstairs as quietly as we could.

Riley had left a hastily-scribbled report in the letterbox for

Burke, saying that Sanchez had done nothing further suspicious, but had gone to bed. Paquita was in her room. Winifred, Mr and Mrs Walcott, Irene Maddox, and all the rest were present and accounted for, and he had decided on resting, too.

Kennedy sent Watkins off to bed, after taking from him the things he had brought back from the city, and the early morning, just as it was beginning to lighten a bit, found us three again in the cellar.

Kennedy carefully reconnoitred the store-room where the telephone outfit had been placed. It was deserted, and he set to work quickly. First he located the wires that represented the number 100 Main and connected them with what looked very much like a seamless iron tube, perhaps six inches long and three inches in diameter. Then he connected in a similar manner the other end of the tube with the wires of Main 101.

'This is a special repeating coil of high efficiency,' he explained to Burke, whom he was instructing, as it occurred to him, just what he wanted done later. 'It is absolutely balanced as to resistance, number of turns, everything. I shall run this third line from the coil itself outside and upstairs through Shelby's window. Before I go to the city I want you to see that the local telephone company keeps a couple of wires to the city clear for us. I'll get them on the wire and explain the thing, if you'll use your authority at this end of the line.'

In spite of the risk of disturbing Shelby Maddox Kennedy finished leading the wires from the coil up to his room and placed a telephone set on a table near the bed. Then he carefully concealed the tube in the cellar so that under ordinary circumstances no one could find it or even guess that anything had been done with the two trunk lines.

Shelby was resting quietly under an opiate and the nurse was watching faithfully. I did not hear Kennedy's instructions entirely, but I remember he said that Burke was to be allowed into the outer room and that Shelby Maddox and Winifred were to talk only over the new line as he would direct later.

Again we retired to our rooms, and I fell asleep listening to Kennedy instruct Burke minutely in something which I think was just as much Greek to the Secret Service man as it was to me. Kennedy saw that it was and wrote down what he had already said, to make doubly sure.

My sleep was dreamless this time, for I was thoroughly tired. Whether Kennedy slept I do not know, but I suspect that he did not, for when he was conducting a case he seemed unable to rest as long as there was something over which he could work or think.

It seemed almost no time before Kennedy roused me. He was already dressed—in fact, I don't think he had taken time for more than a change of linen.

A hasty bite of breakfast and we were again on the first accommodation train that went into the city in the cool grey dawn, leaving Burke with instructions to keep us informed of anything important that he discovered.

No one for whom we cared saw us leave and we had the satisfaction of knowing that we should be in the city and at work long before anyone probably knew it. That was a quality of Kennedy's vigilance and sleeplessness.

'It's just as important to guard against prying ears at this end of the line as the other,' remarked Kennedy, after hurriedly mapping out a course for ourselves, which included, first of all, calling out of bed an officer of the telephone company with whom he was intimately acquainted and whom he could therefore afford to take into his confidence.

Without a moment's more delay we hurried down-town from the railroad station.

Shelby Maddox had given Craig the names of two Curb brokers with whom he was dealing in confidence, for, although Maddox Munitions was being traded in largely, it was still a Curb-market stock and not listed on the big exchange.

'They are in the same building on Broad Street,' remarked Kennedy as we left the Subway at the Wall Street station and took the shortest cuts through the basements of several tall buildings in the financial district. 'And I don't trust either one of them any farther than I can see him.'

It was very early, and comparatively few people were about. Craig, however, managed to find the janitor of the building where the brokers' offices were—a rather old structure overlooking that point where Broad Street widens out and has been seized on by that excited, heterogeneous collection of speculators who gather daily in a corner roped off from the traffic, known as the Curb market. From the janitor he learned that there was one small office in the front of the building for rent at a seemingly prohibitive rate. It was no time to haggle over money, and Kennedy laid down a liberal deposit for the use of the room.

His tentative arrangements with the janitor had scarcely been completed when two men from the telephone company arrived. Into our new and unfurnished office Craig led them, while the janitor, for another fee, agreed to get us a flat-topped desk and some chairs.

'Whatever we do,' began Craig in a manner that inspired enthusiasm, 'must be done quickly. You have the orders of the company to go ahead. There's one line that runs into the office of Dexter and Co., on the second floor, another to Merrill and Moore on the fourth. I want you to locate the wires, cut in on them, and run the cut-in extensions to this office. It's not a wire-tapping game, so you need have no fear that there will be any comeback on what you do.'

While the telephone men were busy locating the two sets of wires, Kennedy laid out on the desk which the janitor brought up on the freight elevator a tube and coil similar to that which I had already seen him employ at Westport.

Though the telephone men were as clever as any that the official of the company could have sent, it was a complicated task to locate the wires and carry out the instructions that Kennedy had given, and it took much longer than he had anticipated. At least, it seemed long, in our excited frame of mind. Every minute counted now, for the advance guard of office boys, stenographers and clerks had already begun to arrive at the offices in preparation for the work of the day.

We had fortunately been able to start early enough, so that that part of the work which would have excited comment was already done before the office workers arrived. As for the rest, on the surface it appeared only as though someone had rented the vacant office and had been able to hurry the telephone company along in installing its service.

There was no difficulty about connecting up our own regular telephone, and as soon as it was done Kennedy hastened to call Westport and the Lodge on long distance.

'Shelby has awakened much improved after his night's rest,' he announced, after a rapid-fire conversation. 'Miss Walcott is with him now, as well as the nurse. I think we can depend on Burke to handle things properly out there. It's an emergency and we'll have to take chances. I don't blame Shelby for feeling impatient and wishing he could be here. But I told the doctor that as long as things were as they are he had better humour his patient by giving him an outlet for his excitement than to keep him fuming and eating his heart out in bed, helpless. Between Winifred and ourselves we ought to keep him occupied.'

I do not think that the telephone men had the faintest idea what it was that Kennedy was planning to do, and I am quite sure that I did not. For, in addition to the outfit like that at Westport, he now laid on the table a peculiar arrangement. It seemed to consist of a metal base, which he placed near the telephone receiver. From the base three prongs reached up, and there was attached to it on one side one of those little flat, watch-case receivers such as are used on office telephones.

It was getting late, and Kennedy and the men from the telephone company were working as rapidly as possible, testing and adjusting the connections he had caused to be made.

As I stood by the window, watching the gathering crowd below, I suddenly realised that the market had opened.

It was as Kennedy had expected. Pandemonium seemed to reign on the Curb. Buyers and sellers crowded and elbowed one another, wildly shouting and gesticulating. From the thick of what looked like a huge free-for-all fight orders and sales were relayed by word of mouth to clerks standing on the sidewalk, who in turn shouted them to other clerks in the windows of our own building or others about, or despatched messengers to offices farther away. It was a curious sight, and one never to be forgotten.

Passers-by stopped on both sides of the street to look and listen to the struggling mob, and I soon saw that even the usually electrified atmosphere of the Curb was this morning more than ordinarily surcharged with excitement. Far above all the noise and bustle I made out that there had been overnight a veritable flood of orders from weak holders, as well as others, to sell Maddox Munitions. It was not the weak holders we feared so much as the hidden 'others' who were seeking to manipulate the stock.

Our telephone rang and Craig answered it, while the men still worked on the new line. It was Shelby. He had called up his brokers and had heard of the market opening.

'Not quite ready yet,' hastened Kennedy. 'Go ahead and place your orders over the regular wire with the brokers. I'll let you know when we're ready and what to do. Don't worry.'

Kennedy had stationed me now permanently at the window to report what was happening below. From my eery point of vantage I could now see that the first flood of selling orders was receding, as Shelby's brokers wormed their way in and now and then snapped up a lot of stock offered for sale. The buying momentarily seemed to stiffen the price which before had threatened to toboggan.

Yet no sooner had the buying begun than it seemed as if other blocks of stock were brought up for sale. It was, for all the world, like a gigantic battle in which forces were hurled here and there, with reinforcements held in reserve to be loosed at just the right moment. Who was back of it?

Gradually, in spite of the large purchases which Shelby had made, the price of the stock worked its way down. I began to understand something of what was going on. Actually it seemed as though every time there was an order to buy, coming from either Dexter or Merrill and Moore, there was a corresponding new order to sell by some other broker. Thousands of shares were thus being dumped on the market, recklessly, relentlessly.

It looked as though someone was 'wise'. Were the brokers with whom Shelby was dealing straight? I said as much to Kennedy, but he merely shook his head and plunged into work deeper.

One after another blocks of stock appeared for sale. There could be no doubt now that there was a carefully planned quick assault being made at the very opening of trading to take people by surprise at the suddenness of the bear raid.

More and more frenzied became the selling and buying. I could imagine the strain that it placed on Shelby, miles away, forced to take only the reports that his brokers sent him, and to fling back other and larger orders to buy.

As the trading progressed it became evident that the offerings of stock were coming with more surprising regularity. The more I observed the more I was convinced that there was some collusion here. It was not chance. Someone was informed of each move of Shelby's even before it could be executed, was enabled to prepare for it, to meet it with a decided advantage. It was a game being played for high stakes, but as far as Shelby was concerned, the cards were stacked and marked.

Our telephone rang insistently and Kennedy answered it. It was from Dexter. They were feeling shaky and worried.

Our door opened and a clerk from the Merrill and Moore firm entered. He was suave and polite. But back of it all could be discovered the eagerness to stand from under a possible crash.

'You will readily understand,' the broker hinted, 'that under the circumstances we cannot continue to take Mr Maddox's orders over the telephone indefinitely. Suppose he should repudiate some of them? Where would we find ourselves?'

Kennedy glanced at the two telephone men, one of whom had straightened up and was watching the other.

'I understand,' he said simply, a grim smile flickering about his mouth. 'Just a moment, sir. Walter—keep Dexter on this wire.'

Below on the street I could hear the babel of voices. I knew what it meant. At both ends of Shelby's telephone line were traitors. A panic in the stock was not only threatened. It was here.

Maddox Munitions was on the verge of collapse!

CHAPTER XXIV

THE PHANTOM CIRCUIT

I LOOKED at Kennedy in despair. He was not even perturbed. It was for just this moment that he had hurried to New York and had worked so intensely.

Over the telephone that I was holding, Dexter himself politely informed us that he had reached a point where orders from Mr Maddox to be filled must have some more binding force than word of mouth over the telephone.

'Tell him to wait just a moment,' directed Kennedy, turning to the other broker who had come to us. 'Will you, sir, tell Mr Merrill to step down to the office of Mr Dexter? I shall be there in a moment myself. Walter,' he added calmly, 'ring Dexter off. Get Shelby Maddox and tell him to use the new wire connections.'

I did as I was told. Even over the telephone I could feel that the strain was telling on Shelby's shattered strength. His voice was shaky as he inquired thickly for news. I shouted something encouraging back, and urged him to get on the other wire, at which, at our end, Kennedy was already impatiently waiting.

A moment later I heard Kennedy and Shelby exchange a few words. Shelby was evidently much alarmed over the sudden turn of events.

As I waited, I saw Kennedy jam the receiver down on the little metal base. The three prongs, reaching upward, engaged the receiver tightly, fitting closely about it. Then he took the small disc receiver from its hook and placed it to his ear instead of the regular one.

I wondered what it all meant. Craig's face showed that, whatever it was, it was most important.

'Yes,' I heard him call back, 'give whatever orders you want now to me. I will see that they are delivered. Pay no attention to the other telephone. Let it ring—until I tell you. Go ahead.'

Evidently Shelby was giving orders for stock up to the limit of his resources that were available.

For a moment there evidently came a pause in what was being said over the telephone at the Westport end, and Kennedy gazed impatiently about the room.

'What good will that do?' I objected, seeing that Kennedy was not occupied. 'Don't you suppose they'll hear what is said over this line, too? We know they've cut in on the two trunk lines at the Harbour House, and there is every reason to suppose that someone taps the brokers' wires here—unless the brokers are crooks, too. They'll know what Shelby is going to do.'

Kennedy shook his head. 'No,' he replied calmly, 'no outsider knows a thing about this. You see, I'm not using any ordinary means to prepare against the expert who has brought this situation about. The messages that I am receiving are coming over what we call the "phantom circuit".'

'"The phantom circuit?"' I repeated, mystified.

'Yes. It seems fantastic at first, I suppose,' he pursued, 'but, after all, it is in accordance with the laws of electricity. They know nothing and they cannot cut us off or interfere. You see, I am taking advantage of the fact that additional telephones or so-called phantom lines can be superposed on existing physical lines. It is possible to obtain a third circuit from two similar metallic circuits by using for each side of this third circuit the two wires of each of the other circuits in multiple. All three circuits are independent, too.'

He was growing more and more impatient. Apparently there was some delay at the other end.

'The third telephone current,' he went on hurriedly, covering up his nervousness by talking about his machine, 'enters the wires of the first circuit, as it were, and returns along the wires of the second circuit. There are several ways of doing it. One is to use retardation or choke-coils, bridged across the two metallic circuits at both ends, with taps taken from the middle points of each. But the better method, I think, is the the one you have seen me install. I have introduced repeating coils into the circuits at both ends. Technically, the third circuit is then taken off from the midpoints of the secondaries or line windings of these repeating coils. I don't know what's the matter,' he added, calling vainly for Shelby Maddox. 'Oh, all right. Yes. I'll wait. But hurry, please.'

I could appreciate Kennedy's eagerness, for below on the street the tumult was rising.

'It's working all right,' he reassured. 'I suppose you know that the current on a long-distance line is alternating in character, and it passes readily through a repeating coil. The only effect it has on the transmission is slightly reducing the volume. The current passes into the repeating coil, then divides and passes through the two line wires. At the other end, the halves balance, so to speak. Thus currents passing over a phantom circuit don't set up currents in the terminal apparatus of the side circuits. Consequently, a conversation carried on over the phantom circuit will not be heard on either side circuit, nor does a conversation on one side circuit affect the phantom. You get three messages at once on two sets of wires. We can all talk at once without interfering with one another.'

At any other time I should have been more than interested, but just now the delay was galling. 'What's the trouble?' I inquired.

Kennedy shook his head. 'Shelby is talking to Winifred about something. I can hear only a word now and then. But he said it was important and asked me to hold the wire. Evidently she wants to do something he doesn't want her to do. Yes—hallo— yes, this is Kennedy. Say, you'll have to— Oh, good morning, Miss Walcott. Yes, fine. What? Why—certainly—if he says so, you may. That's right. Go right ahead. I am attending to everything at this end now.'

A moment later when Craig restored the telephone to its normal condition he looked at me with a smile.

'Winifred Walcott is a trump!' he exclaimed, jumping up.

Just then our other telephone rang, and I answered it. 'I'm down here in Mr Dexter's office,' called a voice which I took to be that of the other broker. 'We have been talking the situation over. Of course, if Mr Maddox were here himself, you know,' he went on apologetically, 'it might be different. We could have him sign his name to orders, but—really—well, you understand, under the circumstances—we feel, both Mr Dexter and myself, that we have gone about far enough. It's not that we question Mr Maddox's intentions in any way, you understand, but—perhaps if he were on the ground, he might protect us from loss, which he may not be able to do over the telephone. We're sorry, but—'

'Tell them I'll be right down,' interjected Kennedy, sensing from my look the tenor of what was being said.

I interrupted the broker at the first opportunity, then turned to Kennedy. He had pulled from a compartment of the metal base a little wax cylinder and dropped it into his pocket carefully.

'Come on,' he cried, dashing for the door and taking the stairs, not even waiting for the elevator to come up.

A moment later we burst into the board room of the broker. Customers were standing about in a high state of excitement, while the boys at the board scurried about, replacing the figures on little bits of green cardboard which fitted under the abbreviated names of the active stocks listed on the board at one end of the room. Others were gathered about the ticker, reading the words that the printed tape was pushing forth. All seemed talking at once.

Kennedy did not pause, however, but walked unceremoniously into the private office of Dexter. There already were several men representing the two brokerage houses. Evidently they had been having a hasty conference on what they should do in view of the situation in Maddox Munitions.

I felt a sort of frigidity in the air as we entered. It was not that anything was either said or done, but I have felt the same thing several times when as a reporter it was my duty to be present at some event that marked the freezing out of some person financially.

'Maddox Munitions,' began Dexter, clearing his throat with dignity, 'seems to have occasioned somewhat of a flurry on the market today in which it is the chief sufferer itself. Our latest quotation shows that it has declined steadily—two points, for instance since the quotation before, and twenty-five under the opening of the market. I think you will readily appreciate, Mr Kennedy, our position in the matter.'

Before Kennedy could reply, however, another took up the conversation. 'Yes,' he remarked, 'we have been observing the trend of events for the last few days. Of course, we can readily appreciate the feeling of Mr Maddox in the matter, and, indeed, I must say that at the beginning I thought that all that was necessary was a good strong show of buying and that the run would end. Now, however, it begins to look as though there were other factors entering in. You know the newspapers have given a great deal of unpleasant notoriety to the Maddox family and Maddox Munitions. Perhaps the general public does not like it. At least it begins to seem as though even Mr Shelby Maddox might not have the resources to stem the tide.'

'This is Mr Merrill, of Merrill and Moore, I believe?' asked Craig quietly, reminding them that in their suave haste they had forgotten to introduce him.

'Yes,' returned Merrill, flushing a bit, for he was a great stickler for punctilious etiquette, and his failure had betrayed the anxiety he sought to conceal.

It was a ticklish situation and the brokers, always conservative, were making it worse. Nor could one blame them. The case for the stock looked at its darkest, verging rapidly on panic.

Kennedy knew it all just as well as they did. But he kept his coolness admirably and never betrayed that he was doing a thing more than to drive a bargain, whereas another might have given them an impression of merely stalling for time.

As the downward trend continued, I saw that Craig was indeed calculating how far he would let it go, as though one were letting himself down a hill and testing just how little he needed to apply the brakes not to have the car run away from him.

It seemed to nettle the brokers. They wanted to close the whole matter up brusquely. Yet Kennedy's commanding personality checked them. I felt sure that they would even have ridden rough-shod over Shelby. Kennedy was another matter.

Dexter rose decisively. 'This must stop,' he frowned.

'I have orders from Mr Maddox to buy shares—well, I shall not say what it totals, but the first order is for ten thousand,' cut in Kennedy quietly.

There was a moment of silence during which the brokers looked at each other, waiting for one to take the initiative.

'That is just the point,' began Merrill finally. 'You see, we have been buying steadily for Mr Maddox. If he had authorised us by letter—or if he had handed us a cheque, certified—'

'But he could not well have foreseen this raid this morning,' temporised Kennedy.

'True, no doubt. But it does not protect us. For example, where is your authority, something, anything, that may be binding on him for this new order of ten thousand shares?'

There was an air of triumph about the way he said the words. It was evidently intended to be a poser, to leave Kennedy floored and flat.

'Authority?' repeated Craig quietly, looking about. 'I wonder whether you have one of those dictating machines, a dictaphone, in the office? Perhaps someone in the building has one.'

'We have one,' returned Dexter, still coldly. 'I do not see how anything you might dictate to it and which a stenographer might transcribe would have any bearing on the question.'

'It would not,' agreed Kennedy, blithely. 'That was not what

I intended to do. There is another use I wished to put it to. Ah—I see. May I use this transcribing apparatus? Or better yet, would you gentlemen be so kind as to listen to what I have here?'

He deliberately drew from his pocket the cylinder I had seen him detach from the instrument upstairs and slid it on in the proper place in the new machine.

As it began to revolve I studied the faces about me, intent on listening to what would be said.

'Is that good enough?' queried Kennedy. 'It is a record on an instrument devised for just this purpose with you brokers who wish to hold your customers to an agreement over the telephone.'

The needle of the machine sputtered a bit as Craig added, 'It is the telescribe—a recent invention of Edison which records on a specially prepared phonograph cylinder all that is said—both ways—over a telephone wire. As nearly as I can make out someone—unknown—has been playing animated telescribe in this case. Let us see now whether your utmost demands for safety and security cannot be satisfied in this modern way.'

Not a word was said. The novelty of the turn of events seemed to leave them no objection.

In Shelby's own voice came, clear and distinct, the order to buy ten thousand shares of Maddox Munitions. Then Kennedy stopped the machine.

'Let us see how that works before we go any further,' he said significantly. 'His buying orders seemed forestalled by selling orders when they were given over the regular telephone. Before the next is given perhaps we may find we have stopped part of the leak.'

Kennedy's calm assurance seemed to have completely changed their attitude. They were not convinced, but at least silent.

Out on the Curb we could hear the shouting as brokers with stock to sell crowded about the man with the order to buy.

Whoever was back of it, it was a well-planned raid. The

order for ten thousand scarcely stemmed the flood. Quickly Kennedy let the little cylinder revolve. Another order was placed, and another.

I could not help noticing, however, that each succeeding order was smaller than the rest and it was hard to escape the implication that Shelby was really reaching the limit of his available resources.

Anxiously I listened to the turmoil on the Curb. Now it would abate, only to start up again. I glanced at Craig. What would he do?

Just then word was passed up that another block of stock had suddenly been hurled on the market. The brokers looked sceptically at Kennedy. Would Shelby be able to meet this final assault?

Craig released the revolving cylinder again. I gasped as I listened, remembering the pause over the wire upstairs, the apparent reluctance of Shelby over something, and Craig's remark that followed.

Winifred Walcott was placing orders—two of them—one to Dexter, the other to Merrill and Moore. They were large orders, too, a great deal larger than the selling order which had last bombarded the market. I glanced at Kennedy. Not for a moment did he betray the anxiety I know he now felt. For the orders must have involved a large part of Miss Walcott's own private fortune.

In his abstraction Kennedy had forgotten to stop the telescribe and I heard over it another voice that sounded like Burke's.

'Oh, say,' he announced. 'I've got a clue on that store-room in the cellar. I—'

'Never mind now, Burke,' I heard Kennedy answer over the telescribe. 'That will keep. Just now there isn't a minute to spare.'

I heard no more, for Kennedy realised what he was doing and shut the reproducer off, pulling off the recording cylinder

Would Miss Walcott's order be enough to turn the scale? The stock was down. Her money would purchase more shares than before. If it did and the stock rose, she stood to win. If it went lower she might lose all.

I jumped to the window again.

The news of the order, two orders, in fact, and large ones, came like a bombshell on the overwrought market. Was the supporting power of Maddox unlimited? One could feel the air tingle with the question. I saw some speculators hold a hasty conference. Though I did not know it at the time, they decided that an interest that could weather such an assault could weather anything, that someone had been buying all the way down, to boost back the stock far above the old high mark. They wanted to share in the upward turn, and were ready to take a gambler's chance. Others caught the spirit, for if the Curb is anything it is a driven herd.

Slowly the stock began to climb. The speculative public were in it now. Selling orders almost fell off. Up jumped the price.

Kennedy drew a long breath as he pulled a Westport time-table from his pocket, to cover his revulsion of feeling.

Maddox Munitions was saved!

CHAPTER XXV

THE ADVENTURESS

THERE was no use in our staying longer in New York, for the turn in the market had come, and it was able to take care of itself.

Up in our little office, Kennedy began hastily to pack up what of the stuff he wanted to save, and was just finishing when the telephone rang.

It was Hastings, who had been trying to locate us all the morning. The flurry in the market had very much excited him, and the final upward turn had not served to decrease his excitement.

'There don't seem to be many trains to Westport in the middle of the day,' I heard Kennedy consider over the wire. 'Your car is here? Well, can you go back there with us? Yes— right away.'

As he hung up he turned to me. 'Poor old Hastings hasn't been able to practise his profession for the last few days,' Craig smiled. 'He wants me to hurry up the case. We'll see what we can do. He's coming up for us in his car, and then we'll shoot out to Westport.'

It was a beautiful day, but none of us appreciated it much as we slid along the splendid roads from the city. There was only one subject uppermost in my mind, at least. Whence had come this new stock-market attack? Who was back of the series of violent deeds which had taken place in less than a week? Above all, where were the precious telautomaton plans?

At least it was some relief, when we swung into Westport, to know that we were back again at the main scene of action, and I felt that now events would develop rapidly.

Burke was waiting impatiently at the Lodge, though it did not seem as though our arrival was the only thing he had on his mind.

'What was it you found in the little store-room in the cellar?' demanded Kennedy, jumping from the car as we pulled up at the Lodge porte-cochère.

Without comment, Burke pulled a crumpled bit of paper from his pocket and handed it to Craig. We crowded around and read:

> If a hair of her head is harmed I will have revenge, though it sends me to prison for life.

We looked at the Secret Service man inquiringly.

'Not a soul has been near the store-room since we began to watch it this morning,' he explained hurriedly. 'It must have been left there before we got up—just tucked under the telephone instrument. Paquita's disappeared!'

'Disappeared?' we exclaimed, almost together, as Burke blurted out his startling budget of news.

'Yes—and not a trace of her. She must have got away before you fellows were up.'

I looked again at the crumpled bit of paper. What did it mean? Was it that someone had actually kicked over the traces in working for one higher up?

To whom did it refer? Instantly there flashed through my mind the picture of Winifred as we had seen her borne off by the abductors whom we had foiled. Could it be she?

Taught by Kennedy, I did not allow a first impression to rule. Might it be anyone else? I thought of Irene Maddox, of Frances Walcott. It did not seem to fit them.

Paquita? Perhaps the note referred to her. If so, who would have sent it? Sanchez? And if from Sanchez, to whom was it sent?

'How about Sanchez?' I queried.

'As much surprised at her disappearance as the rest of us,' replied Burke.

'How was that?'

'I picked him up and had him shadowed. I know that her disappearance mystified him, for he had no idea he was observed, at the time. He got away again, though. If we are ever to pick that girl up again, shadowing Sanchez may be the best way. I have had Riley out—'

'Not the same hand that wrote the cipher,' interrupted Kennedy, studying the note. 'I beg pardon. What of Riley? Any word?'

'I should say,' burst out Burke. 'Down in the cove—Little Neck they call it—in a deserted barn we've found a racer— answers the description of the one seen in New York the morning of the robbery and on the road out here. It's my dope that you made the little garage here untenable, Kennedy, and that whoever it was took the car to the cove to hide it.'

He paused, but for want of something to say. Before we could urge him he added: 'And that scout cruiser, too. She's been scuttled, out past the point, at the entrance to the cove. Whoever it is, he's been wiping out all the evidence against him that he can.'

'No word of Paquita or Sanchez?' inquired Kennedy again. Burke shook his head.

'How is Shelby Maddox?'

'Much better. I was in the room during the flurry. You should have seen him when the turn came. We could hardly keep him in bed. He was frantic.'

Kennedy had continued studying the anonymous note very carefully as we talked.

'It squares with my theory,' he mused, more to himself than to us. 'Yes—it is time to act. And we must act quickly. Burke, can you get all the Maddoxes up to Shelby's room—right away? Perhaps by that time we may have word from Riley. At any rate we shall be ready.'

Shelby was propped up in bed with pillows, quite reconciled now to being an invalid, when we entered.

'The best little nurse ever,' he greeted us, scarcely taking his eyes from Winifred. 'And a financier, too,' he added, with a laugh; 'a power in the market.'

'You mustn't forget Professor Kennedy's machine,' put in Winifred, welcoming us with a smile that covered the trace of a blush which glowed through the pretty tan of her cheeks.

Shelby grasped Craig's hand. 'You said you wouldn't work for me,' he grinned, 'but you certainly didn't work against me. Just let me get on my feet again. You won't regret, old man, that you—'

A knock on the door cut him short. It was Frances and Johnson Walcott.

For a moment the two women looked at each other. Not a word was said, but each understood. Whatever differences had kept them apart seemed to have been swept aside by the emotions of the moment. Frances whispered something in Winifred's ear as she flung her arms about the girl, then turned to her brother and bent over him.

Man-like, Johnson Walcott stood awkwardly. His wife saw it.

'Congratulate them, Johnson,' she cried. 'Don't you understand?'

Before he could reply there came another tap on the door. It was Burke again, escorting Irene Maddox, reluctant and suspicious.

Surprised, she glanced from the Walcotts to Shelby, then at us.

'Congratulate whom?' she asked quickly. 'What is it all about?'

There was a moment of embarrassment, when Kennedy came to the rescue, stepping forward and looking at his watch.

'I'm waiting word from Señorita Paquita and Mr Sanchez,' he interrupted, 'but that is no reason why I should not at least begin to tell you what I have discovered.'

We watched him as he slowly drew from his pocket the crumpled note which Burke had discovered that morning, and the apparently blank sheet of paper we had picked up in Paquita's room.

It seemed as if Kennedy's words had recalled them all to their former selves. In an instant each seemed to be on guard, even Shelby.

'I suppose you have heard of what we call the science of graphology?' he inquired, motioning in pantomime to me to fill a basin with warm water. 'It is the reading of character in handwriting.'

Into the basin he dropped the blank sheet. We waited in silence. I, at least, was not surprised when he held up the wet paper, now covered with figures scrawled over it.

'Even though there is writing on this sheet,' he observed, holding up the note, 'and figures on the other, I think anyone could tell at a glance that they were not made by the same hand. This was by no means my first clue.' He was waving the wet paper with the figures. 'But it decided me. Though the message was hidden both by sympathetic ink and a cryptogram, still, in the light of this new science, the character of the writer stands out as plain as if it were shouted from the house-top.'

He paused again. 'Graphology tells me,' he proceeded slowly, 'that the hand that wrote these figure is the hand of one who has all the characteristics of a spy and a traitor. Before we go further, let me call to your mind some rather remarkable deductions and discoveries I have made. By the way, Burke, you left word where we were, in case we get any news?'

The Secret Service man nodded, but said nothing, as if he did not wish his voice to break the thread of Kennedy's disclosure.

'The plot against Maddox Munitions and particularly the wonderful telautomaton,' continued Kennedy gravely, 'was subtle. Apparently all was to be accomplished at one coup. The plans were to be stolen on the *Sybarite* the same night that the model was to be taken from the safe in New York. How the latter was accomplished we know well enough, now, for all practical purposes. Marshall Maddox's keys were to admit the thief to the office. The burglar's microphone did the rest.

'How it was accomplished here I know, too. Without a doubt, the Japanese, Mito, admitted the plotter to the *Sybarite*, at least signalled so that it was possible to creep up quietly in a cruiser and throw a chlorine-gas bomb through a marked port. Marshall Maddox was overcome—killed. Through the same port-hole his body was thrown.

'Thus at once both the plans and the keys that gave access to the model were obtained.'

As Craig spoke, my mind hastily reviewed the events of what seemed now weeks instead of days past. It was as though he had failed in an explanation of the events in a silent drama.

'Mito was seen ashore that night,' he resumed. 'He was suspected. I was watching him. Worse than that, he knew too much. He was a weak link, an ever-present danger. Therefore he must be got out of the way. He was killed. But his mute lips tell quite as eloquent a story as if he were here before us now. There is another who played an even more important part. She is not here, but I know you all know whom I mean.'

Kennedy had thus deftly shifted the picture to the little dancer. As he spoke, Irene Maddox leaned forward, her face burning with indignation at the mere mention of her hated rival.

'Paquita,' Kennedy continued, carefully choosing his words, 'has been an enigma to me in this case. There is no use mincing matters. There had long been a feud in the family, before she appeared. I think there is no need for me here to elaborate how she has brought matters to a crisis, or the enmity which she stirred up.'

Mrs Maddox murmured something bitterly under her breath, but Kennedy quickly changed the subject.

'We know, also, that Paquita met Shelby Maddox,' he hurried on. 'In the minds of some it looked as though she might break Shelby, too. But it was just because of the reasons that made them think so that precisely the opposite happened. Strangely enough, the little dancer seems to have fallen in love with him herself.'

Out of the corner of my eye I was watching Winifred. Her face was set in deep lines as Kennedy went ahead in his merciless analysis of the case. Shelby coloured, but said nothing, though his manner was of the man who might have said much, if he had not learned that defence was worse than silence. Winifred's face questioned as plainly as words whether there must always be present that sinister shadow of Paquita. I wondered whether she was yet convinced that he had never loved the little dancer.

Kennedy seemed to feel the situation. 'But,' he added slowly and significantly, 'in the meantime something else had happened. Shelby Maddox had met someone else.'

He had not dwelt on the gossip about Paquita. I could almost feel the relief of Shelby, for Paquita had been a cause of disagreement even between Mrs Walcott and the others.

'Even this new turn of events was used in desperation by the criminal. In aiming a blow at Shelby, after having been defeated at every other point, as a last desperate resort an attempt was directed at Winifred Walcott herself. It was as though someone had tried to strike at Shelby himself, and had decided that the surest way to control him was through someone whom he loved. Who was it,' he concluded, facing us pointedly, 'that kidnapped Winifred, and why?'

As far as I am able to answer it might have been anybody. I had even considered the possibility that Shelby might have carried her off himself in order to make her turn to him for protection. In fact, I had never been able to account for the presence of Sanchez with us at the time. Had I been mistaken in Sanchez?

'Attack after attack on those who were getting closer had failed,' continued Kennedy. 'That being the case, those who might talk must be silenced. Mito was dead. Still Paquita remained. She, too, must be silenced. And so my suspicion, in turn, was thrown on her. By this cipher which I have here she was ordered to go to New York, in order to mislead me. The plan failed. Always in the most clever schemes of crime, they fail at some point. Unless I am very much mistaken, Paquita has seen through the designs. What she will do I do not profess to know. For, in addition to the mixed motives of her hopeless love for Shelby Maddox and jealousy of Miss Walcott, her disappearance this morning indicates that she is in mortal fear of an attack inspired by the plotter.'

Unavoidably my mind raced ahead to Sanchez, who had followed her so jealously. Had he really been in love with her—a love as hopeless as her own for Maddox? Or was he a more sinister figure? Had they been playing a game, each having an insight into the weakness of this unhappy family? I recalled the conversation I had had with Henri in the cabaret and his non-committal shrug. Perhaps Sanchez and Paquita had been deeper than we had thought.

'And now,' resumed Kennedy, evidently temporising in the hope that word would soon come from the searchers whom we had out, 'now we find that a final effort has been made to remove all incriminating traces of crime. The car which we could not locate in the garage here has been found hidden miles away. The fast motor-boat which escaped us last night lies at the bottom of the bay. At the same time an insidious stock-market attack has been wrecked, for it was a final purpose in this ambitious scheme evidently to wreck Maddox Munitions in order to gain control of it. Even my own resources of science must have failed if it had not been for the loyalty of one who cast all into the balance at the final moment.'

We were following Kennedy intently now, and I did not betray that I saw Shelby's hand steal out and clasp that of Winifred, which was resting on a table beside his bed. She did not withdraw her own hand.

The telephone rang and Burke, who was nearest it, answered. The conversation was brief. Evidently the party at the other end was doing most of the talking, but as we scanned the detective's face we could see that something important had happened.

'You do not know where Sanchez has gone?' asked Burke finally, adding, 'Keep the boys on the trail, then, until you get some clue. Goodbye.'

He hung up the receiver slowly and turned toward Kennedy, but I do not think any of us were prepared for his message.

'Paquita has committed suicide!' he blurted out suddenly.

We looked at one another in amazement at this startling turn of events.

What did it mean? Had she seen nothing more to live for, or had someone pursued her and was she anticipating fate?

'It was Riley,' recounted Burke briefly. 'Evidently she had taken poison. They found her body in the woods not far from where we discovered the car and the sunken boat. Some children say they saw a man there—he answers the description of Sanchez. Riley is following the clue.'

'What drove her to it? Was there no word, no note?' asked Irene Maddox, awed by the tragedy.

'Yes,' replied Burke. 'On a piece of paper she had written, "I have mailed a letter to Shelby Maddox. May God forgive me for what I have done. There is nothing left in life for me." That is all.'

We gazed at one another in consternation.

'Poor girl!' repeated Kennedy in a low tone. 'She was merely a pawn in the hands of another. But it is a dangerous game—this game of hearts—even with the heart of an adventuress.'

'I think we should organise a search for this fellow Sanchez before he can get away,' proposed Johnson Walcott, taking a step toward Kennedy. 'My own car is below. We can get up a posse in no time right at the Lodge.'

Before anyone could take up the suggestion the door of the room flew open.

There stood Sanchez himself—pale, his eyes staring, his

whole manner that of one who had reached the last point of desperation.

Half-way across the room he stopped, faced us, and tossed down on a table before Kennedy a package wrapped in oiled silk.

'That is my revenge!' he exclaimed in a voice almost sepulchral. 'I found it in the boat before I scuttled it.'

Craig tore it open. There, unrolled before us, at last lay the plans of the deadly telautomaton.

Of a sudden I realised that the model had destroyed itself in sinking the *Sybarite*. With the plans in our possession the secret was safe.

Slowly Sanchez raised an accusing finger, but before he could utter a word Craig had backed against the door and stood holding it.

'Someone has been keeping undercover here,' Craig shot out suddenly, 'hiding behind others who were his tools—first Mito, then Paquita, who has been driven to her death, now Sanchez.

'Graphology first betrayed his fine hand of crime to me. The stock-market attack confirmed my suspicion. Sanchez has completed— Don't shoot! Burke has you covered already. Walter—will you be so kind as to disarm Johnson Walcott?'

THE END

THE DETECTIVE STORY CLUB

FOR DETECTIVE CONNOISSEURS

recommends

"The Man with the Gun."

THE DETECTIVE STORY CLUB

FOR DETECTIVE CONNOISSEURS

recommends

"The Man with the Gun."

MR. BALDWIN'S FAVOURITE

THE LEAVENWORTH CASE
By ANNA K. GREEN

THIS exciting detective story, published towards the end of last century, enjoyed an enormous success both in England and America. It seems to have been forgotten for nearly fifty years until Mr. Baldwin, speaking at a dinner of the American Society in London, remarked : " An American woman, a successor of Poe, Anna K. Green, gave us *The Leavenworth Case*, which I still think one of the best detective stories ever written." It is a remarkably clever story, a masterpiece of its kind, and in addition to an exciting murder mystery and the subsequent tracking down of the criminal, the writing and characterisation are excellent. *The Leavenworth Case* will not only grip the attention of the reader from beginning to end but will also be read again and again with increasing pleasure.

CALLED BACK
By HUGH CONWAY

BY the purest of accidents a man who is blind accidentally comes on the scene of a murder. He cannot see what is happening, but he can hear. He is seen by the assassin who, on discovering him to be blind, allows him to go without harming him. Soon afterwards he recovers his sight and falls in love with a mysterious woman who is in some way involved in the crime. . . . The mystery deepens, and only after a series of memorable thrills is the tangled skein unravelled.

LOOK FOR THE MAN WITH THE GUN

THE DETECTIVE STORY CLUB

FOR DETECTIVE CONNOISSEURS

recommends

"The Man with the Gun."

The Murder of Roger Ackroyd
By AGATHA CHRISTIE

*T*HE MURDER OF ROGER ACKROYD is one of Mrs. Christie's most brilliant detective novels. As a play, under the title of *Alibi*, it enjoyed a long and successful run with Charles Laughton as the popular detective, Hercule Poirot. The novel has now been filmed, and its clever plot, skilful characterisation, and sparkling dialogue will make every one who sees the film want to read the book. M. Poirot, the hero of many brilliant pieces of detective deduction, comes out of his temporary retirement like a giant refreshed, to undertake the investigation of a peculiarly brutal and mysterious murder. Geniuses like Sherlock Holmes often find a use for faithful mediocrities like Dr. Watson, and by a coincidence it is the local doctor who follows Poirot round and himself tells the story. Furthermore, what seldom happens in these cases, he is instrumental in giving Poirot one of the most valuable clues to the mystery.

LOOK FOR THE MAN WITH THE GUN

THE DETECTIVE STORY CLUB

FOR DETECTIVE CONNOISSEURS

"The Man with the Gun."

recommends

THE PERFECT CRIME

THE FILM STORY OF

ISRAEL ZANGWILL'S famous detective thriller, THE BIG BOW MYSTERY

A MAN is murdered for no apparent reason. He has no enemies, and there seemed to be no motive for any one murdering him. No clues remained, and the instrument with which the murder was committed could not be traced. The door of the room in which the body was discovered was locked and bolted on the inside, both windows were latched, and there was no trace of any intruder. The greatest detectives in the land were puzzled. Here indeed was the perfect crime, the work of a master mind. Can you solve the problem which baffled Scotland Yard for so long, until at last the missing link in the chain of evidence was revealed?

LOOK OUT

FOR FURTHER SELECTIONS FROM THE DETECTIVE STORY CLUB—READY SHORTLY

LOOK FOR THE MAN WITH THE GUN